AGGIE
the
HORRIBLE

vs. Max the Pompous Ass

AGGIE

the

HORRIBLE

vs. Max the Pompous Ass

LISA WELLS

Entangled Publishing, LLC
10940 S Parker Rd
Suite 327
Parker, CO 80134
rights@entangledpublishing.com

Amara is an imprint of Entangled Publishing, LLC.

Edited by Lydia Sharp, Liz Pelletier, and Robin Haseltine
Cover illustration and design by Elizabeth Turner Stokes

Manufactured in the United States of America

First Edition July 2021

Content Warning

Aggie the Horrible vs. Max the Pompous Ass is a fun, witty interoffice rivalry romance. However, the story includes elements that might not be suitable for some readers. Alcohol consumption, drunkenness, and various sexual acts appear in the novel. Child abandonment, emotional abuse, extreme poverty, and death of a loved one are mentioned in the characters' backstories. Readers who may be sensitive to these, please take note.

This book is dedicated to all my readers who are living on the wrong side of the proverbial tracks. You are beautiful. You are wonderful. You are powerful. Be defined by your values not your address. I, too, grew up on the wrong side, and I believe the experience made me a better person. In fact, there are many in my town who would say I'm still on the wrong side of those all-powerful tracks simply because I live north of a major street that supposedly divides our town from the haves and the have-nots. To them, I say, whatever.

Chapter One

Max Treadwell carefully weaved his way through the posh gathering at the newly opened Ties & Stilettos Cocktail Lounge. An overnight success located on the second floor of a forty-two-story office building in downtown Kansas City. A development Max had spearheaded.

His destination—the corner table where his best friend, Grant, waited on him for their ritual Friday night, five o'clock unwind drinks. Ritual unless one of them had a date, then it switched to Friday morning coffee.

"Dude," Max said to Grant the minute he reached the table, "prepare to pay our tab tonight." He dropped his credit card on the table next to Grant's. The one with the best worst story of the week drank for free.

"No fucking way." Grant leaned back in his chair, loosened his tie, and unbuttoned the top button of his dress shirt. "The boss assigned me a sexual harassment case between a married couple. And it's the nerd-alert husband suing the hot-as-fuck wife. Your life can't beat that shit. I mean, dude, she's hot. Let her ogle you while you're in the shower."

The Kansas City law firm where Grant worked boasted a team of young up-and-coming lawyers and was in the same building on the eighteenth floor as the bar. His boss, a lively woman about forty years older than the rest of the team, had the final word on what cases her lawyers accepted, and her choices leaned on the bizarre side. Grant's last one had been a guy who wanted to sue a café for putting too much ice in his coffee.

Max took a seat that allowed him a view of the door. He agreed. As a rule, his days were a lot calmer at his office than his friend's days. But not this week. "As messed up as that sounds, it doesn't compare to my sad-ass story of the week."

"What can I get you, gentlemen?" the regular Friday night waitress said as she placed cocktail napkins in front of them. Her name was Sam. She was single, had a child, and was like a sister to the two of them.

"The usual," they said at the same time.

She rolled her eyes. "I don't know why I even bother asking."

"Because we're cute," Max said, giving her a friendly wink.

"More likely it's because the two of you math-challenged charmers always over tip," she countered.

"You're worth it," Grant replied.

"What he said." Max didn't let his face or tone show any signs of pity for her less-than-perfect life. Been there. Done that. Ended with a drink in his lap and a word of warning from her to save his pity for someone who truly needed it.

Even so, no matter what their tab was at the end of the evening, he and Grant always made sure their tip covered the cost of a week's worth of diapers and baby food.

"Let's hear it," Grant said once she had moved on to the next table.

"Remember I told you about how Grandmother talked me into letting her fill in as my assistant while my actual assistant is out on maternity leave?"

"Don't even think about bad-mouthing Ms. Grace," Grant said, his tone all-on serious. "She's a saint, and I'll kick anyone's ass, even yours, who tries to say otherwise."

Grandmother was not a saint, but he, too, would kick anyone's ass who bad-mouthed her. "One week in as my assistant and Grandmother has decided the position is far too time consuming and it's interfering with her social life. At four forty-five this afternoon, she gave me her notice. Monday is her last day."

Grant's lips twitched. "I've heard the one-day notice is the new two-weeks' notice."

"Maybe in your Mickey Mouse world."

Grant looked unimpressed. "Didn't you cover exit expectations in your interview with Ms. Grace?"

No, he hadn't. Grandmother didn't do job interviews. "I covered how time-consuming it would be to work for me as my assistant before I agreed to her idea."

"I'm not hearing anything that can beat my sexual harassment story," Grant said. "Cry uncle already. I'm thinking you should even add on first-year college expenses to tonight's tip."

"Listen, I haven't even gotten to the bad part." He slipped out of his jacket, laid it over the chair next to him, and loosened his tie. The club's dress code required either a tie or stilettos, but it didn't require ties to be notched tight.

Some of the cockiness went out of Grant's expression.

Max placed his elbows on the table and leaned in. "Grandmother's new best friend has a granddaughter who has had a string of bad luck in the workplace. A granddaughter I've heard a lot about this past week. And I thought all the chatter about her was because the grandmothers were trying to fix us up. That wasn't it. Grandmother has arranged for the granddaughter to come in for an interview Monday morning for the position of my new assistant."

Grant crossed his arms. "Now we're getting to something fun. What kind of bad luck in the workplace?"

"Something like a hundred fifty jobs over the last eighteen months. Which isn't that surprising when you learn she graduated bottom of her class from Kansas State with a degree in liberal arts." It had been seven jobs, but if he wanted Grant to pay, exaggeration was necessary.

"I know I'm the brain in our friendship," Grant said, giving him a cocky grin, "but surely even you have thought of the fact you can interview the grannies-in-cahoots' Chosen One and not hire her. Tell her she came in a close second, but you've decided on another with more experience."

Max scratched his cheek with his middle finger. "That's exactly what I planned to do, but Grandmother must have read it on my face, because right before she left for the day, she called in a favor."

Grant stilled. "A favor or *the* favor?"

"*The* favor."

He threw his hands in the air surrender-style. "Shit. Then you *have* to do it. I don't care if it's fucking murder."

Grandmother had bailed Max and Grant out of jail when they were sixteen. Not only had she bailed them out, but she'd also managed to make the "minors in possession" charge vanish. All without either Max or Grant's parents knowing any of it happened. Max leaned his chair back on two legs and nodded. "You're right. I have to offer the job to Agnes."

"With that charming of a name, she can't be too bad. I'm sure you and Agnes will get along like fuzzy socks on your old frigid feet."

"A hundred fifty jobs in eighteen months says otherwise."

Grant waved to someone in the crowd—the guy knew everyone—before continuing, "You can handle anyone for a few months."

"Normally, I'd agree with you." Max lowered the legs of his chair to the floor. "But right now is the worst possible time for me to have a hot mess running my office. I'm preparing a bid on the biggest contract of my career. If I don't get it, I'm going to lose my bet with Father." The deadline was less than three months away, on his birthday. And if he lost, the personal cost would be huge.

The laughter in Grant's eyes vanished. "Shit, man. I thought you had the win on that bet locked in with the Rugger Contract. How did you screw it up?"

"It fell through one hour before we were scheduled to sign. I'm convinced Father pulled some type of behind-the-scenes bullshit to make it happen."

"Why in the hell am I just now hearing about this?"

Because it had happened on the anniversary of Grant's divorce. Max wouldn't throw shit on a man who was already having a shitty day. "It's not like you tell me every time you lose a case at trial."

Grant ignored the comment.

"Maybe you'll get lucky and Agnes won't accept the position."

Max let out a loud sigh. "My shit aside, at some point, if I hire her, she'll figure out she's in way over her head, and she'll ask why in the hell I hired her. I'll tell her the truth, and that answer will fracture what must already be a low self-esteem. I mean, can you imagine what it feels like to fail at that many jobs in a year and a half?"

"Here you go, boys." Sam placed a dry martini in front of Grant and a scotch in front of Max.

"Drinks are on me tonight." Grant handed his card over to start their tab.

She glanced at Max. "You having a bad week?"

"How can I be having a bad week when I have the best-looking waitress in town bringing me drinks?" He slid his card back into his wallet.

She smirked. "Yeah, save your smooth talking for someone who actually likes men."

Once she was gone, Grant cleared his throat as if about to give a closing argument. "The bottom line is Ms. Grace called in *the* favor. You have to hire Agnes. The two meddling grandmothers can deal with the consequences of her getting her feelings hurt if it doesn't work out."

They each sipped their drinks and sat in silence, staring off into the distance. The rules were simple during this time. No talking, only unwinding. Max's brain didn't get the unwind memo and continued to spin out worst-case scenarios on what would happen if he caved and hired the *Chosen One*.

Right on cue, the waitress brought their second round. This was always a pitcher of draft beer made at a local micro-brewery.

Grant filled his mug. "I've been wondering, were there any other terms to this agreement that you would hire the Chosen One?"

"None." Max tipped his mug at an angle and filled it. A trick he'd learned from a barmaid he'd once dated. The angle kept you from getting a glass full of foam.

"I have an idea, but if Ms. Grace asks, I will deny knowing anything about it, let alone being the brains behind the storm."

"What do you have in mind?"

"You should conduct a covert piss-off-the-interviewee operation."

"What—"

"Oh. My. God." A brunette stopped at their table and plopped down in the empty chair between them. "I can't believe it's the Magnificent Two from high school."

Max glanced at the woman. It had been twelve years since anyone had referred to him and Grant as the Magnificent Two, their nickname from being the stars of their senior-year football team. Not that he needed to look at her to know who it was. He recognized her New Jersey accent. She'd been the hot new girl on campus their freshman year in high school. "Tiff Baker, is that you?"

"One and the same. Home after a five-year stint in Vegas." She glanced at Grant. "I heard you got a divorce and were back in town. Sorry about that. Divorce is a bitch. I should know. I've had two of them." Her gaze swiveled to Max. "And I heard you are an in-demand land developer that all the elite single girls in this town are vying to date." She pulled out her phone. "I want both of your numbers so we can stay in touch."

Five minutes later, Tiffany left on the same whirlwind she'd arrived.

"Are you okay?" Max asked Grant.

Tiffany had done an inordinate amount of talking about Grant's ex-wife. A woman who'd cheated on him and broken his heart. A woman they had never discussed when he moved back to Kansas City.

"Never been better," Grant said in a low voice. "Back to Operation Piss-Off-the-Interviewee. We have a hiring instrument all potential candidates fill out before we interview them. It gives us information on an individual's personality, their general knowledge and intelligence, and their ability to handle pressure. It takes a good two hours to complete, and it's brutal because it requires short answers. Why don't I send you a copy? Then you can make the Chosen One take it, and hopefully, that will set the mood for her to be less than inclined to want to work for you."

"If she's desperate for a job, I'm not sure that alone would get her to say no."

Grant refilled his mug. "I'm ahead of you, man. Have her take the exam in the outer office and turn off the airflow for that room. It's a miserable enough test without being all sweaty while you do it."

Max chuckled. "You have the mind of a budding criminal."

"Of course, to really sell the idea to her that she doesn't want to accept your job offer, you're going to come across as a real dick of a potential boss. The bigger the dick you are, the more likely she'll tell you to shove your job before you ever get around to offering her the position."

"A dick?"

"If you don't want to destroy her self-esteem down the road by admitting you were coerced into hiring her, then yes, a dick. And, most importantly, if she turns down the job, it will allow you to hire an assistant that can take care of business while you take care of winning that damn bet once and for all."

Max pinched the bridge of his nose. He was a lot of things, hardcore and driven being the most prominent. But not an asshole. Especially to women. "I'm not sure I can play the part of a dick."

"Sure you can. Just channel your father and how much of an ass he's going to be if you let him win the bet because you were too nice to play a little dick-fuckery."

. . .

Aggie Johansson stared across the kitchen table at Meemaw as horror did a jarring jig in her already throbbing brain. "You got me a favor-interview with Ms. Grace's grandson? The same man who has discouraged your friendship from the get-go?" She pushed her plate aside. Suddenly, she no longer had an appetite for the meatloaf and mashed potatoes. She picked up her sweet tea and took a sip, wishing it was something much stronger. Like a scotch on the rocks. Hold the rocks. Leave the bottle.

"He hasn't discouraged our friendship." Meemaw leaned across the table and pushed Aggie's plate back in place. "He just did a background check on me to make sure I wasn't a con-woman."

"That makes him an asshole." She picked up her fork and scooped up some mashed potatoes that had butter oozing out of them. "Why would I want to go to work for someone like that?"

"Watch your mouth, young lady. You're not too old for me to scold."

She swallowed her food before replying. "Yes, ma'am."

Meemaw pointed her fork at her. "And I'll have you know, Ms. Smarty Pants, that's how things are done when you rub elbows—as friends, not the hired help—with people who know people. They run background checks on you, and if you pass, they do favors for you now and then."

Meemaw and Ms. Grace had become friends a few months back after meeting in a long line at a coffee shop.

"But…" The window-rattling racket of a freight train passing by on the tracks that weren't more than a hundred feet away from their backyard fence forced Aggie to stop and wait to finish her sentence. They were the tracks that separated the bad zip code areas of Kansas City from the good zip code areas of Kansas City.

Aggie and Meemaw shared a two-bedroom duplex on the wrong side of those tracks. Had their address been on the other side, Maxwell Treadwell wouldn't have felt the need to have Meemaw *looked into*. Aggie couldn't wait for the day she could afford to move them to a better neighborhood. And to make enough so that Meemaw wouldn't have to work. If anyone deserved retirement, it was her.

While the train blasted its horn, Meemaw hopped up and got the butter dish off the cabinet and brought it to the table, where she proceeded to smear a thick layer of it over a slice of white bread. Then she folded the bread in half and took a big bite.

She always waited to do this until the dinner train rolled by, because the noise prevented Aggie from cautioning her on making healthier eating choices.

Three minutes and ten seconds later, the noise outside stopped. At midnight, it would be the same song and dance.

"What was it you were saying?" Meemaw prompted before Aggie could mention the butter situation.

"What if her grandson thinks this job interview proves the only reason you've pursued this new friendship of yours with his grandmother is to get something out of her and not for the simple reason the two of you hit it off?"

Meemaw scowled. "Because I didn't ask her for the favor. She asked me if I thought you might be interested in helping Little Maxi out of a jam."

"Little Maxi?" The throb in her head lessened as she laughed.

"That's what Ms. Grace calls him."

What an unfortunate nickname. All Aggie could think of when she heard Maxi was maxi pads. She bit her lip to keep from laughing, because Meemaw wouldn't appreciate her fourth-grade humor. With much difficulty, she refocused. "Are you sure this isn't just the two of you scheming to get your grandchildren hooked up?"

"Why in tarnation would we do that?"

"Umm...because you think I'm perfect, and she thinks he's perfect. And the two of you have decided that would make us perfect together."

Meemaw dropped her fork, and a flush stained her

withered cheeks.

The only time Meemaw blushed was when she'd been caught. Which was seldom because she could scheme with the best of them. "That's really what this is about? You two old broads are matchmaking."

"Bless your heart. Don't you just think you're too smart for your britches? Well, you listen to me, missy, you don't have a job. He's got a job that needs filled. Don't you go and embarrass me by not going in for the interview Ms. Grace went to a lot of trouble to set up for you. The fact we'd like to see the two of you hit it off has nothing to do with this opportunity."

Aggie rubbed her temples with her index fingers. The throb was back. This whole conversation was her fault. She should have never told Meemaw this morning she was once again unemployed. Meemaw, who'd never been without a job since she was fourteen, didn't understand Aggie's lack of commitment to the jobs she had held since graduating from college. And that was partly Aggie's fault as well, because she didn't want to hurt her feelings by explaining her need to find a career. One she could see herself staying in for thirty years and getting a pension from. Keyword being a pension. A job that would keep her from ending up like Meemaw.

In eighteen months of looking for the perfect job, so far, she hadn't found a workplace that whispered in her ear, "This is your forever home." And if there's one thing she'd learned from watching Meemaw work herself to the bone all these years—in jobs she didn't even enjoy—and still not able to retire, it was that the endgame was all about the quality of your pension plan. She lowered her hands to the table and picked up her fork. "Fine. I'll go in for the interview." She stabbed the meatloaf, picked up her knife, and sliced off a bite.

For a few seconds, they ate in silence.

"If he does offer you the job," Meemaw said, "I expect you to take it." Instead of looking at Aggie, her concentration was on seeing how many green beans she could stab onto her fork at one time. She managed four and ate them.

"Of course you do."

"I'm not fool'n now. I wouldn't be able to hold my head up around Ms. Grace if you shunned her grandson's offer after she got you an interview."

There were some arguments Aggie could win with Meemaw. This wasn't one of them. Not outright, anyway. "Fine. If he offers, and the benefits are agreeable...I'll accept."

Meemaw's gaze snapped away from the remaining green beans on her plate and speared Aggie to the spot. "I'm sure he pays his assistant quite generously. Do I have your promise you'll accept? Who knows? You might find you're good at it and not quit halfway through the honeymoon phase."

Respect kept Aggie from rolling her eyes. There was no way in hell a nine-to-five office gig would be her forever type of job. "If Little Maxi offers me the job," she said, sugared-tea sweet, "I promise to accept."

That didn't mean she wouldn't do everything within legal limits to keep him from offering her the position. And she had the whole weekend to devise the perfect plan. A plan so perfect only a fool would offer her the job after she put it into motion.

Chapter Two

Max Treadwell hated surprises. Especially on Monday mornings. He'd walked into his office, expecting to find Grandmother fulfilling her one-day notice, and instead found, he was fairly certain, the source of his current headache. The Chosen One was shockingly thirty minutes early. She stood at his desk with her back to him, thumbing through a stack of his papers. She had arrived for her interview wearing the type of short dress women wore at the clubs he frequented. And she had topped it with a scarred bomber jacket. Interesting choice for an interview.

He'd dug into her social media presence over the weekend. Under her biography she'd written the quote:

Life's a journey to ping-pong through in a haphazard fashion.

No wonder she couldn't hold a job. The asinine life philosophy would leave all who followed its wisdom mutilated and defeated.

"I take it you're Agnes Johansson?" he said.

She whirled around, a look of bemusement—not

embarrassment for having been caught snooping through papers on his desk—in her lavender-blue eyes. She batted her long lashes at him. "You can call me Aggie. And you must be Little Maxi Treadwell."

He scowled. "It's Max. You're not on my schedule for another half hour. Do you happen to know where my assistant went?"

"She called last night and asked me to come in early. She said you really put a lot of stock on punctuality, and I do oh so want to make a good first impression. Speaking of good first impressions, Ms. Grace is such a sweet woman. Anyway, when I got here, she told me to tell you that she's meeting my meemaw for coffee and she'd try to be back in time for you to take your lunch break."

He swallowed the dismay he felt over Grandmother's lack of professionalism and…well…almost everything about the woman standing in front of him. "I see."

"Oh, and she said to tell you that she's had the phone forwarded to your desk, so answer when it rings. And to remind you that you're expecting an important call from a client."

He rubbed the back of his neck. "Let me get this straight, she called you in early and then still left you here unattended and the phones unmanned?" Grandmother's one-day notice hadn't even made it past hour one.

Aggie's eyes narrowed a fraction, like maybe she found the comment a subtle dig. "Your phone has rung twice, and since you're expecting an important call, I took the liberty of answering. I left your messages for you there by the phone."

"Thank you." The initiative didn't mesh with his view of her as an employee train wreck. She could have just as easily let the calls go to voicemail. He picked them up and grimaced. The handwriting was horrific. "I can't read these."

"My bad." She plucked them out of his hand then held

one up. "This one's from Grant. He said to tell you to check your email before interviewing me."

Damn. "What?"

Her lips pressed together in a firm line. "Well...he didn't say my name, but he described me."

Max pinched the bridge of his nose. He should've grabbed a cup of coffee after his morning run instead of showering and rushing to work. "What did he say?"

"He called me *the chosen one*."

"And the second message?"

She glanced at the other one. "This was from a fun-sounding Tabitha, who said to tell you she really hated that she had to *hurry* off." She dropped the messages into the trash bin and picked back up his papers she'd been thumbing through before.

His first impression of the Chosen One was cementing his decision to implement his and Grant's plan. He strode to his desk, swiped the résumés out of her hand, and motioned for her to have a seat in the chair across from his desk. The scent of her perfume tickled his nose. Not strong. Subtle. Flirtatious. He ignored the asinine desire to linger so he could inhale her deeply.

"Didn't anyone teach you it's impolite to snoop?" He did a quick glance around to see if anything else looked out of place. The blinds that he closed every night before leaving had been opened. One of the chairs in the seating area had been turned to face the view of Kansas City out the floor-to-ceiling wall of windows from his third-story office. He refocused.

"Snoop?" The Chosen...Aggie stuck a loose strand of hair behind her ear. She had a lot of loose strands, like maybe she'd yanked up her ponytail in a hurry. "For your information, your grandmother, Ms. Grace," she said, "handed them to me before leaving and asked me to alphabetize them." Instead of taking a seat, she leaned the curve of her hip against his desk. "Since this is a courtesy interview that won't end in an offer, why don't I help you find the best candidate?"

Oh hell no. It *would* end in a job offer. An offer he needed her to refuse. "Not a courtesy interview at all," he said. "I know all about your employment history, and I'm willing to cut you some slack. Do you have a résumé?"

"My employment history?" Traces of steel hardened her tone. "Since I haven't yet given you my résumé, how do you know anything other than my name and who my meemaw is?"

"Grandmother mentioned that you've had a run of bad luck job-wise."

"Oh." She leaned down, picked up a bag that was way too large to be a purse, and set it on the chair. For a few moments, she rifled through it before pulling out a tube of toothpaste, a Rubik's Cube with all the correct colors on each side, a bag of gummy bears, and a rather heavy-looking hammer.

He cocked his head. Should he ask?

She straightened. "Damn. I knew I forgot something this morning. If I could borrow your computer, I'll pull up my Aggie's Assets and print it off for you. It will only take a jiff."

He raised an eyebrow. "Aggie's Assets?" Did it include her bra size along with her typing speed?

She cheerfully nodded.

"That won't be necessary. You can email it to me later today."

"Thank you." She shot him a bright fake smile. "Meemaw said you were a peach." Her tone was suddenly purely Southern in every way possible. The accent. The sweetness. The thinly veiled insult.

"I do try to be a peach every chance I get," he said drily.

One by one, she put everything back into her duffel bag of a purse. How did she even manage to carry that thing?

Once she'd finished repacking, she gave him a saucy smile and then took a seat.

"I'll start the interview by asking you to fill out a questionnaire." He walked around his desk and sat. His knees hit the desk. Damn it. She must have sat in his chair and jacked up the height.

"Like a test?" She retrieved a gummy bear from her suitcase and popped it past her bright red lips.

"More like a personality survey." He tore his gaze away from her mouth and reached under the chair to adjust it.

"You're *testing* my personality?" She eyeballed him. "Why?"

"The job as my assistant is demanding and somewhat odd at times, so I need someone I'll mesh with. After the impressive number of employers you've burned through, you would agree meshing is a good thing. Right? Even for a temporary position."

"Temporary?"

"What? Did Meemaw forget to tell you?" he asked in a patronizing tone that came out sounding just like his father. Good. That was the plan, after all. Channel dear old Dad during this interview.

Her nostrils flared. "I must have missed that memo."

"My permanent assistant, the one Grandmother was filling in for, is out on maternity leave. And I'll be honest with you, her shoes will be hard to fill."

"Your permanent one or your grandmother's? Because...I mean...Ms. Grace left me alone in your office. I'm thinking I can slide into her shoes just fine and dandy."

Did she mean to downplay her abilities just now? If so, what game was she playing? "My permanent. My competitors have tried to lure her away for years. Lucky for me, she's loyal." He opened his laptop, shook the mouse awake, found the email from Grant, then clicked the link and hit print.

"Are you not interested in a two-month job?"

"Temp work is my favorite." Aggie crossed her legs at the knees, causing her already short skirt to slide up ever so slightly, showing off her slender, toned calves. "Especially if it pays well. Meemaw said she was sure you would be super generous with my compensation, considering I'd be doing you such a huge favor and all, helping you out in this bind."

"Bind?"

She leaned in, her eyes twinkling like a person privy to insider information. "You know... Since you knocked up your *permanent* assistant. You know, the Loyal One."

He coughed. Damn it. "I did *not* get her pregnant. She's happily married. And I have plenty of candidates to choose from for this position, so there isn't any bind here for me to get out of." Where in the hell had she gotten that misinformation?

Aggie gave a delicate shrug and settled back in her chair. "Right. My bad."

He grabbed the pages of the survey off the printer without looking at them and handed them across the desk to her. He glanced at the pencil holder. Empty. His germophobic Grandmother must have confiscated his writing utensils for a thorough disinfecting. He sighed. "Do you have a pen?"

Once again, she rummaged in her purse, this time pulling out a condom. She glanced up at him, and for a moment, a hint of red flushed her cheeks. Then she gave him a wicked grin. "I have an extra if you want this one. It's glow-in-the-dark pink."

He said nothing. What could one possibly say to a job candidate who had just offered you a condom? If it weren't for the fact he knew Grandmother hated pranks, he'd think this was all one elaborate prank.

She dropped the condom back into her purse and pulled out a pen. "You don't mind pink, do you? It's my lucky color."

And all this time he thought it was hideous orange. Like

what was on her eyelids. "It'll be fine. Fill this out and return it to me when you're finished. You'll have one hour." He held out his hand. "I'll need your phone so you can't contact anyone for insight on how you should answer a question."

She handed over her cell. Easily. *Too* easily. "And your bag." She could be hiding a dictionary in that thing. Or an entire library.

Aggie lifted her purse and placed it on the edge of his desk with a *thump* and then flipped through the pages of the document. "Do you have a clipboard, or should I use the corner of your desk?"

"Follow me." He marched out and pointed at the receptionist's desk.

"Won't your receptionist need her space?" Aggie asked.

Don't even get me started on the receptionist fiasco. "I don't have one of those at the moment."

Aggie chuckled softly. "Is it just me or is there a pattern forming that doesn't reflect well upon you as a potential employer?"

"It's just you." Grandmother was supposed to have hired him a receptionist last week. Not only did she not get that job accomplished, but to make matters worse, over the weekend, she called and asked him not to fill the opening until she'd made up her mind if it was a position she might want to tackle. After all, it wouldn't be as demanding as that of his assistant.

Aggie studied him as if looking for a sign of lying. Then she shrugged. "My bad."

He snapped his mouth shut, pivoted, went back to his private office, and turned off the air for the receptionist area.

• • •

Aggie watched the great Max Treadwell stomp back to his office and shut the door with a defined *click*. His expression when she accused him of getting his last assistant pregnant had been priceless. For a moment, she thought she might have given him a heart attack. There was no way in hell he'd offer her the job now.

She scanned the personality quiz. *I'm in search of someone whose personality meshes with mine.* Jeez. She was applying to coddle to his office needs, not his heart needs.

She read the first question. Laughed. Read it again.

Explain zymology. Why did his assistant need to know the chemistry of fermentation? Did he have a side hustle making beer? Or did he want to assess if she was the *personality type* to have a beer with him after hours?

What is pneumonoultramicroscopicsilicovolcanokoniosis? Well, duh. It practically gave you the answer in the word itself. Who didn't know that the longest word in the English language was a name for a lung disease?

She rolled her shoulders and glanced at the next question. Another easy one.

Which letter of the alphabet is most often used to start words? Anyone who watched *Wheel of Fortune* knew it's the letter *S.*

The smirky bastard views me as brainless. She'd show him. *Blondes can kick trivia ass. Get ready for a rude awakening.*

If he truly needed an assistant with this type of knowledge, he'd be lucky to have the *Chosen One.* Meemaw had been stuffing Aggie full of odd facts since she'd been in kindergarten.

She looked around for a cooler spot to sit. This room was a lot hotter than his office. She walked to the air vent, but nothing came out, and there wasn't a temperature control on any of the walls.

"It takes a lot more than a little heat to beat Agnes Johansson." She grabbed several tissues out of a box on the desk, stuck them between her boobs where she always sweated first, and reclined onto the cold tile. With her back against the wall, she got busy.

She quickly made her way through the questions. Most of them were easy. A few were more thought provoking. Like questions number ninety-five, ninety-six, and ninety-seven. Until this point, she'd kept her answers beyond reproach, but these just begged for jazz hands.

What do you think about when you're alone in the car? *I remember things while I'm driving. Like this one time I was speeding down the highway on the back of a Harley, when the hum between my legs got to be too much. I unbuttoned the top button of the guy's jeans I was with and slipped my hand inside his boxers. You can tell a lot about a man in that kind of situation. I think about his erection a lot when I'm alone in a car.*

She chuckled. Let him squirm over that one. If he was going to make her sweat, she could make him do the same. That answer alone should keep him from offering her the job. She moved on to the next question.

What would your autobiography be called? *Reckless in the City.*

How would you describe yourself in three words? Fabulous. In. Bed.

Fifty-five minutes later, she knocked on Max's office door, ready to hand him all the ammo he needed not to offer her the position. Of course, by now, he should have already firmly made up his mind not to make the offer. Hell, she'd worn spiked heels to the interview.

If there was a part of her that kind of, sort of, maybe wanted a job that required this kind of knowledge, well… she just ignored it. She didn't take handouts. Not even job handouts.

• • •

Max's mood had deteriorated from amused to annoyed then pissed to damn right ready to strangle someone, and it was Aggie's fault. He had plenty of work to keep him busy, but her damn phone kept mooing every five minutes. After the third moo, he checked to see what in the hell all the farm noises were about. It was her sound choice for new text alerts. The sound choice of an adult delinquent. Curious, he read what he could see on the screen without opening her messages.

Tim: *Are we on for tonight?*

Bob: *Thinking of you.*

Bill: *Hey, do you want to ride my Harley later, or just me?*

After that one, he'd turned her damn phone facedown. But that didn't keep him from wondering how she'd reply to Bill. Which kept him from concentrating on the contract he was reviewing, which—

A firm knock pulled a curse out of him. "Come in." He glanced at the time on his computer. Fifty-five minutes. She couldn't possibly finish a two-hour test so quickly.

Aggie opened the door and stepped inside. She didn't appear flustered.

He frowned. "Did you need more time?"

"Nope." She strode over to him and handed him the survey. She'd removed her jacket, displaying a sleeveless dress.

"Have a seat while I check these." He glanced at the first question. Fuck. He didn't have a clue if she'd answered it right or not. He read the next, and the next, and the next. Hell. Were these personality questions or trivia questions? Did

Grant send him the wrong form?

He pulled up Grant's email and smiled when he discovered he'd attached an answer guide. Not wanting her to know he was checking her work against a key, he picked up her phone and held it out. She didn't notice. She was too busy...pulling tissues out of her pink lace bra and stuffing them in her purse.

He cleared his throat. "Before I forget, here's this. You've had a few thousand moos."

She laughed. "Sorry about that. I should've put it on silent."

There wasn't one apologetic bone in her distracting body.

She happily thumbed through the messages, stopping to laugh and reply to a few as he reviewed her responses. While she aced all the answers, he only fathomed about half. Her graduating in the bottom of her class had nothing to do with her brain.

He flipped to the last page and settled in to read her pink loopy script.

What would your pet say about you if we asked for a reference? *My human is puurrrfect as long as you don't expect her to procure you anything until she's fetched herself a cup of coffee.*

In other words, if he hired Aggie, he'd probably end up making and bringing her coffee instead of the other way around.

On a scale of one to ten, rate yourself on how weird you are? *Zero. I'm perfectly normal. Anything I do wrong has nothing to do with an abnormality in my personality and everything to do with my mood.*

A well-thought-out response. Mature.

How do you weigh an elephant without using a scale?

Max hissed in a breath. *What an asinine question.* He glanced at her response.

Calculate the volume of the water in the pool and make a note of the water level. Once you've got the elephant in the pool—good luck with that—the Archimedes' principle says the volume of water dislocated is the same as the object's weight.

What is the temperature when it's twice as cold as zero degrees? *Depends. Are you asking Fahrenheit or Celsius?*

Are your parents disappointed with your career aspirations? *I don't know my parents.*

Shit. He was playing dick-fuckery with an orphan. He shut down the guilt and moved to the next question.

Why is a manhole round? *Any other shape of a manhole cover could be moved in such a way that the cover would fall in. No one wants that to happen, because it would probably land on an important rat and kill it, and then PETA would get involved and there'd be protests, and the surviving gutter rats would get all worked up and invade the city to avenge the death of King Rat Face. The circular one can't fall in and it doesn't require exact placement and it's easy to move and roll out of the way.*

If you don't get this job, what is your back-up plan? *Blame you for being unrealistic in your expectations.*

He groaned and then smiled.

How would you describe the man who is interviewing you? *Cocky. Handsome in a pretty-boy way. Not my type. But I'm sure we'll mesh on a professional level.*

He'd bet his trust fund Grant added that question. The next time he saw the guy, he would kick his ass.

Not her type. He didn't ask to be her type. He glanced her way. She was clicking away on her phone with what he'd bet was a real smile stretched across her face. No doubt answering her messages.

He read the next question.

What do you think about when you're alone in the car?

By the time he finished reading her response, he was hot, hard, and horny. Now he knew her type. It really wasn't him. She went for the bad-boy brand. But God help him, at this moment, he wished he were. Which pissed him off, because he knew that's exactly what she'd meant to happen.

He shifted in his chair, trying to ease the discomfort of having a hard-on, and immediately felt her gaze on him. He stopped squirming and glanced up. They made eye contact. Contact that lasted longer than it should have. Her lavender eyes darkened a fraction, and she slowly licked her bottom lip. He shook his head, as if to tell her no, or himself no.

"How did I do?" She lifted a brow at him.

Time to pull out the big-dick guns. "I'm relieved to know I'm not your type. You're not my type, either."

She sat up straight. "I'm not?"

"Not enough drive. Too...casual." That part was true. He planned to take the world by its balls, and when he was ready for love, he'd need a strong woman by his side. Not someone known for quitting. Like his mom had.

"Whatever." Aggie flicked a piece of gummy bear off her dress, leaving it on his carpet where it landed.

He raised a brow. "Brain food of choice?"

"My man's breakfast food of choice." She bent forward to pick it up, giving him a clear view of her cleavage.

He gulped. Damn.

. . .

Aggie watched Max and waited. There was nothing left for them to say to each other except the one very important thing. *You'll be hearing from me.*

"One more question," he said in a voice that sounded forced, while twirling a pen between his fingers. "Are you willing to work evenings and weekends? Is there anything, short of getting naked or illegal activity, you would not be willing to do?"

There was something going on with him. Something she couldn't put her finger on. Yet.

"Well?" He sounded annoyed. With himself.

She squared her shoulders and stared straight into his slate-gray eyes. The color of a moody, moonless night. This was her last chance to prove to him she did not fit his needs. "I'll do anything to make this job work, short of robbing a bank, lying to old ladies, or blowing you." That should seal the no-deal spiel.

He dropped the ink pen.

It took everything inside of her not to laugh. His expression was priceless. "I'm sorry," she said in her best contrite voice. "I didn't mean to say that last part." She reached for her purse and was about to stand when he made a noise. She glanced up and caught his lips twitching. The guy was trying to be a gentleman. How sweet.

"I can live with those terms." He wiped at his eyes.

He had a nice face. Not nearly as uptight as most of the words that came out of him. Maybe he was slightly good-looking...in a handsome-and-he-knows-it kinda way. She raised her chin, waiting for the punchline. None came. Realization seeped in.

Are you freaking kidding me? "You can?"

He nodded. "I'm impressed with how you conduct yourself under pressure. The job is yours. For the next two months."

Noooooooo. "With benefits?"

His eyes widened. "With benefits."

She sighed internally. A deal was a deal. Meemaw would be happy. "I'll need you to put that in writing."

The nostrils of his arrogant nose flared. "You need a contract for a two-month position?"

"I do." She'd not lasted that long anywhere since graduating from college. She'd done her best not to get hired here, but since that failed, she had to go all in to make Meemaw proud. Hopefully, a contract would solve her quitting problem.

Chapter Three

An hour after the interview from hell, Max sat in his car at a job site and released a long, slow breath. All the tension in his muscles started draining away. He liked to spend his days out of the office and in the thick of things. He lowered the window to catch a breeze, grabbed his cell, and called Grandmother while he waited for his client to arrive. As soon as she answered, he got to the point of the conversation.

"You'll be happy to know I've hired Aggie to be my assistant." And given her a contract and benefits that included a five-hundred-dollar IRA fund.

"Why, of course you did, darling. And I'm so happy she invited you to call her Aggie instead of Agnes. She's perfect for you." Her tone implied she meant the statement in a much more personal manner.

He let the insinuation slide. "She's on a one-week trial. I need to determine if she's capable of keeping up with my hectic work pace." A white lie meant to minimize the amount of gloating he'd have to listen to from Grandmother. Why had he agreed to an actual two-month contract?

Hell. He knew why.

The minute Aggie said "blow job," his brain had exploded like a firecracker tent hit by lightning. At that moment, she could have asked for him to wear nothing but boxers and stilettos into his and Grant's favorite lounge and he would have said yes.

"It wouldn't hurt you to slow down and smell something other than money," Grandmother said. "Like roses, or orchids, or a woman's perfume."

Oh, he'd smelled a woman's perfume. Aggie's. Soft with a hint of Satan's seduction. "Considering I'm allergic to roses, that's probably not the best suggestion you've ever made."

"Aren't you still taking shots for all of your allergies?"

He saw his client's car pull into the parking area. "I quit once I turned eighteen and had control over my environment."

Growing up, his dad had insisted on keeping bouquets of roses in the foyer despite how allergic Max had been to them. *No boy of his was going to have a girly weakness.* The only area Dad had given him an inch was his plan to bring a cat home and cure Max of that particular allergy.

"It gives me a reason to avoid going to Dad's penthouse."

She harrumphed loudly. "Ever since you and your father made that angry bet, you've been nothing but business. It's not healthy."

Time to cut the call off. "I'm not all business. I met Grant just last night for drinks. Listen, I have a client waiting on me."

"And I'll wager the two of you talked business after your rebound drinks."

"Unwind drinks, and you'd be wrong. Grandmother, I really need to go."

"I am not done talking to you, young man. When was the last time you took a woman out for more than one date?"

Not this again. "When was the last time you accepted a

man's invitation to go out on a second date?" He waved at his client who'd gotten out of his car and now waited on him.

"You can't answer a question with a question." She spoke in a hushed tone, which meant she must be in a public setting. Grandmother believed firmly that people shouldn't talk on their phone for all to hear. He was surprised she had taken his call at all. If Ms. Manners had a sidekick, it would be Grandmother.

"Why can't I?" He held up a finger to his client.

"Because there are rules of etiquette when it comes to carrying on a polite conversation. Do you not recall any of what you learned from that finishing school your dad sent you to?"

He closed his eyes and took a breath. *The Art of Being a Gentleman* had been one of those last-minute additions Dad put on his schedule. Which prevented Mom from getting Max during the entire month of July. "I remember what I want to remember." He remembered being pissed Mom didn't tell Dad to reschedule.

"Well, I would hope you'd want to remember how to carry on a titillating conversation. You're never going to find a woman to fall in love with if you're lacking in manners."

"Since I don't plan on falling in love until I'm thirty-five, I'd say I have plenty of time to brush up on my etiquette between now and then."

"Thirty-five? That's almost five years from now." Her voice now at an everyone-can-hear-you level.

She meant well, but that didn't keep him from stiffening at her command. As a minor, he hadn't had control over his life, but as an adult he did. What others viewed as a rigid personality, he saw as peace of mind. "I'll be fine. I promise."

An image of Aggie popped into his head. He shook it off.

When he did get around to marriage, it would *not* be with someone like Aggie or his mother. It would be with someone known for following through on their commitments, not quitting when the going got rough. Not that he blamed his mom for quitting on his dad. The man was an ass. But Max did blame her for quitting on her son.

His client tapped his watch. "Grandmother—"

"Darling, Hazel just arrived. I must disconnect. It's rude to keep a person waiting."

Before he could say "goodbye," or "wait a minute," or "when exactly can I expect your decision regarding my unfilled receptionist position," the phone went dead. He stared at it in bemusement. Ms. Hazel was Aggie's Meemaw. If the two hadn't already met for coffee this morning, why had Grandmother rushed off earlier? She could have easily stayed and answered the phones while he interviewed Aggie.

Shaking off the thought, he got out of the car. Time to beat his father at his own low-handed game.

Chapter Four

Aggie jumped in her car, cranked up the air, and called Meemaw. Her insides hummed with giddy satisfaction and nerves and dismay. Mr. Dick-in-the-Mud had actually offered her a job after everything she did to stop him. Her clownish makeup, her inappropriate attire, and her off-the-wall comments would have given Meemaw the shakes.

In what world did that happen? Not hers. Only it did. And now that she'd had a few minutes to let it sink in, she wasn't devastated. How could she be when she now had the start to a retirement fund? Of course, the money wouldn't go into the fund until she'd successfully completed her two months with him. But the contract should make sure that happened.

"I got the job," she said when Meemaw answered. Her words came out loud like a drunk at a funeral.

"Bless your heart, of course you did." Meemaw had the prettiest Southern drawl when it suited her needs. The woman was not from the South. And she always misused the term *bless your heart*. "I told you not to fret. Tell me all about what he's like in person, and don't leave any detail out."

Aggie took a long, calming breath. "You mean tell you about the job description."

Meemaw knew better than most that men who were born with a silver spoon clutched in their privileged hand mostly believed themselves to be out of league from girls who lived on the wrong side of the tracks. Aggie knew those men were wrong. It was she who was out of their league. Or at least, that's what she told herself during her rare moments of self-affirmation practice.

Only problem was Meemaw, thanks to Max's grandmother, believed the world had changed since her own across-the-tracks love affair that ended with a baby and no husband. Ms. Grace assured her the attitudes of today's young and rich had evolved past Meemaw's ridiculous notion. Especially where Max was concerned.

"Sure, you can tell me about the job, too," Meemaw cackled. The laugh she always belted out when filled with joy. Which was very seldom, so when it happened, it made Aggie happy. "But tell me first, is he as handsome in person as he is in the photos I've seen?"

"He's not ugly, but he is pompous. And more rigid than a dead man's hard-on." To be fair, that part wasn't quite true. He had smothered a laugh over her blow job comment. Which had been a pleasant surprise. But Meemaw didn't need to know about that. "And he comes to work smelling like an expensive ad for a night out."

"What in tarnation is wrong with a good-smelling man?" Tarnation was one of Meemaw's favorite cuss words when flabbergasted. Otherwise, she'd strive to use five-dollar words. Words meant to protect her from ever again being called lower than dirt by another living soul.

"Nothing, other than it's a red flag that he hits the bars right after work, trolling for women."

"Agnes Johansson, I've never known you to utter such

gobbledygook. I raised you to be smarter. I think Maxi's got you all in a dither, or you're trying to throw me off my bone."

Despite herself, Aggie grinned, remembering his face when she called him Maxi. "What bone would that be?"

"You know exactly what bone that would be, smarty pants." The Southern drawl had lost its charm.

A hefty twinge of guilt over saying something that took some of the happy out of Meemaw's day tried to squeeze through the cracks of Aggie's conscience. Luckily, its plump ass got stuck before it could do any damage, and she held firm on the need to squelch Meemaw's romance angle. It was for the best.

Meemaw sighed. "Tell me about the job."

"I think I'm going to like it." The truth lurched out before Aggie contemplated the pros and cons of admitting that. She floundered for a moment then recovered. "That is if he doesn't ruin it by injecting his personality into my duties."

"Interesting. I don't remember you ever mentioning liking any of the other jobs you've held this year. That's a sure sign you connected with your new boss."

"Meemaw, please don't read something into nothing. He was born into money. What could we possibly have in common besides the paycheck he signs and I deposit?" This was a two-month job. Not her life's career. Or the beginning of a beautiful love story.

"Honey, I've got to get back to work," Meemaw said, "but before I go, I want you to listen to me and listen good. I've told you that times are changing. You've got a real shot with someone like him."

Aggie knew that wasn't true, but for the first time she could remember, she found herself wondering what if it was? What if men like him no longer thought her inferior because she was the bastard child of a bastard mom?

Chapter Five

Tuesday morning, Aggie arrived at work at exactly eight o'clock. Not an easy task for a night person. What she wouldn't give for a job starting at noon and ending before rush hour traffic jams. She stifled a yawn.

"Good morning," she said to Max.

Max had already removed his tie and draped it over the edge of his desk, unbuttoned the top two buttons of his shirt, and rolled up the sleeves. A guy ready to get down to business, and not in the fun way.

While she waited for him to acknowledge her existence, she drank in the man-skin on display. Nice forearms with sexy, sinewy muscle threads. The sight pulled a soft sigh of pure female appreciation from between her lips. Her gaze continued to linger there as she pondered another place he might have a sinewy male part. Would it be as impressive? She yanked her mind back from the gutter and shifted her gaze to his wrist. Shock of all shocks, the guy had a tattoo. It looked like a date.

"Good morning." Thank God the greeting didn't come

with eye contact, or he would have noticed her yanking at her blouse to allow cool air on her body. Instead, a blueprint spread out on his desk held his attention.

Two minutes later, she cleared her throat, reminding him she still existed.

"Oh. Yes. Right. Why don't you have a seat at the desk in the outer office?" Still no eye contact. "I've left papers there for you to fill out. Tax withholding, insurance, non-compete agreement."

Non-compete? Intriguing. None of her previous jobs required one of those. "What would I compete with you in?" She shifted her purse to her other shoulder. She should clean it out. Lighten the load. But one never knew when one might need a hammer.

He sighed and rested his clasped hands on his desk. Their gazes clashed. His eyes appeared to darken right before his gaze skimmed down. He lingered on her pink blouse. She'd buttoned it all the way to the neck, because Meemaw insisted Aggie appear as highfalutin' as the women she'd heard Max liked to be seen with at the fanciest of restaurants in town.

Aggie's stomach tightened.

His gaze shifted onto her black pencil skirt, her pink high heels with sassy bows on the back straps, before making an upward journey to her face. Today her makeup was as subtle as her outfit. All of this occurred with the slowness of a lover's hand. She'd been ogled by plenty of men in her life, but none of them left her feeling...hopeful.

Did he like what he saw? Professional enough? She'd left her hair down. It was straight and boring. She'd long ago given up any hope of it holding a curl. Maybe she should have twisted her locks into a spinster bun again and this time left tempting wisps around her jawline. A combination of 99 percent hardcore career girl and one percent flirt, the flirt part to remind him, and herself, that even though she was *beneath* his social and economic standards, she could still get a man like him. If only short-term.

"You'll learn many of my secrets. I don't want you to run to one of my competitors when you're done working for me and trade them for a job."

What a first-class pompous ass. "I've actually found trading sex for a job is the most efficient way of obtaining one." The words popped out and couldn't be unpopped. Not that she wanted to. He'd hired her knowing her mouth was a loose cannon, no reason not to continue to let fly the wayward side of herself. At least until he chilled a degree or a hundred.

"What?" He sounded like his airway had collapsed.

She sighed. Then again, eight weeks was a long time, and Meemaw really liked Ms. Grace. "I'm teasing." She set her bag on the corner of his desk. "If I have to sign one, then I see no reason you shouldn't have to sign a non-compete for me. I can't have you teaching your permanent assistant, once she returns, everything I do that leaves your mind royally blown."

His eyes narrowed on the word blown.

"My methods are copyright protected." She smiled blandly.

"What?"

While he had an excellent poker face in place, his Minnie Mouse voice gave him away. *He freaking believes I've copyrighted my blow job technique.* Heat crept into her body. Not in her cheeks. Between her legs. Which just went to prove she wasn't his type of woman. A well-bred woman wouldn't get excited so easily. Or at all. She warred with the desire to let him believe what he thought and her drive to make Meemaw proud.

Pleasing Meemaw won.

"I'm talking about the techniques I use to wow your potential clients. With my words. Not my mouth. Well, with my mouth but—"

His cheeks took on a red tint. "I didn't…you don't…"

When nothing else came out of his mouth, she said, "I missed that last part. You were saying…"

He groaned. "Fair enough. I'll sign a non-compete agreement for you."

She unbuttoned the top buttons of her blouse so she could breathe. Teasing him seemed to impact her own airway. "After I've finished with the paperwork, what is my first task?" She picked up her purse and strode to the door, ready to get out of his office and consume her stash of emergency, nerve-soothing chocolate. She never started a job without a fresh supply. Usually, when it was gone, she was gone. Not because the chocolate was gone, but just because, weirdly, the two events usually timed out to happen simultaneously. But not this job. This job she'd signed a contract.

He leaned back in his chair and crossed his legs at the ankles. "You're going to make over my offices. Give them a facelift. You'll need to hire a decorator, and they will report directly to you."

"How fun." She'd completely expected him to give her the most boring task possible in the hopes she'd quit. Maybe she'd been too quick to judge. "Thank you for trusting me with this undertaking."

He moved a stapler a few inches to the left and then back to its original position. "There's a catch."

She leaned against the doorframe. "There always is."

He sat up straight and glanced around his office. "I have several important meetings next week. One has a lot of potential. Everything about Treadwell Properties has to wow him. That includes not just my proposal but the appearance of my offices. Therefore, you need to do an excellent job and finish it before Friday at closing."

For an average assistant, that probably would be considered an awful catch. Lucky for him, she wasn't average.

"This is your lucky day. I'm an Amazon Prime member, so I can get one-day delivery on what I purchase. Which will help make this impossible assignment possible. Of course, I will need to enter your credit card in my account as a payment option. Did you see on my Aggie's Assets that I'm a decorator? Or at least I was one for a time."

He picked up his stapler. "If you recall, you didn't bring that with you to the interview, so no, I didn't know you were a decorator for *a time*."

She waited for him to make eye contact and then gave him her get-out-of-jail-free grin. "It was one of my many jobs over the past year. Trust me, I may not have been in the position long, but I learned scads while there." Her boss had been in the midst of a breakup with his boyfriend. The breakup had been ugly, and her boss could barely function. As a result, Aggie had been given a crash course on how to do what he'd spent years learning and then told to do it. She'd really liked that boss. Too bad he'd ended up going out of business.

"Be that as it may..." Max dropped the stapler on his desk and picked up the pencil. "I prefer you hire a professional decorator." His pompous-ass voice was back. "One with more than a few weeks' experience to help you in your decision-making process. Offer to pay them extra to make up for the rush of the assignment."

"Do I get paid extra for the rush part?"

"You do not."

. . .

Max watched Aggie glide to her desk. Her hips swayed hypnotically, and her gorgeous hair swished to the beat, begging him to get up and run his fingers through the thick strands, tugging them until her head tilted back and he had a clear shot at dropping hot, lingering kisses along her slender neckline. *Christ*. He had to get a grip or the next two months would be one long, cold shower. He buzzed her on their intercom. "You forgot to shut the door."

He told himself to get back to work. Instead, he watched as she came back to his door, shot him a scowl, and shut it with a firm *click*. He chuckled. She clearly believed he should close his own damn door.

About ten minutes later, Aggie asked, "How are your legs?" She spoke to him through the walls.

What a strange question. He picked up the phone and pushed the intercom button. He refused to have a conversation between the walls. Mom taught him at a young age if an individual couldn't hear you with your inside voice, you moved closer. "They're fine."

"I'm ordering two desks," Aggie said loudly.

That did not explain wanting to know how his legs were. He once again pushed the intercom button. "Please use the intercom."

A squeaking noise came over the intercom, causing him to wince.

"Mine's broken," she yelled. "Anyway, your desk will be fancier than the other, but they'll match. Is that okay?"

That's right. Grandmother had mentioned spilling her coffee the other morning and how some of it might have gotten on the phone. *Might my ass*. He glanced at the wall between him and Aggie. Imagined her sitting on the other side and how her tight skirt would have ridden up on her legs, showing off their breathtaking length. Hell. At least today's skirt covered her knees, and he much preferred today's choice of neutral eyeshadow. He considered his options.

One, ask her to come and have the conversation with him face-to-face. If he did, he'd get no work done.

Two, boorishly answer through the walls. No matter which choice he went with, the actual answer to her question wasn't an answer he wanted to commit to. But…it had to be said. "Make that three desks?"

Silence.

Did she leave?

Where did she go?

Did she slip out for a—

His office door opened, and Aggie stood there holding a tape measure. "I just measured, and the reception area doesn't have space for a second desk along with all the file cabinets and the coffee bar I plan to add. Where shall I put the spare desk?"

Of course she had a tape measure. "Two of the desks will go in here. One for me and one for my assistant. One desk will go in the outer office for the receptionist." Be that his grandmother or someone else. With every word he spoke, he had the gut-clenching feeling of losing control over his life. Personally and professionally. "Once I hire a receptionist, you will have a desk in my office." He wiped his palms on his slacks. "It's not an ideal situation, but it is what it is until I'm able to obtain what I'm looking for in office space."

Aggie leaned against the frame and folded slim arms under her ample breasts. "*Your* office space is *my* office space?" Did she mean to look so damn sexy?

His groin thickened. He ruthlessly reminded both of his heads of the details of last month's workplace sexual harassment case Grant had regaled him with over drinks. After hearing the sordid details, Max knew there wasn't any way in hell he should ever allow himself to get involved with an assistant. "You'll have a desk. Nothing more."

She glanced at the wall of windows. At the space next to his desk where a low table sat with a wobbly stack of rocks as its centerpiece.

He'd thought about having the rocks cemented together but hated to lose the ability to pick one up when in the mood to reminisce about a dear deceased friend.

"Where will my desk go?" she asked.

He pointed to the corner farthest from him. A corner that his back faced. "Over there. In the empty spot." Which, to be fair, was also where his permanent assistant's desk used to sit. He'd had her clean it out before going on maternity leave and promised her a shiny new one when she returned, along with an eventual office of her own. He was working on that. But the space he wanted to buy had yet to come on the market.

Aggie pondered the spot. She tilted her head left and right and far right. Then she straightened and gave him a charming smile. "That's the most boring spot in your office. Be a peach and let me put it where the table is."

"Not there."

"But—"

He rubbed the tattoo on his wrist. "Please close the door on your way to the reception area." He didn't need to explain to her the importance of the rocks. "And please, no more conversations through the wall. Call and get an order in to have your intercom fixed."

He glanced back at the rocks. Gifts from Mandy. Growing up, her family lived on one side of his family home. On the other side lived Grant and his family.

In sixth grade, Grant, Max, and Mandy started a band and called themselves The Three Rocks Stars. They played at middle school parties.

Their junior year in high school, Grant fell in love with Mandy. Out of fear it would ruin their friendship if she didn't return his feelings, Max talked Grant out of telling her. Unbeknownst to Max, the next day, Mandy told Grant she'd fallen in love with Max. Grant gave her the same argument Max gave him. She also didn't declare her love.

When they graduated, Mandy wanted to travel and see

the world, so she enlisted in the Marines. Every new place she went, she'd send Grant and Max a rock.

Those gifts stopped coming three years ago when Mandy died from a roadside bomb. After her funeral, they got drunk and had the date of Mandy's death tattooed onto their wrists.

"I really don't get a sense of style from your current furnishings," Aggie mused. "They're generic. Tell me, are you looking for modern like me, or vintage like our grandmothers, or stuffy like...you?"

He stiffened but didn't comment on the insult. She was cheekier than a Kardashian ass.

She raised her eyebrows, reminding him he hadn't answered. He seemed to forget to answer a lot around her.

"Something that will speak to my clients. Make them aware I have my finger on the pulse of the future. Someone who can provide them with exactly what they need before they know they have the need."

"What is it you do?"

Most potential job candidates would have discovered that before sitting down for an interview. Aggie was not like most...in more ways than just that. "I repurpose property."

Her eyes lit up. "That sounds deliciously sketchy. Give me the deets."

He jerked. If sketchy was what got her all hot and bothered, he wouldn't have to worry about a work affair. That thought should have soothed him. It didn't. "There's nothing sketchy about what I do." Did she do sketchy things with Bill the Harley guy?

"Oh." The spark left her eyes. "Tell me in layman's terms what it is you do."

"Last year, I bought a grain silo in the downtown area. I repurposed it into lofts and left the bottom floor equipped for a business. Then I sold the property to a young entrepreneur."

"Oh. You're a flipper."

"Mostly. But there are times, the land—along with my idea for how it could be repurposed—is sold 'as is,' and the new owner brings it to fruition," he said. "The entrepreneur I sold the silo to turned the first floor into a wine bar."

A spark of interest returned to her eyes. "I know the place. Love going there. Or at least I did until Meemaw decided it was her new hangout."

"I believe Ms. Hazel and Grandmother met there for drinks last night." He chuckled. "My source tells me they were celebrating us working together."

"Those two," Aggie said, her tone implying she thought they were a handful.

He nodded. "Those two."

Glancing back at his rock garden, she said, "Did you know artists have used the colors held inside some rocks for thousands of years?"

The comment reminded him of her answers on the test. "I didn't." How many unusual facts did she have stuffed inside her brain? "How does it work?"

"Artists would crack them open and used their powder for painting. For example, the mineral rock called cinnabar has a brilliant red center. They used its powder for painting religious art in the Middle Ages." Her eyes caught a twinkle. "I have a hammer in my purse. Let's crack one of yours open and we can see for ourselves."

He blanched. "We should probably get back to work, but if I ever find myself in the mood to paint and have none, that information will come in handy."

She lifted a shoulder. "Too bad. It would have helped me justify carrying my hammer in my purse. Marie Kondo, you know who she is…don't you?"

He shook his head.

"Oh. Well. She's this famous decluttering expert. Anyway, she advises if something doesn't still give you joy, you should get rid of it." She tilted her chin up a fraction. "Between you and me, my hammer hasn't brought me joy since I got drunk and cracked a guy's knuckles with it."

"You cracked a guy's knuckles with a hammer you carry in your purse?"

"When you say it that way, you make it sound weird. But it wasn't. We were in a bar, he groped my ass without asking, I hit his knuckles without asking."

He laughed. "That sounds more than fair." He was willing to bet none of the women he'd ever dated would ever consider cracking a guy's knuckles with a hammer.

"Unfortunately, the judge didn't agree, and I had to pay his medical bills."

"The ass groped you and then sued you for medical bills?" That sounded like one of Grant's bizarre court cases.

She perched on the corner of his desk. Leaned toward him. "I prefer not to dwell on that matter."

His skin heated and a desire to reach across his desk and touch her grabbed him by the nuts. "About your assignment."

She straightened and tucked a strand of hair behind her ear. "Just to be clear, you want your office to shout to potential clients you have your thumb on the pulse of possibilities and you, the great one, can see in property what others can't even imagine?"

He was fairly certain the term *great one* had been a dig at his personality. "Can you make that happen?"

"Is my favorite color pink?" she quipped, removing her cute ass from his desk.

Images of her pink bra careened across his brain like an out-of-control train. "I have no idea what your favorite color is." He had a sudden desire to know the color of her panties.

Her eyebrows shot up. "Did you forget already? I told you my favorite color at my interview." She shook her head in disbelief. "It's pink. Are you okay with me donating the furniture I don't keep to charity?"

He nodded, impressed she hadn't asked to sell it on eBay and keep the profits to pay the groper's medical bills. Perhaps underneath all of her flippant—

Her phone mooed, and she pulled it out of the waistband of her skirt. She sent a text and then glanced up at Max, a large grin on her face. Different from the other smiles he'd pulled out of her so far.

He didn't know who the text went to, but he wanted to elicit that kind of high-wattage smile out of her for him. For something he said. Who had been the lucky recipient? Tim, Bob, or Bill the Harley driver? He fucking hated Bill the Harley driver.

She stuck her phone back in her waistband. "On it, boss man."

Chapter Six

Wednesday late morning, Aggie stood in the middle of the outer office and surveyed the controlled chaos. She couldn't remember the last time she'd had so much fun on the job. Being given carte blanche on her task to refurnish the offices left her giddy. She didn't normally do giddy. Cynical was more her style. In that way, she and Max were a lot alike.

This morning, they delivered the new standing desks. This afternoon, everything else. She'd banned Max from the office until further notice. She wanted everything to be a surprise.

He had grumpily agreed, but only after he informed her in his uptight voice he had several parcels of land and old buildings to check in person and now would be as good a time as any to take care of the matter.

While he did his thing, she'd transformed their offices into something you might find at Apple or Warby Parker. Very current. It turned out magnificently—if she did say so herself. Meemaw would be pleased.

Aggie had painted the outer office walls a pale gray, and

a matching rug covered the floor. A faux fireplace now sat flush against the back wall, and on either side were cabinets for all of their files. Two royal blue ottomans sat in front of the fireplace, and two matching plush chairs sat on one side of a coffee table. On the wall opposite of the chairs, she'd put the coffee bar, complete with state-of-the-art coffeemaker, grinder, and mini-fridge.

The receptionist desk, a large white rectangle on funky legs, could be raised to allow for standing and working. On the other side were two square chairs in a gorgeous shade of red.

In Max's office, she'd painted the walls a dark shade of gray. His desk was black and hers a lighter shade of gray. Her desk, because of space limitation, was about half the size of his. Both could be raised or lowered.

The new furnishings for the sitting area hadn't yet arrived. They'd come tomorrow. She couldn't wait to get them all in place. The *crème de la crème* piece for the sitting area would be a gorgeous white leather couch. It would go in the space currently hosting his lackluster rock garden. Across from it, she would place two module chairs that shouted a modern-day man works in this office. She'd modeled his area off of a picture she'd found on Google of what Apple's offices looked like.

She couldn't wait to see his reaction when it was complete. She grabbed her phone and called him.

"Hello." His phone voice gave her a delicious shiver. It was like he'd forgotten to add the thread of disdain he normally added when talking to her. The result...yummy.

"Hi, it's me. Aggie." Did he know her voice without her telling him? Did she sound stupid announcing herself? It's not like he didn't have caller I.D. Of course, he probably didn't even have her cell number in his phone. She really should get her asset sheet to him. He'd asked for it a couple of times now.

Next time, she'd just say hi.

"What can I do for you?"

She twirled a strand of hair around her finger. "Did I get you at a bad time?" What just happened to her voice? She didn't do coy. "I can call back?"

"Now will do." And there it was. His normal voice.

She let go of the strand of hair. He really wasn't her type. "I'm calling to remind you not to come back to the offices until given the green light."

"I made no promises."

"Do you take pleasure in being difficult?"

"I take pleasure in being the boss. The one who gets to make the rules, not follow the rules."

The UPS guy showed up in the doorway. His name was Smith. She waved at him. "Oops, got to go. There's a hunk flexing his arm muscles here to see me."

"Does the hunk have a name?" If Aggie weren't so attuned to Max's normal voice, she might not have picked up on the thread of jealousy. But she did. Weird.

She glanced at Smith. He'd heard the question, because she had Max on her cell's speakerphone. "He does." She winked at Smith and placed a shushing finger to her lips. "It's Bill." Who knew mentioning Bill on the interview questionnaire would come in handy later? She clicked off before Max could make a public response and quickly explained to Smith she was messing with her boss.

Too late, she remembered her decision this morning to start behaving 100 percent respectable instead of continuing to yank Max's chain. She had decided to let some other woman teach him how to loosen up and have fun. Part of the reason for this decision was to make Meemaw proud, but not all of it. While she could and would—if challenged—defend her career impacting choices over the last eighteen months, she had realized she'd gotten into something of a bad habit.

Perhaps pulling the quit trigger a tad prematurely.

She wasn't going to do that this time. She would prove to Meemaw and herself that she did have it in her to see something through. The good. The bad. And the grumpy.

Chapter Seven

Max stared at his phone. Aggie had disconnected before he got to ask why Bill showed up during her work hours. As a result, he had an uncharacteristic urge to break someone's nose. Bill's in particular. A guy he'd never fucking met.

He put his phone away and glanced around at the crowded restaurant. If he hadn't already ordered, he'd leave and surprise Aggie with an unscheduled drop-in at the office. Had Bill stopped by to take her to lunch or take her on her desk? He knew, for a fact, which he'd be doing if Aggie was his girl.

Damn Aggie and her...ability to get under his skin?

While waiting on his food, he turned his attention to all he'd accomplished today. Luck had been on his side. The property connecting with the land he'd purchased several years ago had gone on the market today, and he'd snatched it before his competitors could blink.

This purchase put him in the perfect position for winning the bid with O'Reilly Hospitality. They'd announced in January they were taking bids on potential new areas for a project. They needed a one-mile-square radius of land that would house a boutique hotel and several clothing shops.

A set of old college dorms occupied a couple of the acres Max had just purchased. They could be refurbished and then pitched to O'Reilly Hospitality as an opportunity to offer guests a unique hotel experience, an experience allowing them to leave a smaller carbon footprint. Young people today fretted about the environment like old people fretted about the manners of *today's* generation.

He had Aggie to thank for this deal. If she hadn't pushed him out of the office, he would have never driven around and discovered it went up for sale today. The spitfire might end up being his good-luck charm instead of his death bell.

Of course, he'd have to work overtime to put a winning proposal together by the quickly approaching deadline. Which meant spending more time with her. He would need her help. He glanced at his watch. One fifteen.

He could go home and work from there. Or, Bill aside, he could drop by and check Aggie's progress on the redecorating of his offices. Make sure his walls weren't now her favorite shade of pink. Not to see if Bill was there.

One hour later, Max stood in the hall doorway of his outer office and stared. The smell of paint, which tickled his nose the moment he stepped off the elevator, turned pungent, causing his eyes to water. Eyes astounded by a room full of color.

Music came from his office, and Aggie sang offkey along with some country song. Funny, he wouldn't have pegged her for a country girl. He refocused on the outer office. The woman was full of surprises.

To be honest, he didn't know what he'd expected, but not this. Certainly pink. But not this. Not only had Aggie met his expectations, but she had also far surpassed them. Which was hard to do.

She must have hired an expert.

Aggie walked through his office door and squealed. "What the hell, boss man?"

"I wrapped things up quicker than I planned."

She frowned and pushed at the strands of hair coming loose from her ponytail. From the smears of gray paint on her face, she must have done that more than once today while painting.

"This was supposed to be a surprise."

"I am surprised." He waved a hand at the reception area. "It's a bold color choice. I like it." It impressed the hell out of him she'd done the painting herself. It could have easily been contracted out.

Uncertainty crept into her eyes. "Are you just saying that to be nice?"

"I never say something I don't mean. I take it you hired a decorator." He stepped toward his office door, and she met him halfway, blocking his access.

"You can't go in there. Your office is a work in progress. All the furniture hasn't arrived."

He sidestepped around her, but she blocked him again. He raised an eyebrow. He had no intention of trying to outwit her next move to get into his own damn office. "Let me be perfectly clear. I am going in there. All I need is a desk. Do I have a desk?"

Her lips pinched together. Then she stepped aside. "Fine. Spoil the surprise. And remember, you gave me carte blanche."

His gut twisted. *Here comes the pink*. He stepped into his office. Stopped, stared, and shoved his hands in his pockets. Plastic covered the floors. Paint brushes were propped on cans of paint. The walls were a rich shade of gray. *Nice choice*. He glanced at his desk. Also covered in plastic, but from what he could tell, there was a problem with the desk.

It didn't adhere to the standards of an executive's desk. More like a tabletop with weird legs. A lot like the one in the reception area, but larger and a different color. It would have to go back. "This room is coming along nicely. It appears to be mostly done." *Whenever you're about to disappoint someone, start with a positive.*

She shook her head like he was an idiot. "Far from it. I'm still waiting for furniture for your sitting area. And the pictures need to be hung, and—"

"I stand corrected." He removed the plastic from the strange desk. Tried to look at it with an open mind.

"Speaking of standing," she said, picking up a remote from his desk and handing it to him, "your desk is a standing desk."

"A what?"

"A standing desk. You can stand to work instead of always sitting. It's good for you. The boss at Google has one just like this one. Same color and all."

"And you know this how?"

"I Googled it."

"I see." He seriously doubted the CEO of Google had a desk like this. Max gave Aggie a bad-news-is-about-to-come softening smile. "I like how you did your research and colored outside of the box with this idea."

"Thank you."

He pressed on. "But I prefer a more traditional desk. One with drawers and a—"

She moved her hands behind her back and lifted her chin. He was beginning to realize that chin of hers might be the window into her soul. Or at least her emotions. Different angles meant different things.

Like right now, it meant hurt.

"Why didn't you point this out before I bought desks? Before I designed a room around these desks?" And to prove his deduction, her voice wobbled, like the words surfed out of her throat on a wave of tears.

He hated tears. Mother cried a lot when he was a kid. Not that she knew he could hear her through his bedroom wall. "Can't you have it exchanged? I love everything else you've done."

"If I return yours, I must return mine." She pointed to the other desk in the room. "And I like mine." Hers was the same design but smaller.

"Yours can stay."

She rolled her eyes. "Our desks have to be similar or it will look like an amateur did this room."

Hell. He couldn't let her emotions dictate what he wanted her to accomplish with this task. "Then exchange both of the desks. I'm sure my real assistant will be fine with a normal desk."

As if he'd slapped her, she jerked.

"What? What did I say? Why are you making this so difficult?" His words came out gruffer than he intended. He blamed it on memories of his mom crying.

"Your *real* assistant has just had a baby. She's at risk of having blood clots if she sits for too long. A standing desk is good for her health. Believe it or not, I thought about your *real* assistant when I chose standing desks."

He ran a hand through his hair. She had a point. "The desks can stay. But I'll need filing cabinets and drawers, and—"

She placed her hands on her hips and tapped her bare foot. "I told you, your office isn't done. I, obviously, have all of those things ordered. Why don't you take whatever it is you need and leave so I can get back to doing what you're paying me to do?"

He didn't want to leave. He wanted to sit right here in his office and watch her do whatever in the hell she was doing in those damn short-shorts. Which made him a first-class creep. How old was he...thirteen? Damn it. He dragged his eyes away from her legs. "Any calls?"

"Ms. Grace called. She said to tell you she has a fun idea for the two of you to do together."

Hopefully, not some weird double date she'd concocted as a result of Meemaw's influence in her life.

"Funny enough, Meemaw left the same message for me on my phone."

"Fuck," he said. "Should we be worried?"

Chapter Eight

Aggie stared at Max. "I'm not worried. Meemaw loves to come up with fun surprise ideas for me." Of course, she *was* worried, but he didn't need to know that.

"You're not worried that they're trying to throw us together?"

She shook her head. "Meemaw knows you're not my type." This caused him to scowl, but he let the comment stand. "Shall we get back to the desk fiasco?" No surprise he didn't like the desk. It required a certain amount of coolness to see the fun of a standing one. Well, he'd asked for something to impress his clients, and these desks would impress clients.

These days, you couldn't just sell a great product or service, you also had to be green, into a healthy lifestyle, and a visionary of what today's youth would want in tomorrow's markets.

"It's no longer a fiasco. I caved and said they could stay."

"Touché." That was not boss-man-like of him. She wasn't sure how to process the information. "You should leave. The paint fumes will make you lightheaded." She bent down to pick up her white face mask and slipped it over her face.

His long legs carried him swiftly to his temporary desk. "Where's my Rolodex? I need a number."

She lowered the mask and eyeballed him. A vein had appeared in his forehead. It hadn't been there a few moments ago. "Your what?" Was he about to pop a gasket?

"The thing on my desk holding all my phone numbers?"

"Oh. I tossed it. Not worth giving to charity. No one, and I mean NO one, uses those anymore." She'd have to ask Meemaw if she'd used a Rolodex back in the old days.

"I do." The vein turned a bruised-blue color. "It belonged to my grandfather."

"Then put it in a memory box where it belongs and move your office practices into this century." According to the stubbornness in his eyes staring back at her, he didn't give two flips about her suggestion. "You really don't care if customers call you an ol' fuddy duddy behind your back?"

He gave her a lackluster smile. The kind you give the checkout lady at the grocery store when they ask if you're having a good day, and you're not, but you don't want to burden them with your problems. "I can always hide it in my desk when customers are in my office. Dig it out of the trash and bring it to me. It holds numbers I don't have written anywhere else."

"Not necessary. I saved all the numbers. I created a Google Docs for you."

"I prefer my grandfather's Rolodex. It's super easy to find a number in it."

"For a guy who wants to appear young, you sure have some ancient habits. How about we compromise? Lend me your phone, and I'll insert the numbers into your contacts."

"You can't have my phone. I'm expecting a call."

Did he seriously think she meant to drop everything and do it right at this moment? Could he not see how busy she was? Reminding herself she wanted to impress him, she responded accordingly. "How about Monday morning? I can enter the information while you're in your meeting. That's a time you'd have your phone turned off anyway. Correct?"

He stepped over to the windows and looked out. A position that gave her an inordinate amount of time to take in his ass. And since today, he'd been roaming land with a surveyor, he'd worn jeans and boots. And, lucky her, those jeans were singing the chorus to "Sexy and I Know It." *Girl, look at that body.* They gloved his ass in a caress, making her want to forget all about trying to appear as grandiose as the women Meemaw said he normally dated. Those jeans were practically shouting in her ear, *Ask him if he wants to break in his desk with some good old-fashioned sex.* Which she wouldn't do even if he were the type. Right? Well, maybe on the last day of the contract. Meemaw liked to say Aggie had more balls than a herd of bulls.

"I guess that will work." He twisted and caught her eyes focused where they shouldn't be.

Instead of raising her gaze and seeing his no doubt sardonic smile, she pivoted and picked up a bucket of paint. There were places on the back wall she planned on touching up whether they needed it or not.

"What in tarnation do you have on?" Meemaw's voice slammed into Aggie's back, causing her to stumble and some paint to slop out onto the floor and her foot. "Where are the rest of your shorts?"

Aggie spun. Meemaw and Ms. Grace stood in the doorway of Max's office. Meemaw's eyes shot daggers at Aggie, and Ms. Grace's mouth hung open.

"These are my painting shorts." Aggie spoke slowly, as if explaining to a child. "You know that. You've seen me wear them while painting."

Meemaw clutched her heart. "Those are your *home*

painting shorts. Not your work painting shorts. What in the world must Max think having you show up to work in those child-size things?"

They all turned and stared at Max.

He cleared his throat. "I hadn't noticed."

Aggie read his face for signs of lying. Of course he was. Her legs were her best feature. She just wanted to figure out his tell. That kind of information could come in handy.

"Bless your heart," Meemaw said to Max. She hiked over to Aggie and blocked Max's line of sight and Aggie's line of sight, which meant she didn't have enough time to get a good read on his tell. "I'm inclined to believe you, because if you had, you surely would have died of a heart attack. Or had her arrested for indecent exposure."

"You're exaggerating. They're not *that* short. I have shorter ones." Aggie stepped out from behind Meemaw. "In my defense, he's not supposed to be here. He promised me he wasn't coming back to the office until told it was safe to do so." She glanced toward Max to see how mad he was, because she'd just thrown him under the Grandmother Bus.

He chuckled, the vein in his forehead gone.

Ms. Grace snapped out of her stupor. "Maxi, dear, is that true? Have you broken a promise to this poor child and thus placed her in this embarrassing social situation?"

All three ladies once again turned their full attention on him.

His mirth died the quick death of a spider smashed to smithereens by an arachnophobe. "What brings you two beautiful ladies to my office today?"

His grandmother moved over to him and laced her arm through his.

Meemaw did the same to Aggie.

"What are you two up to?" Aggie smelled a scheme.

"What Aggie asked," Max said, directing the comment

to Ms. Grace.

"Why do we always have to be up to something?" Meemaw patted Aggie on the cheek. "I wanted to come by and see your progress on the office transformation project." She turned toward Max. "You know, she's talked my ear off ever since you hired her. Your name's been mentioned a thousand times. I can't remember the last time she dithered so over a job or boss."

Aggie nudged Meemaw. "I'm sure Max couldn't care less about our personal conversations." Max did not need to know she found herself liking him more than she'd thought she would. While, yes, she wanted to impress him, at the same time she didn't want to appear like a conquest falling all over herself to please him. According to Meemaw, who'd heard it from Ms. Grace on more than one occasion, he'd had too many of those types of women in his life.

"On the contrary, what you say about me when I can't hear is of utmost importance to me," he said in a smooth voice. The one she'd liked earlier from on the phone.

Goose bumps popped on her arms, but she didn't rub them. No way did she want to draw Meemaw's attention to her body's reaction to Max.

"The reception area looks like a million dollars," Ms. Grace said. "The color is stunning."

Aggie smiled. Going with a bold blue instead of a tame white had taken a leap of faith in her ability as a decorator. "Thanks. That means a lot coming from you."

"And I like the color scheme in here," Meemaw added. "Very manly. Yet not caveman manly."

"Ladies, why are you here?" Max asked, interrupting the love fest. Did he not like it when he wasn't the center of attention? Or did he also smell a scheme and wanted the lowdown?

"Maxi, dear, remember the other day when you asked me

what I wanted for my birthday?"

"Aggie, dear, remember the other day when you asked me what our next new thing to learn should be?"

Aggie and Max glanced at each other. Max looked like a fly caught in honey and just noticing the golden syrup was in the pathway of a descending flyswatter. Aggie was pretty sure she looked like a thief caught in floodlights.

They looked at their grandmothers and nodded.

"Well, we know what our answers are," the ladies said in unison.

"We?" Aggie asked.

"As it turns out," Ms. Grace said, beaming up at Max, "our answers are the same."

"Sugar Britches," Meemaw said, "we're going to learn to play Bridge. Isn't that just as nice as a sweet Georgia peach in the summer?"

Aggie untangled herself from Meemaw's arm. "Bridge? As in the card game? The one you called—"

"Fun," Meemaw said, cutting Aggie off from saying the actual word she'd called the game. "You always were so smart."

"Maxi, darling, I'd like for you to help me teach Ms. Hazel and Aggie how to play Bridge."

Aggie shook her head. Nope. Spending more time in the presence of Max was a terrible idea. She couldn't quite pinpoint why. It wasn't like he was her type. But still... "Meemaw, I thought we'd finally take those motorcycle driving lessons we've been talking about. I know a guy who said he'd teach us for free. And this is a good month for him."

Max gave her a squinty-eyed stare. One she had no idea how to interpret. If only she could crawl inside his brain for a few hours and hear his thoughts. Did he or did he not want to help teach her and Meemaw how to play Bridge? If he didn't, she could stand back and let him be the bad guy and squash their grandmother's latest bad idea.

• • •

Max waited for Ms. Hazel's response to her granddaughter.

"Bless your heart, you know you prefer being the plus-one on the back of Bill's Harley versus actually driving a Hog," Meemaw said to Aggie. "And at my age, well…I'm not sure I want to wear leather past the age of sixty-four."

"Sixty-four?" Aggie said in a teasing tone, drawing a pinched-brow expression from Ms. Hazel.

Bill and Aggie were an item. Not just a hookup. Women didn't tell their grandmothers about hookups. Max flipped that information around in his brain. Every way it landed caused him heartburn. "Grandmother, what happened to your Bridge partner?" Bridge brought up old memories he'd prefer to not dwell upon.

"Her husband transferred to the Dallas office." Grandmother sighed as if they'd done so just to spite her. "And Grace and I ran into Dottie Monday night while out…having a cocktail, and she suggested I should ask Hazel to be my partner for the upcoming tournament, only Hazel doesn't know how to play. It's so hard to teach someone if you don't have another couple to play against."

"Meemaw, is this something you really want to do?" Aggie asked, worrying her bottom lip with her perfect white teeth. "I didn't think you particularly cared for Ms. Grace's Club friends."

Ms. Hazel propped her hands on her hips. "Sometimes you have to do what you have to do to prove what you want to prove."

Aggie angled her chin to the right. "What does that mean?"

"Dotty implied the reason I didn't want to learn was

because I wasn't capable of learning, because I dropped out of school."

"You told her you dropped out of school?" Aggie's words came out a high-pitched squeak as if she'd been goosed.

"I most certainly did not," Meemaw scolded. "Which means someone else did. And when I find out who ratted me out, I will give them a good piece of my mind and just possibly a knuckle sandwich with that hammer of yours."

Max looked at Grandmother. How did she feel about being friends with a woman who'd give anyone a knuckle sandwich with a hammer? Strangely enough, he didn't feel at all bothered. He liked a woman who stood up for herself against men who behaved like pigs.

Grandmother stared off into the distance. He immediately forgot about the other two women in the room. Something was bothering her. Something big. She should have had ladies begging to become her new Bridge partner if her old one had moved. Grandmother had a record of winning that tournament. Why had it come down to her asking Ms. Hazel? The two of them were great friends, but they weren't club friends. "Grandmother?" he prodded gently.

She gave him a bright smile. "Maxi, are you going to give your grandmother what she wants for her birthday?"

"If I say yes, how would this work?"

"You'll partner up with Aggie, and I'll partner up with Hazel."

"But—"

She gave him a look of reproach. "A sentence starting with the word 'but' is never worthy of a Treadwell. Especially when it's being used in reply to when a seventy-five-year-old woman tells you what she wants for her birthday."

"Yes, ma'am." Maybe he should run this idea by Grant, make sure he wasn't crossing a line that would get him slapped with a sexual harassment charge down the road.

"Perfect. Our first lesson will be next Wednesday evening at my place," Grandmother said. "And, by the way, I've invited your dad over for dinner tomorrow night, and I told him you'd be there."

Max's good mood dissipated. Hell, he was going to win "worst story of the week" two weeks in a row.

Chapter Nine

Thursday night family dinner came quicker than divorce gossip makes the rounds in a country club. Now Max, Grandmother, and Father all sat at one end of Grandmother's formal dining room table.

"Max, Mother's been full of enthusiasm over a new employee you've hired. Did you steal her from your competition or find a treasure all on your own?"

Max placed his fork on his plate and picked up his wineglass. The thought of Aggie being referred to as a treasure amused him. "She's more like a diamond in the rough."

Father would stroke-out if he knew he and Aggie were pairing up as Bridge partners to help Ms. Hazel and Grandmother shore up their signals before the big tournament.

Disappointment filled Father's eyes. "Do you think it's wise hiring from the bottom of the pile instead of the top?" Condescension oozed from his tone like pus from an infected scab. "Surely, by now, you can afford to pay enough to attract the top-tier candidates. By your age, I had at least four well-paid employees on my payroll."

If only Father knew just how far on the bottom Aggie's work history placed her. "Actually, Grandmother connected us."

"Mother, who exactly is this woman you've brought into my son's life?" He tugged at his tie, not to loosen it, but to no doubt make sure the knot sat perfectly in the middle of the collar of his pale blue dress shirt. His way of pointing out to his son that he, too, should be wearing a tie and a jacket.

Grandmother dabbed her lips with her cloth napkin. Of course, she had changed for dinner. But, unlike Father, she didn't do it for status reasons. Dressing for dinner was simply a tradition hardwired into her brain she never chose to ditch. Max, on the other hand, discarded it the moment he turned eighteen. Unless it was a special occasion, he showed up to dinner at Grandmother's wearing slacks and a pullover shirt.

"If you must know, she's Hazel's granddaughter."

Father slammed his palm on the table, causing the china to shake. "Of course that woman's involved in this fiasco."

Max and Grandmother both glanced at their watches. They had an ongoing bet on the number of minutes it would take before Father did his table slapping. The loser had to buy the other breakfast the next time they met. Tonight, he made it a full ten minutes. His record, fifteen.

Grandmother gave Max a slight nod of her head in acknowledgment he'd won tonight's bet. He'd guessed nine minutes. She'd gone with four minutes. "What does 'of course' mean?"

"That woman has tried to weasel herself into this family ever since you've met."

Max didn't intervene—Grandmother could handle her own battles. Hell, she's the one who taught him how to stand up to Father.

"And what does *that* mean?" Disapproval dripped like a slow-leak from her words. "Hazel has not once asked me for money."

"Not yet. And why should she, if she has a bigger picture of setting her nobody granddaughter up with your somebody grandson?"

Like a piece of driftwood doused in kerosene and lit with a blowtorch on a windy day, Max's anger ignited. "Aggie Johansson is a lot of things, but a nobody isn't one of them. She's funny. She's energetic. She's a force that will turn your world upside-down and make you glad for it. She's not an invisible nobody." He abhorred how the man judged the world by the size of their bank account or the status of their parents. "She's efficient and enthusiastic. Bold and proficient. Those, Father, are not the fucking traits of a nobody. Make no mistake, Aggie Johansson is not a nobody. She's very much a somebody."

Father narrowed his eyes and peered closely at him. Like he saw or heard something Max hadn't meant to disclose. "She has the same last name as her grandmother. That alone tells you she's quite likely a bastard child."

Max bolted to stand. He hadn't given much thought to Aggie's birth status. Probably because he didn't give two cents if she carried her father's last name or not. Not to mention there were a couple thousand holes in Father's absurd assumption. And, besides, the marital status of her parents when she was born was irrelevant. "Bastard child" should have never crossed Father's lips. "You're so fucking unbelievably snobbish. Grandmother, please tell me you didn't raise him with these views."

"I blame them on his father."

"May he rest in peace," they said in unison.

"I'm a realist," Father snapped. "If you want to get somewhere in this world, you surround yourself with people with shirttails you can ride. Not with people looking for handouts."

"How can you accuse Aggie of anything?" Hell, she had singlehandedly painted his offices. A task she could have easily hired out. That wasn't a sign of someone looking for a handout. "You've never even met her."

"I—"

"Hush. Both of you." Grandmother's voice cut through the tension like a judge calling for order in the court. "I didn't invite you to dinner just to hear you attack each other."

"Sorry, Grandmother." Max shot her an apologetic smile and sat down. If it wasn't for her, he'd only see his father on the holidays, and maybe not then. She so longed for them to get along. For her sake, he'd strive to do better next time.

"Son," Grandmother said to Father. "Aggie can't help it if her parents never married. Max is right. She's a lovely child. Smart as a whip. Went to college on a full scholarship. It's sweet of Max to give her a chance."

He hadn't known Aggie went on a full scholarship. Interesting.

"At least, she's a college graduate." Father picked up his fork and cut a pea. "What was her major?" He directed the question at Max.

He quickly dismissed the idea of lying. He'd stopped caring about the man's opinion the day his father sued for full custody of him and won. "Liberal arts."

"Of course that's what it would be."

Max hated he'd had the same reaction when he found out Aggie's major. He wanted to have nothing in common with Father. "There's nothing wrong with a liberal arts degree. It makes her a well-rounded individual."

"Just remember she's an employee. Treadwells don't fuck the help."

He resisted an urge to slap his own hands on the table.

Who in the hell did Father think he was fooling? According to Mother, he fucked the help every chance he got. Another reason to keep Aggie at arm's length. He didn't want to be like Father in any way. Other than successful. "Did I mention I have a meeting with Richard Harris on Monday?" Max hadn't planned on telling his father about the meeting. It wasn't like they were business confidants.

"You sound very proud of yourself for doing something most would consider boorish manners." Father raised his nose in the air like a proper snob. "You do know stealing clients from your own family is deemed low-class?"

Max refused to feel guilty. "You said it's every man for himself when I told you I was going into competition with your company." The decision to be the asshole son happened after Father refused to hire him right out of college. He insisted Max learn the business elsewhere and then come to work for him when he had experience the company could benefit from. Father delighted in the fact he hired no one straight out of college. Not even his heir. "Some would say I'm a chip off the old block," Max added.

Father's nose came down, and he gave a calculated chuckle. "Our bet on if you will...or will not...net a million before you turn thirty-one must be eating at you if you're willing to steal from my list of clients to achieve it."

It had been a while since either of them mentioned the bet. "I'm not stealing anything. Mr. Harris came to me. He requested our first meeting." Max refrained from ruining Grandmother's lovely dinner by telling Father his oldest client had jumped ship long ago. Max and Richard's upcoming meeting wasn't their first.

"Just remember, if you don't make your first million by your thirty-first birthday, we have a deal."

"That deal is nonsense," Grandmother said. "I demand both of you agree to drop it right this moment."

"Mother, a bet's a bet. Right, son?"

Max nodded. All the more reason he had to win the O'Reilly bid. "Don't worry, Grandmother. According to my accountant, I'm almost there." Not exactly a lie, but not exactly the truth.

"For your sake, I hope you are," Father said in a mock-fatherly tone. "Your birthday is in only a couple of months."

Chapter Ten

Monday morning, Aggie purposefully arrived at work before Max. Getting up early hadn't even been torture. She actually awoke before her alarm. That never happened. She was more like a three-snooze-buttons kind of gal.

Now, while waiting for Max, butterflies were unexpectedly dancing in her stomach. Like they used to on Christmas mornings while she waited for Meemaw to open the gift she'd handmade for her. Handmade, because their budget didn't allow for store-bought gifts. Aggie always worked extra hard to make sure what she made was special, because it would be the only gift Meemaw would receive. Her favorite gift from Aggie had been a small wrapped box with a handwritten note saying it was full of kisses and hugs. The tiny box still sat on her bedside table.

Now, she couldn't wait to see Max's face when he laid eyes on his newly redecorated office.

When she couldn't find anything clsc to adjust— every pillow had been fluffed to perfection, every picture straightened, and both desks arranged with eye-catching arrays of office supplies—she forced herself to stand still and take in her creation. Was this how the creator of the world felt when preparing to show the first human what he'd done?

Aggie double checked her appearance in the mirror she'd bought for her desk. Whereas on Thursday, she'd looked anything but the professional Max wanted working for him, this morning she oozed flawlessness. Her hair smoothed into a bun, her suit a chic black with a gentleman's white shirt underneath. The skirt of her suit hit below her knees. She'd even worn pantyhose. He would find nothing to ridicule.

A knock at the door stalled her inspection. "Coming." She hurried into the front office and opened the door. "Welcome," she said to her boss. Her nose twitched. He'd changed his cologne. Something a tad sexier. Why?

"Thank you." He handed her the sticky note she'd placed on the outside of the door directing him to knock before entering. "You're looking lovely today."

Her breath caught in her throat, and her insides went all wonky. And all that wonkiness caused her to want to simultaneously smile and cry? Since when did a flattery make her emotional? "Aren't you a peach for saying that."

"Why did I have to knock to come into my offices?"

The smile she'd been trying to contain under a facade of sophistication broke free. "Follow me. I have something to show you." She forced her black kitten-heels to carry her at a normal pace to his office door. "Close your eyes."

Surprisingly, he obeyed.

She twisted the knob and pushed the door open. She stepped through first and did a quick overview.

His raised desk, the white couch, the alternative seating chairs, the paintings on the walls by a local artist. All were ready for admiration.

"Open your eyes and enter your new office."

He did. His face remained impassive as he slowly glanced

around.

"What do you think? Do you love it?" She glanced at her creation. "Better than you could have ever imagined? Magnificent, right?" She glanced back at him and her happy rambling stumbled.

His face had changed. Not in a good way. It was as if a bucket of ice water had just been tossed on him in the middle of an ice storm.

The dancing butterflies in her stomach fled the dance floor. He didn't like it.

"I don't see my rocks." His tone was low, with a heavy thread of something she couldn't decipher. Not anger but something heavy. Something worse than anger.

"They are safely tucked away," she quickly assured him.

He closed his eyes. Mumbled something. Then his eyes opened. "Tucked where?"

She stepped away from him to give herself a beat while a breath forced its way past the lump forming in her throat. This was not how she'd imagined this morning's unveiling would go. "They're in the storage closet across the hall."

Max strode to the storage room. She followed. Didn't he believe her?

He twisted the handle, but it didn't open. "The key," he said through what sounded like gritted teeth. "Please."

She hurried into their office and grabbed it off her desk. She thrust the key at him. "What's so special about the rocks?"

"They were a gift from a friend." He opened the door and stepped inside. The room was empty.

Sweat broke out on Aggie's upper lip. Shit. This wasn't good. "Ummmm. The janitor must have accidentally grabbed them along with all the things I told him to repurpose. I promise, I had them sitting way aside in a different box labeled...well, not labeled *someone's soon-to-be treasure*."

Max whirled and glued her to the spot with a gaze that hinted at a pending storm. "Find them."

She laughed. More from nerves than actual humor. "And if I can't?"

"I have every faith you'll find a way to recover my rocks," he said quietly. But the impact on her insides was the same as if he had shouted the words. Her body was currently considering flight or fright. Flight would mean quitting.

She inhaled. Nope. Not happening. She was going to fight, and the best way to fight was to treat the problem like it wasn't a big deal. This was a small issue that could be easily rectified. The janitor would know where she could find his precious rocks. She stood up straight, giving another inch to the inch her heels gave her. This wasn't a quitting moment.

"You're right. I will. But first, if it's not too much trouble, can we go back over to our office, and you actually take the time to see that I worked my ass off to give you an office with a butt-load of cool-factor?"

He yanked at his shirt sleeves, showing off gold cuff links. "I'm sure you did, and we'll discuss it just as soon as you recover my rocks."

"And if I can't locate them?"

His eyebrows lowered and pinched together. "I'll have no choice but to fire you." Without waiting for her response to that kick-in-the-teeth threat, he strode back to his office. To his desk.

You'll what? This is not how this morning was supposed to shake out.

She trailed him. "Damn it, Max, I got up two hours early to surprise you with all I've done. You can't fire me over something I worked so hard to do...for you. And, must I remind you, you have a big client this morning. You need me here to answer the phone."

Max stared so intently Aggie swore she heard crashes of

thunder coming out of his ears and saw lightning spit from his eyes. "Had you left them alone like I told you, he would have never gotten his hands on them."

She swallowed her pride. It meandered going down and, when it finally landed, soured her churning stomach. She should just grab her purse and leave. Only she'd promised Meemaw and herself she'd stay employed. "You're right. I'm sorry. I was out of line."

He didn't respond.

"I'll do everything within my power to find your rocks, but if I don't, you can't fire me over it, and I'll tell you why."

"I'm listening. Please do explain why I can't fire you."

"Because I am part of the birthday gift you gave Ms. Grace for her birthday. Who knows how many more birthdays she'll celebrate?"

He paled. "Don't say something like that." He knocked on the wood of his desk. "It tempts the Universe."

She laughed. "Do you mean to tell me the Great Maxi Treadwell is superstitious?"

Her humor seemed to knock something loose in him, and he exhaled hard. "Are you always such a smart-ass?"

Why yes. Yes, she was. "Around some people more than others." An image of Meemaw standing in the room listening to this conversation popped into Aggie's brain. Ugh. She hated when that happened. Meemaw would not approve of the way Aggie was handling herself. "Tell me about the friend who gave you the rocks."

His shoulders slumped. "She…" His words trailed off, but his gaze didn't waver.

"She?" Aggie echoed. "Is that what this temper-tantrum has been about? Are you all in a tizzy because your current girlfriend gave you those rocks? Someone you're in love with. Does Ms. Grace even know about her?"

Max raked a hand through his hair. "How in the hell does

that matter?"

All of her calm blew into a tornado. "Because Ms. Grace has been encouraging Meemaw to fix me up with you since they met."

For months, Ms. Grace had been giving Meemaw false hope Aggie might marry up in society. That Max was unlike other high-society boys. That he actually liked a person based on their personality, not their bank account. That he wouldn't loathe falling in love with someone like Aggie.

Granted, the odds of that happening were slim to bankrupt. But Meemaw was what most would call a gambler riding the highs of a year-long lucky streak. One in which she won a Mustang convertible in a poker game.

Meemaw's wants were few, but at the top of her list was to see Aggie break the cycle of unwed mothers in the Johansson women and to marry a good man.

"Grandmother knows."

"Then why is she trying to fix you up with someone like me?"

"Like you?" His eyebrows raised.

No way would she spell it out. "Out of your league."

The joke didn't register on his face. "The friend who gave me the rocks is dead."

The attitude whooshed out of her. "Damn it, Max, you could have freaking led with that."

His phone buzzed.

While he spoke into the phone, Aggie attempted some clear-headed soul searching. Max hadn't corrected her when she said *someone like me*. And didn't laugh when she said out of his league. Then again, his girlfriend was dead, so she really should get over herself. At least, she was breathing.

Max clicked off his call and turned to her. "My client is downstairs. Please meet him and bring him up." He pulled a list out of his suit jacket and handed it to her. "If you're not getting fired today, the least you can do is complete this to-do list for me. And, please, try to complete the list without ripping my soul from my body again."

Was that what losing the rocks felt like to him? A soul wrenching. No one had ever stolen her soul. "I thought you wanted me to find your rocks?" Max loved a dead girl. He'd earned the right to be stiff over some damn rocks.

"I'll search for them myself."

Aggie didn't argue with him. On the bright side, once she updated Meemaw on Max's heart situation, she'd stop thinking she and Max were perfect for one another. "What's his name?"

"Whose name?"

"The client downstairs."

"Richard Harris."

She sucked in her cheeks. Rocks and souls and dead girlfriends forgotten. "You're kidding. Richard Harris? As in Missouri's wealthiest bachelor. Richard Harris, who is in the top ten on the Forbes list of wealthiest individuals for this year? That Richard Harris?" He'd been a topic of conversation on more than one occasion between her and Meemaw.

Max sighed. "Is having you meet him going to present a problem?"

She clasped her hands behind her back and managed not to bounce from heel to heel. "Why would meeting *the* Richard Harris be a problem?" She'd never met a billionaire. Never had the chance to pick the brain of a billionaire. And Richard Harris wasn't just a billionaire. He was a self-made billionaire. His youth had been as dismal as Meemaw's. If he could pull himself out of the stigma of being from the wrong side of town, anyone could. Even Agnes Johansson.

"You're not planning on asking him for an autograph or something idiotic, are you?"

Her hands flew apart and landed on her hips. "There is absolutely nothing wrong with asking for an autograph from someone you admire." She might ask him to have coffee with her and Meemaw. That would be like the best gift ever in Meemaw's eyes. "But no. I'm not planning on asking him to sign a piece of paper or my left boob."

Max ran a hand down the side of his face, and his eyes flickered to her cleavage. Her nipples immediately tightened. She hoped like hell he couldn't see her lit-up headlights.

"Why do I feel I've asked the wrong question?"

"There's nothing in my contract that says I can't date one of our customers, is there?" Since Max thought her moral compass didn't work, and he'd ruined her big reveal, he deserved to squirm.

"He's old enough to be your grandfather."

Which made him the perfect age for Meemaw. Hmmmm. Who said grandmothers were the only ones who could try and fix someone they loved up with another? "Haven't you heard men like him only date women my age?" She unbuttoned the top button of her shirt. "And really, I may be too old. When you're scandalously rich, arm candy is expected." She swept out of the office with her head held high and her ass swaying to the rhythm of "Red High Heels" as she sung its lyrics under her breath.

• • •

Aggie sashayed out of Max's office like she'd not only just won the battle but also the war. And, damn it, she had. Temporarily. He didn't have time to figure her out or analyze how his body reacted to her every word as if she were flirting. Right now, he needed to wrap his head around the deal with Mr. Harris, not around Aggie the Horrible. Or his missing rocks.

Three minutes later, while he was trying to lower his damn desk, Aggie burst in without knocking, Mr. Harris standing next to her.

"Mr. Treadwell," she said, "I found this good-looking gentleman in the downstairs lobby, and he said he knows you."

"Considering I sent you down to fetch him," he said, "I'm amused you sound surprised he was there."

Her eyes narrowed. What game was she playing? "He says he has an appointment with you."

Max held out his hand. "Richard, so nice to see you again. I hope Ms. Johansson hasn't caused you too much grief in the short time you've spent with her."

Richard glanced at her and chuckled. "On the contrary, Aggie's a delight."

"You're such a peach." She laid her hand on his arm. "I bet you say sweet things to all the women sent to *fetch* you."

Max stiffened at her flirtatious tone. Something had happened between Aggie meeting Richard and their arrival in his office. Could she seduce a guy in three minutes? Of course she could. Did they already have a date planned?

Richard glanced around. "I must say, I love the changes you've made in your office. By the way, how is Mrs. Deverish? I take it she had her baby. I hope everything went well."

Richard had met Max's assistant many times and still referred to her by her last name, but with Aggie, he was already on a first-name basis. "She's doing great. I'll let her know you asked after her."

Aggie cleared her throat. "Now that I've shown Mr. Harris to your office—"

"If I'm to call you Aggie, then you should definitely call me Richard."

She beamed. "Thank you, Richard. Mr. Treadwell, I'm leaving now." She pulled the to-do list out of her jacket pocket. "This list won't complete itself."

"Don't forget the toilet paper. I added that to the list, right?" The taunt was out before he could stop it. And the reason was pathetic. He wanted Richard to think twice before getting involved with his assistant. He wanted Richard to think of Aggie as somehow beneath his attention. Which made Max a first-class ass. Like the five-star general of asses. He'd have to apologize to Aggie. But right now, he was willing to own the title of ass and do whatever it took to kill any budding romance between the two.

Spots of color entered her cheeks. "All I recall seeing on the list was Preparation H. Extra strength."

He forced a chuckle. She gave as good as she got. If she ever did meet his father, at least she'd be able to hold her own. Then again, why would she ever meet the man? "Be a *peach* and add it," he said.

Richard held out his hand to Aggie. "I'm looking forward to seeing you again." Then he turned to Max. "Before I leave today, I insist you give me the name of the company who redesigned your offices."

"I'll be sure and do that."

Aggie shut his door with a sharp *click*. Hell, he'd been so upset with her over the rocks, he'd forgot to ask her to put the phone on do not disturb. And, now that he thought about it, he should have scratched off a few of the things on the list. Things not necessary for Aggie to do. His gut told him he would come to regret that lapse in memory.

Chapter Eleven

Aggie stood stiffly in the outer office and glared at the wadded list in her hand, a mangled ball of compressed anger, and then at her screeching feet. She'd carefully chosen her shoes to impress Max with how effortlessly she could dress the part of his assistant. Their design was not suitable to trudge around the city, running errands.

First of which would be to locate his damn rocks. Because...well...because they were obviously his tangible security blanket. Meemaw was hers. Even the fiercest of warriors needed a safety blanket to come back to after a battle. She took a deep breath and exhaled noisily. Now that she'd moved events into perspective, he was justified in his downward spiral upon learning of their demise. Understandable. Which meant the guy was still in the ballpark of redeemability.

She carefully unwadded the list and read. Dry cleaning. Grocery shopping. Wine shopping. Drop everything off at the condo. Water plants. Dust. Change bedsheets. She wadded it back up. "Salvageable my ass. I work for a first-class prick."

Only one thing could explain this list.

Max had shown up to work with the preplanned goal of goading her into quitting. Before he even knew she'd screwed up, his intentions were set. For some unfathomable reason, over the weekend, he had decided he didn't want her as his assistant and had come up with this list to get her to abandon her job—contract be damned.

Puzzling the change of attitude, she forwarded the phones to his desk and caught a whiff of Ms. Grace's perfume. It wiggled loose a memory of her mentioning she had invited her son for dinner, and she expected Max to join them. That had been Thursday night. Aggie didn't see Max on Friday because she'd asked him to stay home while she put the finishing touches on the office. Had Mr. Treadwell, over dinner, convinced Max that Aggie wasn't of the right caliber to be his assistant?

That had to be it. He didn't like Meemaw, therefore it made sense that he wouldn't like Aggie, either. Like father, like son. Her first instinct had been the right instinct—Max was a smug bastard.

She stomped to the elevator, cursing him with every step. Fuck him all the way up asshole mountain. It would be a cold day in an Arizona sauna before he provoked her into quitting. Two could play this asshole game.

Standing inside the elevator, she wiggled her toes to make sure she still could. She could, but barely. First stop home. And then the rocks.

Twenty minutes later, she quietly let herself in the front door of Meemaw's and her home.

"What in tarnation are you doing sneaking in at nine thirty in the a.m.?" Meemaw said, causing Aggie to startle and nearly pee herself. "Please tell me you haven't already gotten yourself fired."

She sighed. Meemaw had worked the third shift last night.

Aggie had hoped to find her conked out and snoring. "Not fired. Just changing my shoes." She couldn't blame Meemaw for her lack of faith.

Meemaw glanced at Aggie's shoes. "Why did you wear those shoes to work?"

"I don't have time to explain. I'm in a hurry. I've got lots of important things to do today." Like buy toilet paper. She would buy the cheapest damn toilet paper she could find. Maybe even steal a roll from a hole-in-the-wall gas station. The kind you could read a newspaper through.

"Agnes?" Meemaw followed her inside her bedroom.

"Yes, ma'am?"

"I know I sound like a scratched record, but please do us proud with Max. Prove to him just because we're poor doesn't mean we're trash." Meemaw grew up in North Blue Ridge, in a three-room house with dirt floors. Her dad was mean as a wild pig and her mom a drunk. The town's population stood at seventy-one. Ranked number one worst neighborhood in Kansas City.

At sixteen, after she got kicked out of the fancy school she went to on a scholarship, she quit school and ran away. As far as Meemaw knew, her parents never reported her missing. Maybe because they didn't care. Maybe because they never noticed. Meemaw held three jobs at one time and moved into a one-room apartment located over a dry cleaner in East Blue Valley. A town with the impressive population of 1,595. Ranked number nine on the list of ten worst neighborhoods in Kansas City, so to her that was a step up. That's where she fell in love, got her heart broken, and gave birth to Aggie's mother.

"Meemaw, he doesn't view us as trash, because we're not trash."

Meemaw sat on Aggie's bed. "If he doesn't, he has friends and family who do. Working for him gives you a chance to prove them all wrong."

Aggie laced her fingers with Meemaw's. Her hands were old and worn out from her early years of hard labor as a maid, a cook, and a bartender. "I hate that it matters so much to you what people think of us."

Meemaw drew her into a big hug. "I love that you don't. It means I've done something right raising you."

"Oh, Meemaw, you've done everything right raising me. Anything I do wrong is on me, never you." Aggie stepped out of her grip. Her heart squeezed at the brightness in Meemaw's eyes.

"If I raised you so right, you'll impress him just fine."

She smiled tightly. She would behave at work. She would keep this job. Buy him expensive toilet paper. "I'll prove to him my manners can compete with the best of them. But please get it out of your head that he and I will end up an item. We're not."

"Give me one good reason."

The guy loves a dead person. "I don't go for the asshole types."

"Agnes LaBelle Johansson, have you forgotten who you're talking to? Don't make me put soap in your mouth. I've told you a hundred times, smart people don't need sentence enhancers to get their point across."

Ever since being told she was dumber than dirt by the guy who got her pregnant and then dumped her, Meemaw had been sensitive about the opinions of others. That's the day she vowed to never be called dumb again.

"I know. You're right. I'll remember to use my smart words."

"And one more thing," Meemaw said.

"What's that?"

"I love you, dear."

Aggie's heart squeezed. "I love you more."

Three hours later, Aggie stood in the lobby of Max's condo, arguing with the concierge to let her on the key-needed elevators. "I work for him. I'm his assistant. This is his dry cleaning."

"I'm sorry, ma'am, but not once in all the years I've worked for him has he asked an assistant to bring his dry cleaning to his apartment. That is a task Glenda does for him on Wednesdays."

Aggie bit her tongue. The ass already had someone doing this for him? Regularly? "Fine, call him. He'll tell you I have permission."

She tapped her toes while the guy stepped away from his station and called Max.

"My apologies. You may go up." He didn't look sorry. He looked like he didn't like to be wrong. He handed her a piece of paper with six numbers on it. "This is his entry code. It changes daily."

Of course it changed daily. Max would never settle for an out-of-the-box, Walmart-purchased security system. He'd have one with all the bells and whistles you could only get from companies who offered customized installations.

Max lived on the thirty-seventh floor in a condo in downtown Kansas City. Twenty seconds later, she stood inside the doorway of his home. Luckily, no one could see her face or hear the beat of her heart against her ribs. Ten of Meemaw's and her home could fit inside his open-floor-plan condo.

Aggie followed Instagram posts of the rich and famous. But she'd never been so up close and personal with how the other half lived.

Meemaw had, because she'd once worked for the fifth wealthiest woman in Kansas City, but not Aggie. Meemaw refused to let teenage Aggie work as a maid to help pay the bills. "Holy smokes," she said, taking it all in.

She kicked off her pink Crocs and grimaced at them. They were an atrocity to the fashion-minded. An abomination. But a lifesaver to those who spent hours on their feet. Meemaw owned a closet full of them.

Aggie stuck the whole grocery bag in the refrigerator. Max could sort the food out when he got home. She placed his rocks on his kitchen table. After she finished the other to-dos, she'd arrange them in the memory box she'd bought at Hobby Lobby and then prop her "I'm sorry" card in front of it.

Still carrying his dry cleaning and Dollar-General-sales-aisle toilet paper, she went in search of his bedroom. She might have done the right thing when it came to the rocks, but doing the same with the toilet paper was asking too much.

"This place makes what I did to his office appear about as amazing as a runway model on a diet." No wonder he'd been underwhelmed. "I gave you a Cadillac and you prefer Ferraris." According to Meemaw, Max was thirty years old, and his business was at the start-up stage. How did he afford such luxury?

Realization bitch-slapped her, and she winced. "You're a freaking trust-fund baby." She despised trust-fund men. Meemaw's heart and pride had been broken by a smooth-talking trust-fund baby. A guy who pretended to think Meemaw could fit into his world until he'd gotten what he wanted out of her.

The last door on the left revealed the master suite. A room not in the tiniest bit dominated by the unmade king-size bed, chest of drawers, and a magnificent armoire.

"I could fit two king-size beds and Dolly Parton's wig collection in here."

There were two doors. She opened one, and a dream bathroom greeted her. Clawfoot tub and a shower that could host a major-league baseball team. She placed the cheap toilet paper on the turned-down seat, left the room, and opened the other door. A gasp escaped her parted lips.

The master closet! The *crème de la crème* of any home. Decked out with all the organizers a person could ever dream of owning. Before she left today, she would take the room's measurement and share them with Meemaw. When Aggie was little, she and Meemaw used to dream of the day they had a home with a closet bigger than any Meemaw had ever had to clean. So they had a tiny notebook where they kept the dimensions of the ones she'd cleaned over the years.

Mr. Trust Fund had a whole row of custom suits organized by color. Just for fun, she mixed the two black suits she'd picked up at the dry cleaners in with his blue suits. And then mismatched several pairs of shoes in the shoe organizer.

Smiling, she zipped back to the massive bed. A bed Max Treadwell slept in. She quickly stripped it of its soft white sheets. What thread count were they? Did he wear pajamas? Or go commando? Hmm. That question begged for an answer. One by one, she opened drawers and conducted an undetectable search.

None of them contained pajamas.

One of them held a bevy of boxer shorts. Silk and cotton were represented. She looked at the labels. Ellen. Tommy John. Calvin Klein. Brand loyalty didn't apply to him. Did that filter over into his sex life? Did he have a blonde, a brunette, a redhead on speed dial? Did he change them out the way one did underwear?

She took a pair of Ellen boxers off the top. Watching the Ellen Show was one of her guilty pleasures. She would have never imagined someone who took themselves as seriously as Max did would wear Ellen underwear. Maybe the guy had a hidden fun side.

She laid the boxers on the bed in the spot she imagined that area of his body would be if he sprawled himself there. "How well do you fill these out?" she murmured. "Well enough there'd be spillage when you have a hard-on?"

She climbed up on his bed on all fours and imagined—

Her phone rang. *Max*. Fuck. She scrambled off his bed.

"Hello." She forced herself to sound polite and not guilty of just perusing his drawers and imagining blow jobs. She may or may not have succeeded.

"Did you find what you were looking for?" Max asked.

She stopped breathing. Did he know she'd just been thinking inappropriate thoughts where he was concerned? *Get a grip. Of course he doesn't know.* "If you're asking did I buy your toilet paper, the answer is you'll have to wait and see for yourself." Meemaw would be proud she didn't use the word fucking before the word toilet.

He cursed. Was it because her less-than-stellar attitude toward doing his chores surprised him, or did he simply not like wait-and-see games? Did the rich boy prefer immediate gratification? If that was the case, she pitied his girlfriend.

"I mean, did you find what you were looking for in my drawers?"

The room grew disconcertingly still. She swallowed hot embarrassment, and sweat slid between her boobs. How did he know? She glanced around. "I can't imagine what you're talking about." Oh God. Had her lips opened while she imagined giving him a blow job?

He sighed. "I have a maid cam in my bedroom. What exactly were you looking for?"

Sweet baby Jesus. "Your pajamas." She glanced around the room, trying to figure out where he'd hidden a camera. Maybe…he hadn't…*fuck*…

"Why?" On the surface it sounded like a perfectly normal question, but the strange timber in his voice told her otherwise.

"To lay them out after I turn down your bed."

"Darling," he spoke the words in a smooth honey tone,

making her want to lick him like a coffee-flavored ice cream cone, "I sleep in the nude." Or maybe it was what she'd been thinking of while on all-fours that had her imagining long, languid licks.

Desire ricocheted through her, causing her to squeeze her legs together. Yep. She wanted to lick Max. What was it about this guy who could make her mad and horny at the same time? "Figures."

"What does that mean?" He sounded amused.

She reminded herself he was a trust-fund baby. The enemy. Not someone to lick or have sex with or get all emotionally gooey over. "A guy who has a *maid-cam* in his bedroom is obviously a pervert. Anything you think you saw is off-limits for reprimand."

She had a lot of dreams to accomplish in life before letting loose her gooey side with any man. Like travel outside the country. Live in NYC for a year. Lick a man's coffee-flavored ice cream–lathered cock. Fuck. Fuck. Fuck. That was a brand-spanking new addition to her list of things to do before settling down. Max was changing her.

"My bed is out of the focus range of my camera." The words sounded like they slipped through clenched teeth. "I'm not a pervert."

Her body sagged in relief. Thank God. Remembering he was still there, still watching her reactions, she straightened. "Did you call to harass me?"

"Actually, I called to let you know I need you to work late tonight."

"Tonight's not a good night. I have a date." With her vibrator. This need wasn't going away with a cold shower.

"Cancel it." The demand didn't hold room for argument.

Which was fair, considering their contract. But that didn't mean she had to go down without a soft swing. "All right, but Bill won't be happy," she said and promptly ended the call.

Chapter Twelve

Later that evening, Max pushed back from the conference table. Aggie had finished reorganizing a brainstorming chart they'd been working on for the past few hours. At some point, she'd removed her jacket. Now, her shirt showed signs of coming completely untucked from her ass-hugging skirt. If he wasn't mistaken, she wore a man's dress shirt. And he wasn't mistaken. He did, after all, own a closetful.

Had Bill left it after a sleepover? The thought settled about as well as thoughts of his conversation with Father during Grandmother's mandatory dinner. He'd been replaying his dad's snide comments as a way to keep his mind off of thoughts of Aggie's hands holding his underwear. As a diversion technique, it wasn't working.

He'd give anything to know what she'd done with his boxers when she went out of camera view. The only thing he'd heard during that moment were the words, "*Oh yeah, I bet there's spillage.*"

Max stretched his legs out, and his foot hit something. He glanced under the table and found her Crocs. She'd kicked them off and pushed them out of her way. Nothing like the sexy ones she'd worn to work this morning. Why had she changed footwear?

His gaze drifted to Aggie. A habit it appeared to excel at doing. Her hair hadn't come down from its matronly bun, but enough wisps had escaped to cause his fingers to itch with a desire to let it all loose. Especially with that damn man's shirt.

"I need the rose-petal-pink marker." She turned toward him with a soft smile on her lips. As if very content with spending time brainstorming with him instead of out on a date.

He grabbed the only pink marker he had and held it out toward her. Unfortunately, she leaned forward to take it from the table at the same time. Their timing misfired, and his hand accidentally brushed her full breasts.

His brain short-circuited like a sound system caught in a sudden downpour of heavy rain. The room's oxygen vaporized. He jerked and dropped the marker. He opened his mouth to apologize, but a fog of hot lust settled over his body. Wave after wave after drowning wave.

Words, the ones that made sense, escaped him. Which words were the ones that went into an apology? Not sex, kiss, naked, what-the-hell. *Breathe idiot.*

"Sorry," he finally said.

Her laughter filtered through his murky brain. "Now, we're even." She sounded carefree and nonchalant.

He managed a breath. "We're what?"

"You've touched my boob, and I've fondled your boxers."

Fondled. Hell. "You're killing me, Johansson."

Their gazes locked. Hers danced with humor.

His did whatever in the hell they did while he imagined her stroking his boxers with her hands or tongue while they were on his body. Or pooled at his ankles. Or—

"I've been told that a time or twenty million."

He shook his head. No wonder she didn't sound choked with embarrassment. Flirting was her second language. Having a guy accidentally touch a breast didn't inflame her with emotions. He should say something equally disarming. But for the life of him, he couldn't think of anything.

"Which means the ball's back in your court." A slight smirk accompanied her words.

A smirk implying she was most definitely purposefully messing with him.

Did she really want him to imagine her helping him place his balls back in his boxers…after she'd had her way with them? *Get a fucking grip, Treadwell.* She was probably only implying she thought of him as stuffy.

He dragged his gaze to his watch. He may not be as stuffy as she imagined, but he was a man of integrity. No matter how fuckable she was, mixing business with pleasure was never a good idea. He searched his brain for a mood deflater and landed on a call he should have already made. "Could you get Glenda on the phone?" His low, tortured voice gave him away, but at least it didn't crack like a horny teenager's.

"Now?"

"Unless you have a prior appointment, now would work." He forced himself to use his boss voice. His dick-fuckery voice.

She walked stiffly to his desk and yanked his Rolodex up. "What's her last name?"

"Whose?" Did she want him to kiss her? Was she mad because he hadn't? Was that why the temperature in the room had dropped below freezing? But that couldn't be. On more than one occasion she'd told him *he* wasn't *her* type. Question was…was she his type? Did he have a type?

"Glenda's," she said.

"Oh." He did have a type. It wasn't Aggie. When the time

came to take a wife, he needed a sensible, predictable woman in his life. "Banks. Glenda Banks."

Nothing about Aggie used those two descriptors. Hell, tonight was a prime example of her not being predictable. Instead of coming back to work in a mood because he'd been an ass, she'd sailed in smiling. No sign of being embarrassed she'd been caught going through his underwear drawer. No sign of anger he'd been a jerk to her in front of Richard Harris.

While they had worked, she'd matched him idea for idea. And they weren't weak ideas. They were damn good. And not once had she complained about how she'd spent her day.

"Do you want me to call her," she said, sounding over-the-top annoyed, "or just give you the number?"

"I asked you to complete my to-do list because she needed today off," he blurted.

Aggie's brows furrowed. "Not because you wanted... never mind. Back to Glenda. Did you say Banks?"

Did Aggie think the list was some type of punishment? "She's my maid. Her husband had surgery today. Which is why I needed you to do the tasks she normally does so when she comes back, she'll see they were done, and she won't fret."

Her disdainful expression dug at his conscience. "You have your maid buy your toilet paper? You know that's what Amazon is for...right?"

Suddenly, he needed Aggie to understand he wasn't like his father. He didn't judge based on income. "Since I pay her by the hour, last year, I made up extra things for her to do after her husband was laid off due to an injury. I would gladly have just paid her more for what she already did for me, but her pride wouldn't allow her to take charity. Which left me scrounging for things to add to her list of duties. Which includes buying all of my household needs."

"Of course she didn't want your charity." Aggie set down the marker and turned around. "For the record, I didn't mind doing the tasks, either. It's not like I think I'm too good for menial assignments. Except for the toilet paper. That I minded."

"It was childish of me to throw that into the mix." He raked a hand through his hair. He'd added that item in because... because he was jealous of the effortless camaraderie she'd had with Richard after only knowing him a few minutes. "I apologize for that, and for not telling you what a wonderful job you did with the offices. And for yelling at you about the rocks."

She sighed. "If we're having an apology-fest, then I'm sorry I didn't incorporate them into my design. I should have known they were important because they were the only personal touch you had in here." She padded back to the conference table, handed him Glenda's number on a sticky note, and settled her sweet ass on the corner closest to him. "I—"

"I should have been clearer. You didn't know how important they were to me." That didn't mean he wasn't still reeling from them being gone. "I went to the place who picked them up and they said a woman had already purchased them earlier this morning." He'd asked for the woman's number, but they said she'd paid cash.

A smile tugged Aggie's lip.

He raised a brow.

"It was me. I'm the woman. I tracked them down and bought them."

One of his protective walls crashed. He stood, knocking over his chair. Not a wall meant to keep him from lusting, but one far more important. One meant to keep him from feeling real emotion toward a woman. "You did what?"

She glanced at her fingernails. "They're arranged in a memory box. One you can bring back to the office, and we can hang on the wall, or one you can display in your condo."

"Thank you." He grabbed her hands and pulled her to her feet. Their eyes met in a naked-soul moment. No walls, no preconceived notions, no emotional barriers. Just two people allowing themselves momentary vulnerability. The feeling was both frightening and invigorating.

He ripped his gaze from hers and locked onto her mouth. He waited for her to kill the moment by saying something Aggie-like. Instead, her tongue darted out and slid enticingly along her bottom lip.

Desire rushed him. What in the hell was his next move? Stalling, he laid his forehead against hers and closed his eyes.

He wasn't his father.

Pulling on strength he didn't want to possess, he let go of her hands and took a step back. "I'm sorry I forced you to cancel your date." Best decision he'd made all day, other than it had destroyed one of his relationship-barrier walls. Hell, he wished he'd included no dating in the damn contract she made him draw up.

Her response came slowly. She tucked in her shirt. He resisted an urge to offer to help. His hands really wanted to slide beneath the thin band of her skirt. Then she pushed the stray strands of hair out of her face. Her gorgeous head of hair was one of her many assets. Thick. Straight. Sort of like him at the moment.

She inhaled deeply, exhaled, and said, "You gave fair warning the hours for this job would be cockamamie."

He laughed. A girl using an old-fashioned word like cockamamie was not having problems with gutter thoughts. The laughter released his tension. "I didn't know anyone under the age of eighty still used that word." She wasn't sensible or predictable, but she was such a unique mixture of intriguing characteristics. Characteristics he found himself liking. A lot. Like funny. Outgoing. Interesting. A bit cockamamie with a touch of dazzle.

Aggie grinned, showing off a beautiful smile and also appearing to relax. "It's one of Meemaw's favorites."

That explained it. Meemaw had to be the most colorful character he'd ever met. Obviously, some of that charm rubbed off on Aggie. "Where in the South did your grandmother grow up?"

Aggie returned to her seat at the conference table and picked a red Starburst out of the candy dish. Although the added distance between them was smart, he found himself regretting her decision. "What makes you think she did?" she asked.

"Her thick Southern accent?"

"Meemaw's never been out of Kansas City. But she spent four years working for a sweet woman who'd moved here from Kentucky. A woman who helped Meemaw learn the ways of high society." Aggie carefully opened the candy's wrapper one corner at a time. "Meemaw liked the way proper English sounded rolling off her boss's tongue in a Southern lilt, so she adopted the lady's accent and colorful sayings as her own."

"And you?"

"And me what?" She popped the candy into her mouth. A movement that had him once again thinking of things he shouldn't be thinking.

"Sometimes you sound as Southern as sweet tea." He stopped and cleared his throat. "And other times as soft and smooth as Missouri Spirits Vodka. What's your story?"

She finished chewing and swallowed. "I don't have a story. Meemaw says I'm a magic sponge. I soak in the best of everything and leave behind the worst."

He nodded. The description fit her like a custom-made glove. "Is that why I feel so drained? You've soaked in all of the best of me?"

She rolled her eyes. "You didn't have much, so it didn't

take long."

A chuckle got away from him. "It's a good thing I'm not your type."

She nodded. "May I ask you a favor?" Her usual confident tone had been replaced by one of vulnerability.

He braced himself. "Ask. Can't promise I'll say yes."

"I think we should complain about each other to our grandmothers. Help them realize on their own we're not romantically compatible, so they'll stop trying to fix us up. I feel like the longer it goes on, the harder it's going to be on Meemaw when a romance between us doesn't materialize."

Damn it. The woman was brilliant. Why hadn't he thought of that? Probably because working late with her had his brain scrambled into an undercooked omelet. But still… "Just to be sure we're on the same page, why aren't we romantically compatible?"

Chapter Thirteen

About to reply to Max's question on why she thought their hearts would always be a mismatched pair, Aggie's stomach grumbled. She glanced at her watch. Eight thirty p.m. It had been a long Monday. "I tell you what," she said. "Buy us dinner, and I'll explain to you why we're not compatible—romantically speaking. As a work couple, we're a dream team. That is, when you don't get in the way of yourself."

Tonight had been invigorating. They'd bounced ideas off each other like a smooth-ass spin-out between two people who'd danced together all their lives. While he took his role as the lead man quite seriously, he gallantly took her likes and pleasure into consideration with each smooth move he executed.

Moments ago, when she thought he would kiss her, she'd had a startling revelation—she wanted it to transpire. And not just the kiss. She wanted everything that comes after a kiss.

And she had no idea when that happened. Just this morning, she didn't like him very much. And when she reminded herself he was a trust-fund baby, she still didn't. Yet...

"Deal," he said.

She shook away the unnerving realization and focused on Max. Just because he could dance didn't mean they were romantically compatible. They weren't. He was pompous. She was fun. She wasn't saying sex wouldn't be grand between them, because, well...it would. But beyond that, the touchy-feely stuff had nothing to do with sex. And that's what she meant when she said they weren't romantically compatible.

Thirty minutes later, they sat across from each other at a small mom and pop pizza joint, Pie in the Sky. Max filled the beer mugs and pushed one toward her. "Enough stalling, Johansson. Tell me your take on why we're not romantically compatible."

"What's your Enneagram number?" She picked up a slice of Hawaiian pizza and took a bite. They'd ordered a large. Half her preference. Half his.

"My what?" He took a bite of his all-meat pizza.

She swallowed. "Have you never taken an Enneagram test?" Wasn't taking that quiz like the first thing every middle-school girl made every middle-school boy do the minute they started talking?

"What is it?"

She laid her slice on her plate. "It's a personality test. A really cool personality test. When you take it, you'll get a number that is your primary personality style and a wing number that also describes you. For example, I'm a seven with a loyalist wing."

He nodded like he understood, but his squished brows didn't agree. "What is a seven? And what's a loyalist wing?" He picked up the red-pepper shaker and sprinkled it heavily on his half. Then he glanced at her to see if she wanted some on hers. She nodded. The hotter the better.

"A seven is called an Enthusiast. In general, a person labeled a seven is spontaneous, versatile, acquisitive, and scattered. The loyalist wing means I'm loyal and tend to speak my mind." She paused and let the words sink in. When he grimaced, she continued. "Tell me, have you ever once imagined your dream woman and thought she would have any one of those traits, let alone all of them?"

He studied her as if she were a science project gone wrong. A theory gone wrong. A hypothesis not proven. "You don't come across as acquisitive."

Lots of men she'd met over the years didn't know what the word meant. The fact he did impressed her. "When you grow up poor, you tend to covet materialistic things. If you ever study Ruby Payne's book, *A Framework for Understanding Poverty*, you'll understand what I mean." She took a small bite of her pizza.

"The poor don't have a monopoly on that trait." He picked up his beer and raised it to his lips. "I grew up rich, and I still want things."

"It's different. Don't forget, I'm also scattered."

"I've not seen any signs of you being scattered. You've completed all of the tasks I've asked you to do without me reminding you."

A group of teenagers came through the door, laughing and carrying on with one another. She waited until they'd been shown to their seats before she responded. "We're still in our honeymoon stage. Trust me, when I'm rattled, I become quite scattered. That's one of the reasons I forgot to bring Aggie's Assets to my interview with you."

"I thought it was because you didn't want me to see your work history."

She gave a one-shoulder shrug. "I will neither deny nor confirm your theory. Anyway, the fact I'm scattered is a huge red flag as to why we are not romantically compatible."

"So you've told me why you're not right for me. Why do you feel I'm not right for you?"

He sounded cocky. Like he couldn't believe any woman wouldn't see him as catch of the year. The fact she kind of agreed irritated her. "I'm willing to guess you're a one with a protector wing. A one is a Reformer."

He shrugged. "What does a Reformer do?"

She pulled out her phone and pulled up the website for the Enneagram site. The action gave her a minute to get a grip on the weird hopes trying to filter through to her consciousness. "A Reformer has the three Ps. They're principled, purposeful, and perfectionists." Dear God, that described him to a T.

He reached for another slice of pizza. "And you see those as bad traits?"

"Not bad. Just not suited to who I am. For example, along with the three Ps, Reformers are also known for their self-control. You have that by the buttload."

"And you know this how?"

"Your self-control is what kept you from kissing me tonight, even though you wanted to." She took a bite of her pizza and waited for his response.

He refilled his beer without breaking eye contact with her. "I'm your boss. Just because I want to do something doesn't mean I get to do it." His words whispered up her spine leaving behind a delicious tingle.

She exhaled. She knew it. Her instincts hadn't been wrong. He did find her attractive. "As a Reformer, you didn't even ask me if I wanted you to be all full of self-control and make that decision for me."

"It was the right decision to make. I didn't need to ask."

"Spoken like a true Reformer. That just proves why we're not compatible. I'm spontaneous. I want a guy to kiss me and worry about the consequences later."

"That's not realistic. I have a company to run. I

can't take the chance of kissing a woman who might decide afterward it wasn't wanted and then file a sexual harassment lawsuit."

"You're absolutely right. You'd be crazy to take that chance. But an Enthusiast like myself doesn't always do what's right. We do what feels good—even if it's crazy. I want to be with someone who has enough spontaneity inside of him to keep me on my toes. To not bore me with constant rules."

The sparkle in his eyes dimmed. "I see."

The effervescence inside her belly fizzled. Sometimes being an adult and making decisions based on logic really sucked. "So you agree we're not romantically compatible, and we should join forces to dissuade our grandmothers of their hopes for a budding relationship?"

He scratched the back of his neck and then inhaled and exhaled loudly. "What do you have in mind?"

Chapter Fourteen

Tuesday flew by mostly because Max had her on the phone gathering information for the bid he was putting together while he worked on the finer details of the project. Over lunch at their desks, they discussed their plan to dissuade the grandmothers of their romantic notions where their grandchildren were concerned.

And now, it was already Wednesday night. Learn-to-play-Bridge night. Aggie sat across the square kitchen table from Max in Ms. Grace's lovely kitchen, an area done in white and light blues. On her right sat Meemaw and on her left, Ms. Grace. They were preparing to play their third hand, round, whatever you called it in Bridge.

Aggie had found herself smiling and laughing a lot. Even though she and Max were having their asses handed to them by a couple of senior citizens. Speaking of asses, his had caught her attention when he arrived wearing a pair of black slacks molding his well-built body in all the right spots. Sweet baby Jesus, the guy must work out.

"I say we take a short break." Max pushed back from the

table and speared Aggie with a frown.

Her pulse did a funny jig. He wasn't mad at her. It was part of their plan to dissuade the grandmothers from their plot to match their two grandchildren.

So far, neither grandmother appeared to have picked up on their blatant attempts to demonstrate their bare-minimum liking of one another. Attempts Aggie found herself having to work at because, for some reason, tonight, she had found herself wondering what the exact odds were of an Enthusiast and a Reformer happily coexisting on a long-term basis. Giving herself a mental slap, she pinched the musing off at its skinny neck, which left her returning a real frown right back at him.

Even if the likelihood was 99 percent, and they weren't, it didn't matter. She and Max had much larger factors dooming them. Money, birth circumstances, difference of opinion on which of them should make the coffee at the office.

"Aggie and I need to revisit our strategy." Max's tongue speaking her name in his trademark grumpy voice made her ponder what it would sound like coming off his tongue under different emotions. Lust. Satisfaction. Love. Nope, not love. Her brain did not go there. Only it did. Fuck. It was one thing to secretly wonder about a sordid affair with the guy, a totally different to harbor other ridiculous wonders.

"Honey, I think that sounds like a fine idea." Ms. Grace's eyes twinkled like faery lights in a Mason jar. "Why don't you and Aggie step out on the balcony and get some fresh air?"

Meemaw nodded her approval. "I'm sure you two could use some alone time. And there's a lovely full moon tonight."

"Take all the time you need," added Ms. Grace.

"Alone time with my boss," Aggie said stiffly, "is the last thing I need." The words came out sounding true. And come to think of it, that was probably because they were. She absolutely didn't need to spend alone time with this guy.

"Aggie LaBelle Johansson," Meemaw snapped in a tone more admonishing than a nun with an unruly school child.

She jumped, and her cheeks took on heat. The last time Meemaw used that tone with her, they were sitting in Principal Pomperein's office, and he was explaining why Aggie wouldn't be allowed to go on the eighth grade field trip to Washington, D.C.

Aggie had told her classmates she got to go, even though she knew Meemaw couldn't afford to send her, and then purposely failed two classes so she wouldn't be eligible. Little did she know, when she failed two classes, a parent-meeting ensued.

She hadn't even told Meemaw about the trip, because Meemaw would do without lunch and work twenty-hour days to try and raise the money.

Failing two classes in order to become ineligible, and keeping Meemaw in the dark, was a hell of a lot better than the alternative—admitting to her classmates she couldn't afford to go. Besides, it wasn't like she would have learned anything on the trip Meemaw hadn't already taught her and shown her via virtual tours of Washington, D.C.

Now, she took a breath and exhaled. "I'm not trying to be mean. I simply know what he'll say." She'd tried to spare Meemaw hurt on that occasion by withholding information from her. That hadn't worked. Hopefully, this subterfuge would. She didn't like lying to Meemaw, but if it saved her feelings in the long run, it was worth it.

The kindest thing she could do was stop Meemaw's fantasy of Max and her standing together in a little white chapel in front of a preacher. "It's what he always says. I'm the problem. I'm doing *it* wrong." She did quote marks around the word it. She glanced directly at Max as she made the dig.

He narrowed his eyes.

Just today, he'd informed her that her skirts were the

wrong length for an office setting. "I could apply makeup, and he'd say I did it wrong and would tell me how to do it right. If he does that during sex, no wonder he's single."

"Agnes Johansson, apologize this moment."

Aggie kicked Max under the table. Why hadn't he jumped in and carried his weight in the playing of their hate game? She didn't enjoy being the only one having their full name used.

Max cleared his throat. "Perhaps if you'd take three seconds and listen to directions once in a while, you wouldn't always be wrong. Hiring you certainly counts as a lapse in judgment."

Did he wish he hadn't hired her?

"Maxwell David Treadwell," Ms. Grace said, a hand over her heart. "Where are your manners?"

"Grandmother—"

"You two are getting your knickers in an unnecessary crumple." Meemaw gave Aggie a look of besiegement, as if to say, *Please don't embarrass me in front of my new friend.* "Don't take your frustration with losing at cards out on each other."

Aggie stood. "I'm going out on the balcony to breathe some fresh air." Disappointing Meemaw caused a twinge in her heart, but it was for the best. "Alone."

"Not alone." Max stood. "This argument isn't over. I'm coming, too."

• • •

Max studied Aggie's expression. "If you have a lot of hearts, look at me like you'd look at someone you're in love with." He waited for her to show him that look.

Her right nostril lifted. "What?"

He sighed. "Remember, it's our signal for hearts. I'll look

at you like I'm in love with you if I have a lot of hearts."

"Let me see your I-love-Aggie look."

Max cleared his throat and stared into her eyes, hoping he was giving her his best I-love-Aggie look.

She glanced off to the side. "I'm pretty sure that's your I-want-to-fuck-you look. Not love you. Who exactly were you really thinking of just now?"

He'd been thinking of *her*. Max shifted his weight. "Show me your I'm-in-love expression."

"With you or with anyone?"

Anyone. "Me."

She squared her shoulders, lifted her chin, looked him straight in the eye, and contorted her face into something that looked quite painful.

"What in the hell was that?" he asked. "Your I-love-Max look reminds me of a constipated monkey."

She raised her hand and scratched her cheek with her middle finger.

He pinched the bridge of his nose. "We're doomed. We'll never win a single hand against these women."

"Not true. I now know what your I-love-you face looks like, and you know mine. They may not be pretty, but they'll work."

True. He lowered his hand to his side. "If I haven't told you, thanks for agreeing to learn how to play Bridge just to help Grandmother win a tournament at her club. That club is important to her." Too bad Ms. Hazel and Aggie would never be on their membership list. They'd be a great addition to the stuffy club. Unfortunately, the Johanssons of Kansas City didn't have the finances to inspire the board to overlook their lack of pedigree. A damn shame.

The door behind them opened. They shuffled away from each other and turned.

"Young'uns, are we playing cards or what?" Ms. Hazel

asked from the doorway.

"Give us another minute," Aggie said.

His gaze shifted back to her. Damn, her body could hypnotize a man. And when you paired it with those eyes…

She laid a slim hand on his arm. "You're welcome, and thank you for giving up on trying to talk Ms. Grace out of being friends with Meemaw."

"They're good for each other. Now, let's get back to what it will take to win a hand against those two."

Ten minutes and several attempts at signal-expressions later, they went inside.

Grandmother and Ms. Hazel scrutinized them.

"It's about blessed time," Ms. Hazel said. "Did you get your cheat-signals figured out?"

"Meemaw, were you spying? Do you know our signals?"

Max groaned. "They were speculating. And now you've confirmed their unprovoked suspicions."

Aggie blushed. "Oh."

Ms. Hazel guffawed while Grandmother laughed softly.

"Maxi, honey, you wouldn't be my grandson if you didn't teach your partner how to cheat."

"True."

"I hope, for your sake, you were smart enough not to recycle the signals we used against our opponents."

Max stared blandly at Grandmother. The woman reveled in discovering her opponent's signals. "With Aggie, I had to keep things much simpler."

Aggie punched him in the shoulder. "Whatever."

The two grandmothers, who were sitting at the table, sipping whiskey from fine china teacups with their pinkies out, grinned with pride at their grandchildren. They reminded Max of two happy ducks floating in a pond full of the food pellets sold to tourists. Damn. Aggie's and his plot hadn't worked even a little.

"Why don't we add a little wager to our next hand?" Ms. Hazel said.

"What kind of wager?" Aggie asked, taking a seat.

Ms. Hazel whispered something to Grandmother, who nodded and then whispered something back. This went on for several seconds. When the whispering ceased, they glanced at their grandchildren.

"The winner of the next round has to fix dinner for the losing team," Grandmother said.

"Don't you have that backward?" Aggie asked. "Shouldn't the loser have to do the cooking?"

"Normally, yes," Ms. Grace said. "But Max can't cook, and Hazel said it's not your strong suit, so since we will win, it's best if we keep the bet the way it is."

Max and Aggie studied their opponents and then nodded at each other. "We'll take you up on your bet. But the next bet is ours to make."

Once again, the two ladies grinned in unison.

Damn. Normally, Max realized what Grandmother was up to the moment she got up to it, but not lately.

"Aggie," Ms. Hazel said, "be a peach and deal the cards."

Chapter Fifteen

Aggie added up the potential value of her thirteen cards. Twelve. Five of them hearts. She laid all of the cards facedown in front of her, placed her elbows on the table, framed her face with her hands and gave Max, who was about to start this round of bidding, her I-love-you expression.

His lips twitched, but just for a second, and then they went back to neutral.

"You okay there, sugar britches?" Meemaw said. "It's not like you to prop your elbows on a table when in polite company."

Aggie removed her elbows, picked up her cards, and gave Meemaw a look of pure innocence. "Simply trying to concentrate on the rules of the game."

"Is that what you were doing?" Max asked in a deadpan tone.

She watched his eyes to catch his signal. None came. Why?

"Maxi, darling, start the bid," Ms. Grace said.

"One heart," he said.

Ms. Grace, who sat to his left, studied her cards. "No bid."

Aggie chewed on her bottom lip and tried to recall all the details on deciding your bid. She didn't want to blow this. She needed to impress Max with her brain. She studied her cards. "One no trump."

Meemaw surprised Aggie with a, "No bid." It wasn't like Meemaw to not play aggressively at anything. Even if it meant bluffing.

After the bidding went another circle around the table, Max said, "We have three no bids. A contract has been entered into. And we are about to play a hand in which we must make at least eight tricks with hearts as trumps."

Aggie grinned. This was good. She had hearts. Five of them.

Max surprised everyone by chuckling.

Meemaw glanced from one to the other. "Grace, I do believe our grandchildren have found their rhythm."

Ms. Grace glanced at Max from over her cards. "I do believe you're right."

Sometime later, Aggie released a whoop of joy. "We win!"

"Gosh darn it, looks like the two of you will have to do the cooking," Meemaw said. "Shall we say next Wednesday night?"

Max pulled his gaze from a smiling Aggie and glanced from one grandmother to the other. "You two lost on purpose, didn't you?"

Aggie lost her smile and glowered at Meemaw. "You purposefully threw a game?"

Meemaw grinned. "Someone needed to show the two of you how to lie convincingly. We decided it might as well be us. The very ones you were trying to dupe."

"You know about our plan to hoodwink you?" Aggie asked.

"Oh yes, we do," Meemaw said. "And there's only one logical reason I can think of as to why you'd feel the need to go to such lengths. You like each other a lot, and you don't want us to know yet."

"Grandmother, you're awfully quiet over there. What do you have to say for yourself?" Max asked Ms. Grace.

She folded her hands primly on the table. "It's your own fault. When the two of you went outside in a supposed huff, we happened to see you laughing together. It became obvious to us that you're simply pretending not to get along."

"Oh, we're not pretending. He's quite pompous."

"And she's quite horrible."

Aggie startled. "Horrible? I'm nothing if not fabulous."

"And if that is true, I am nothing if not humble."

They glared at each other.

Chapter Sixteen

Friday, mid-morning, Aggie sat in the chair across from Richard Harris. For the past thirty minutes, she'd regaled him with fun, inspiring stories of Meemaw in the hopes he might want to ask Meemaw out. They were waiting for Max to show up for a meeting. A meeting Aggie forgot to tell him about.

Not that Max knew the mix-up was her fault. When she'd texted him, she made it sound like he'd somehow forgotten about it.

"There was this one time when Meemaw put on a wig and wore glamour glasses and came to an event at my school called Muffins with Mom. She proceeded to introduce herself as my mom to my classmate, Wanda Pratt, who'd been teasing me because I didn't have a mom."

"Your meemaw raised you?"

Normally, this was where Aggie would change the subject. But she didn't because she needed to stall until Max showed up. "When I was four, Mom dumped me on Meemaw's porch while she was at work." Aggie refused to let her brain dwell on those long hours she sat waiting for Meemaw to come home. Afraid she wouldn't. Afraid she'd have to sleep outside all by herself.

"I'm so sorry. I can't imagine how that must have felt. What happened when Meemaw found you?"

"She invited me inside, and we had a tea party. We talked about all the adventures we would have while waiting for Mom to come back and take me home."

"But she never did?"

"Nope."

Richard stood and stepped to the windows. "Do you have any memories of your mom?" For an older gentleman, he was well preserved. He and Meemaw would make a cute couple. Maybe she should just offer him Meemaw's number.

"I remember her dropping me inside a trash bin outside a restaurant and telling me to dig through the trash for food." She hadn't meant to share that memory, but somehow, knowing Richard came from poverty as well, it seemed safe to do so. But she didn't mention she also had to search for half-empty liquor bottles while in the dumpster.

Richard jerked around and swore under his breath. "That's one thing I never had to do."

Aggie shifted and tucked her feet up on the cushions. "Meemaw told me to look at it as a blessing. It made me life tough. I'm practically invincible."

He didn't laugh. "Have you ever tried to find her?"

She glanced down at her hands. "Meemaw is all the family I need." Part of the statement was true. She definitely needed no one else to love her.

Richard sat down and leaned forward. When she looked at him, his expression was intent. "That's not what I asked."

How had they gotten so personal? "I have. But to no avail."

"How hard have you tried?" He leaned back, folded his

arms across his chest.

She dropped her feet back to the floor. Her brain told her to stand up and flee this conversation. But she didn't listen. "Any time I have extra cash, I give it to a detective who uses it to search for Mom." He wasn't actually a detective. More of a dropout with amazing computer tracking skills.

Richard pulled at his earlobe. "Any leads?"

Why did he care? Then again, as long as they kept talking, the less chance for him to get mad because Max still hadn't shown. "Not yet."

"How does Meemaw feel about your search?"

"She doesn't know. It would break her heart." Aggie inhaled slowly to steady her emotions and laced her fingers in her lap. "She would worry she didn't do enough for me growing up. Which is anything but the truth." Meemaw had saved her.

Richard removed a business card from a silver cardholder, scribbled something on the back. "This is the number of a guy I know who is superb at finding people who don't want to be found. Call him and tell him I recommended him. Tell him to give you the Richard Harris discount."

She didn't reach for the card. Temptation and reality warred with each other. It was like taking the packet of information one needed in order to sign up for the Washington, D.C. trip even while knowing going on said trip was nothing but a pipe dream. "Thank you, but I'm sure, even with the Richard Harris discount, he's out of my price range."

"Rubbish. Take my card. I have him on retainer. When I'm not using him, I've been known to loan him out to my friends at no cost."

"Do you have a lot of friends in need of a detective?" Had he loaned this detective out to Max so he could run a background check on Meemaw?

He winked at her. "One. You. Now, please take the card."

She still didn't reach for the card. Free was never really free. What strings were attached? She didn't get the vibe from Richard it would be sex, but she could have a broken vibe detector. After all, she actually liked Max.

Richard leaned forward.

Oh God. Here it comes. Disappointment jabbed her brain with both its middle fingers.

"In return," Richard said, "how about giving me Meemaw's personal number? She sounds like someone I'd like to have coffee with."

Aggie smiled. Her vibe detector worked. He wasn't a pervert. Which meant Max might actually be worthy of taking a chance on. She casually took the card. "Richard Harris, has anyone ever told you you're as sweet as a Georgia peach?"

She grabbed a Post-it and jotted Meemaw's number and real name. "I don't give this number to just any man," she teased. "Guard it with your life." As she leaned across the table to hand it to him, a shadow in the doorway caught her attention.

She jerked her head in that direction. *Max.* Sweet baby Jesus. How much of their conversation had he heard? The last thing she wanted was for him to know the dirty details of her childhood. Or that she'd just set up Meemaw with Richard. Max would for sure think that was as unprofessional as short skirts.

"There you are, boss man." Her words sounded like a guilty person spoke them. "I'll leave the two of you to your meeting."

Max fixed his gaze on Richard. "Please forgive me. I don't know how this meeting didn't stay on my radar."

"Don't fret. Trust me, I'm not," Richard said. "I've thoroughly enjoyed spending time with this lovely, lovely woman. Aggie, please don't forget to consider my...proposal."

"Proposal?" Max sounded like a lion one second away from pouncing on its prey. "Richard, if I didn't know better, I'd think you've been busy trying to steal my assistant."

Richard chuckled. "I never mix business with pleasure."

"Me, either." Max turned his full gaze on Aggie. "Did you get those estimates I needed?"

"Stop barking at your assistant and come talk," Richard said before she could admit she hadn't. "We have business to finish up, and if it works well, there might be another deal."

"Another deal?" Max echoed.

"After listening to Aggie rave about your ability to see the big picture without getting lost in the woods, I'm convinced you might be the right man for a new project."

It was kind of Richard to not tell Max about what they'd been discussing in his absence.

"I'm glad to hear she wasn't boring you with stories about nothing," Max said. "I've discovered she can sometimes be rather chatty."

Was that supposed to be an insult? Because if it was, she didn't care. Being able to carry on an interesting conversation was a valuable life tool. Meemaw had taught her that.

"May I speak to you for a moment?" Max aimed a too-sweet smile at Aggie. Gah. He'd be brushing his teeth for an hour to get all that sugar off them.

"Can't it wait? Richard has been waiting a while already."

Max's expression went perfectly blank. "I'm afraid not."

Chapter Seventeen

Under hooded eyes, Max watched as Aggie glided across the carpet toward him where he stood in the receptionist area. A perfect vision in a pink suit and a pair of black skyscraping heels. The kind she daily kicked off under her desk.

He motioned for her to close the door. He forced himself to stay calm as he asked, "Did you make plans to go on a date with one of my clients?" He wanted to believe Richard wasn't the sort to date someone young enough to be his granddaughter, but if Aggie put her mind to it, she could probably talk a Mormon into skipping their two-year mission trip experience. Or him breaking his vow not to mix business with pleasure. That one teetered daily.

"Why do you always assume the worst of me?" She stomped back to the receptionist desk, grabbed a tissue out of its box, and dabbed at her cleavage.

Christ. She did that to trash his line of thought. "Are you saying I'm wrong?" His hands tightened into fists as a need to crush something took hold of him.

She stared stonily. "Besides the notes you left on my

desk, do you have anything else you need me to do?"

She could cause all of his dealings with Richard Harris to blow up if she went out with him and things went sideways. "I do." He'd planned on doing this task himself. And it was a shitty thing to ask. But she'd just done a shitty thing to him by jeopardizing a business deal. And as a result, he was feeling quite fucking shitty.

"And it is?" Her words were followed with a grade-A smirk. A smirk that sealed her fate.

He released his fists. "I stayed late last night, working on a new project."

"And?" she asked in an impatient tone.

"I threw away a document I still need." Probably because his brain had kept coming back to thoughts of her naked on his conference table. "Right before I left, the janitor came in and emptied the trash bins."

"And...?" Again with the tone.

Was he asking her to do this for the right reason? Absolutely not.

Fuck. Watching her hand Richard her phone number had made him feel something he didn't want to feel. Jealousy.

As a rule, he wasn't the jealous sort. What was it about Aggie that brought that emotion out in him? It couldn't be simply she was beautiful and sexy. Hell, he'd dated his fair share of that type of women.

The obvious answer to the puzzle didn't escape him. There's brain jealousy and then there's heart jealousy. Just because his brain didn't do the jealous thing didn't mean his heart was immune.

If his heart was attempting to get involved, he needed to shut it down.

There was a saying the heart wants what the heart wants, but all you had to do was look at the divorce column to know more times than not the heart wanted the wrong person.

She had said herself they were incompatible.

If he couldn't stop his own headstrong heart, he would stop hers. When hers crashed and burned, his wouldn't have any choice but to give up. Which meant asking her to do something unforgivable. Something far worse than toilet paper pickup. Something that would take any shine off how she was feeling about him. "I need you to go out to the dumpster and locate my office trash bag and bring it back in." He'd just cemented his asshole status. There would be no recovering from this.

Assholes don't win the love of the lady. His heart was safe.

Her chin jerked. "You want *me* to dumpster dive?" Instead of anger or distaste, her voice held an odd hint of panic.

"Afraid Richard might see you out there and decide not to ask you out on a date?" Yep, asshole-of-the-year award was his for the taking.

Her eyes narrowed. "*He's* not that shallow."

"Good for him."

She shrugged. "If I say no, are you going to fire me?"

If you're going to be an asshole, be a grade-A asshole. No soft underbelly. "I recall you saying, short of blowing me, there wasn't anything you weren't willing to do." Hell. This might qualify him for dick-of-the-year as well. This was far worse than anything Father had ever done to secure the title.

She gave a succinct nod and kicked out of her heels. "I'll change shoes and go look for your bag of trash."

Grandmother would be appalled. Ms. Hazel might shoot him.

Damn it. What in the hell was the matter with him? You didn't make a woman hate you just so you didn't have to deal with the risk of falling for her. He swallowed hard and backpedaled. Not all the way back, but far enough to save his soul when he some day met his Maker and had to defend his actions in life. "Ask the janitor for a hook to dig it out with." He'd find another way to keep her at arm's length. "I don't want you to actually get in the dumpster. If you can't get it with a hook, don't worry about it." If nothing else, he'd revamp her duties so she became his virtual assistant. If she wasn't underfoot, his heart should be safe.

Hell. Why hadn't he thought of that idea before now?

"Right. Lucky for you, I ordered trash bags to match our interior, so it'll be easy to find."

Jealousy aside, he really did need the paper. "Great."

"Great." She swept out the door and, not even bothering with a low voice, muttered, "Jackass."

Fair enough.

Chapter Eighteen

Aggie stood outside the dumpster and concentrated on the sights and sounds and smells until the panic attacking her like a tsunami eased, allowing her to see and breathe and think. She wiped the sweat from her forehead and strategized.

Her memories of doing this were as fresh as yesterday's bread. Mom's strategy had been simple. She'd lower Aggie inside the bin with a toddler strap attached to her back. Once she found a treasure, Mom would hoist her and the item out of the bin. Only to drop Aggie back in to discover more gems.

The smell of those memories still burned Aggie's nostrils. And the panic of having to hurry so no one caught them and stole their treasures away still tightened her chest. Once, someone else had been in the bin. An old guy with no teeth. He'd spat at her. Yelled at her to get out of his dumpster. And when Mom pulled her out, he'd taken Aggie's shoes off her feet and laughed like a mad clown.

Aggie slogged back inside the office building and located the janitor, who was mopping the foyer with a big machine. She waved her arms at him to get his attention. When he stopped, she asked, "Would you happen to have a ladder, and a hook, and some coveralls I could borrow?"

"Not in the business of loaning out stuff." He went back to his mopping.

She waved her arms again. He stopped, his face a ruddy red. Either sunburned or high blood pressure. "Please." She gave him her award-winning smile. At least Meemaw called it her award-winning smile.

"What do you need with a ladder?"

She glanced around to see if anyone could hear their conversation. "My boss accidentally threw something away. I need to dig it out of the trash bin before the truck comes and hauls it off."

The guy looked her over from head to toe and laughed, clutching his oversize belly while he did so.

She waited for his hilarity to pass. Who could blame him? Today, she wore her favorite power suit. One that screamed corporate bitch. "Well?"

"Let me get this straight. You've got a boss who expects you to dumpster dive, and you said yes?"

"He's kind of a jerk like that." Normally, she would have told Max to piss off. But she'd made it a full two weeks as his assistant, and she was determined to ride this contract all the way to the finish line. Besides, if she quit, Richard might decide it would be somehow disloyal to Max if he pursued a date with Meemaw, and Aggie really wanted him to pursue that date.

The janitor turned off his machine and walked away.

She followed. "Where are you going?"

"To get you what you asked for." He pulled a pair of coveralls out of a supply closet and handed them to her. "Pull the door closed when you leave. It will lock on its own."

She watched him walk away carrying the ladder under one arm as if it weighed nothing.

Inside the closet, she slipped on the coveralls. They were about ten sizes too big, but they were way better than nothing, so she rolled up the arms and legs. Leaving her purse tucked under an empty mop bucket, she stepped into the hallway and firmly closed the door, then double checked that it was locked. It was.

About to hurry outside, she heard her phone moo. It was in the closet. She forced herself to ignore the siren call. No way would she bother the janitor for the keys to get back into the closet.

Outside the dumpster, the janitor had propped the ladder in place. "I'll hold it while you shimmy up there and over," he said to her. "Can't have you falling off. Boss would fire me for sure if I allowed that to happen. Probably going to fire me for letting you use the ladder."

She glanced around for a big stick. No trees in sight. "I don't suppose you have one of those trash picker-upper thingies?"

"Nope. Don't do outdoor trash duty."

She sighed. Kicked off her Crocs—no sense ruining them with the smell of garbage—and climbed the ladder. At the top, she glanced down. It was empty of other human beings. According to all of the cop shows she watched, this was not always the case. What it lacked in dead bodies it made up for in its foul odor. She glanced around, her hopes high she would spot Max's trash bag immediately and not have to rummage. Maybe nab it with an outstretched hand. No such luck.

"I should have kept my job at the Estée Lauder Counter," Aggie said. Applying makeup to rich old ladies who wanted the appearance of rich young ladies no longer seemed dire. Gah. Hindsight and all that shit.

"Ain't got all day. Get 'er done," a disembodied voice said. The janitor's. Still safely anchored to the ground on the opposite side of the bin's metal wall.

She sat down on the edge of the dumpster and considered her options—tell Max to go fuck himself or prove to him she didn't always quit when things got rough. She lowered herself onto a black bag. Her foot immediately went through the thin material. "Eww," she screamed, as she sunk knee deep into what smelled like a poopy diaper but was probably just rotten food. Right? Right. "I should have left my Crocs on." It's not like they were Prada. And she could have probably expensed them out to Max.

"What is it? Dead body?" The question was asked with 100 percent sincerity and zero percent concern her answer might be yes. Like the phrase, been-there-done-that-have-the-dead-body-to-prove-it was his to legit recite. The janitor obviously also watched cop shows. If it was the last thing she did, Aggie would see to it Max Treadwell paid for this humiliation.

"No dead body," she shouted so he could hear her. "Just immense grossness."

"I'll be back in ten," the janitor said. "It's my break time. Need to take a piss."

Panic crawled up her throat. She'd never been left alone while inside a bin. Mom always talked to her. Sometimes sang "You Are My Sunshine" to Aggie to help keep her calm.

Humming the tune in her head, she added new lyrics. "You are a dick prick. A lowly dick prick. You make me angry when the skies are blue. You'll never know, Max, how much I loathe you. Please someone take my dick prick away." She bellowed out the words over and over as she poked around for Max's trash bag.

Chapter Nineteen

Max took a breath before striding into his office. Richard stood at the window, looking out. If he looked down, the trash bin would be in clear sight. Aggie would appear there in no time. If the guy liked her, he'd be upset with Max for asking her to dig through trash even if she did utilize a long stick in the process. "I'm so sorry to keep you waiting."

Richard turned.

Max chose a seat at the conference table, and Richard joined him. "Tell me about this new project on your radar?"

Richard looked at him speculatively. "Actually, it's my partner, David Long, who's taking the lead on finding the right property for the venture."

Was she out there? "I haven't yet had the pleasure of working with David." He glanced at the window. Damn it. What in the hell had gotten into him? He'd behaved like a fucking coward.

"We'll see if you still see it as pleasure once you've met the man. He can be disagreeable."

"I've been told I can be disagreeable, too." Max stood.

"I'm going to grab a bottle of water. I've had a tickle in my throat all morning." Not waiting for a response, he hurried toward the outer office. As soon as he was out of view of Richard, he sent Aggie a text telling her to abort her mission. Then he grabbed two bottles of water from the mini-fridge and went back to his office.

"You were saying?" He handed a bottle of water to Richard.

"If things go well with the current project you're working on for us, I'll have Aggie set up a meeting between you two."

Had his lateness to this meeting caused Richard to worry he wasn't up for a bigger task? Or was he pulling back, handing him off to his partner, because he wanted to date Aggie and didn't want to mix business with pleasure?

"Things are going to go better than well with this project. No sense in waiting."

Richard opened his briefcase and pulled out a file. "As great as you are, it will probably be out of your league. In fact, I'm considering your father's corporation for this project."

Max grimaced. "Our styles are nothing alike." Father hired out the diminutive details. Max, on the other hand, bought commercial property, designed a blueprint to best make it shine, and then flipped it.

"I'm well aware of that fact."

"I can assure you, there's nothing Father can do that I can't."

"That's what Aggie told me when I floated the idea by her. She said you're the most brilliant man she has ever known." Richard smiled as if talking about her made him happy.

"She said that?"

"Among other things."

He could only imagine. "Shall we get down to business?"

Their meeting lasted only fifteen minutes. As soon as Richard left, Max walked to his desk to grab a file. When he picked it up, a single sheet of paper lay underneath. The missing document.

Thank God he'd told Aggie to abort the mission.

Chapter Twenty

"Aggie?" a guy's voice said.

Aggie stopped singing and jumped, as much as one can jump while in a sea of squishy plastic sacks, and lost her balance. This time she went backward, landing ass down in the array of bulging bags.

Swiping her hair out of her face, she glanced up into the bright sunlight. Toward the direction in which the voice came. When she saw who the voice belonged to, she was engulfed with true humiliation.

"What?" The word came out more a dog growl than a human sound. Which any sane person would deem appropriate, since it wasn't the janitor whose eyes she met. That left only one other soul who knew where to find her.

Her horrible, horrible boss man stared, with what looked suspiciously like disgust, from over the safe edge of the bin.

"What in the hell are you doing in there?" he snapped. "Didn't you get my text?"

"What text?" she bit out.

He leaned across and down a little and whispered, "To

abort the mission."

"Obviously not!"

"Well, I sent it. Get out of there."

She tapped the fingers of her right hand on a discarded Captain Crunch cereal box. She'd eaten a lot of generic Captain Crunch growing up. "I haven't found what you sent me to find."

He cleared his throat. "Funny story. I found the page. I hadn't actually thrown it away." In what looked like an effort to not touch his body to the bin, he held out a helping hand.

A loud ringing filled her ears, and a red haze blurred her vision. "I'm ass-high in trash for no reason?" She struggled into a standing position. It was a damn good thing for him she hadn't brought a gun with her to this trash party.

He wiggled his fingers at her, as if in a hurry to get her out of the trash and himself back into his office before someone saw them. "To be fair—"

"Fair." Was he really about to try and justify his part in her current predicament? "If I were you, I'd choose my next words exceptionally carefully." She reached out to grab his hand and got nothing but air. On purpose. The last thing she wanted was for him to try dead-lifting her ass out of this bin. He could give it his best shot, with all those muscles that bulged under his dress shirts, and she'd still not leave the ground.

"Come closer," he ordered. "We can talk about the events leading up to this later."

"Did you know there are five million trillion-trillion germs on our planet? That's a five with thirty zeroes after it."

"Can't say I knew that."

"Well, there are. And for every step I take forward, I'm introduced to at least a gazillion of those germs."

He sighed. "Aggie, move closer. I can't reach any farther and maintain my balance."

"Call the fire department, then. Ask them to send a rescue unit. Preferably the one with the crew who modeled for this year's sexy firemen calendar. I'm sure one of them would get dirty to save a damsel in distress."

He shrugged off his suit jacket and removed his tie. "Damsel, huh?" He used his charming voice.

"Fuck you."

"Fair enough." He bent farther over the edge of the dumpster, allowing his white shirt to touch the green metal and, this time, reached out with both hands. "Why not a princess?"

"When you're a princess, your options are limited. Not so when you're a damsel. Any hunk can save a damsel. A princess has to wait for a prince."

He wiggled his fingers as if enticing a one-year-old to waddle toward him. "This is your lucky day, damsel in distress. I'm the hunk who came to save you."

She didn't budge. "The hunk who puts a damsel in danger can't be the same hunk who saves her." *Dick prick. Dick prick. Dick prick.*

"Why not?"

"Fairytales don't work that way."

"Damn it, move closer. Grab my hands." His boss man voice came out to play.

She shuffled a few steps and reached for his hands, but they still didn't connect. Again, that was by design on her part. "What's the hurry? Is Richard waiting for you to get back to your meeting? Did you tell him what you asked me to do?"

"He left about five minutes ago."

"So you waited until your meeting ended and he'd cleared the building before checking to see if I received your text?"

Max huffed out a sigh as if he stood in trash instead of her. "I don't blame you for being mad. I'd be mad, too. But right now, we need to get you out of there."

"Mad doesn't even begin to describe what I'm feeling." Humiliated. Hurt. Scared. Stupid.

"Be resourceful. Stack some of those larger bags on top of each other and then climb up on them."

She screwed up her hands into balls, causing her nails to dig into her palms. "That's a bloody brilliant idea." The guy was practically begging for payback. She stacked four bags on top of one another and climbed her way up. Once she had her balance, she placed her hands in his.

If there was one thing Aggie Johansson was good at, it was payback.

When he relaxed and smiled, she yanked. Not a light yank. A yank of a woman trying to get her vibrator away from a Rottweiler.

She didn't need a fucking hunk to come to her rescue. This damsel would save herself.

• • •

Max realized her intent at the same moment she yanked him down. The option to save himself from the fall didn't exist. For such a slender thing, Aggie possessed the strength of a body-building demon.

Part of him, a small part, admired her tenacity. No wonder she hadn't lasted longer than two weeks at any job until this point. She didn't understand what to do with authority or an apology. He had apologized...right?

The majority of his parts—including the part that gagged at the sight of maggots—stared in horror at the rotting trash gleefully awaiting his magnificent belly flop.

"Agg—" Her name cut off at impact, which didn't hurt. Unless you count the Alaska-sized bruise to his ego.

"Get off me." She pushed at his shoulders, and in a

late attempt not to hurt her with his weight, he rolled. They struggled to their feet, grabbing at each other's arms for balance, resulting in sways and wobbles.

Following their final wobble, their gazes crashed into each other like a high-speed car wreck. Hers held a mixture of revenge and, well...not fucking remorse. Oh, hell no. Aggie, who should have been preparing to grovel, apparently didn't suffer from second-guessing regrets. Instead, she held her sides as if to hold back a laugh.

"You're fired—"

Sure enough, laughter burst from her clenched lips, flooding the dumpster with its lyrical hysterics. "I know. I know. Oh. My. God." Tears streamed down her cheeks, and she rubbed at them, leaving streaks of black mascara in their place.

Unbelievable. She really wasn't sorry. *Damn it*. Even if he was an asshole, he was still her boss. Maybe his gaze wasn't telling her how much trouble she'd landed herself into with this prank. He tried to summon self-righteous indignation. "If you were pissed, you could have just sued me for tasks unbecoming an assistant. I could have even recommended a good lawyer to you." He was certainly not going to have to pay for drinks tonight.

"I prefer to leave the courts out of the matters of my anger when dealing with my colossally privileged boss."

Without warning, laughter bubbled up inside of him and spilled from his lips. After a few seconds, she joined him.

For several minutes, raucous, childhood-like laughter, the kind you got when absolutely nothing was funny, but you and your best friend couldn't stop laughing no matter how many warning frowns your teacher sent your way, bounced off the walls of the trash bin.

The kind of laughter between a guy and the girl who had stolen his heart. *Son of a bitch*.

She reached up and pulled a piece of lettuce out of his hair. "I'm pretty sure you will have to unfire me or face the wrath of Meemaw and Ms. Grace."

A leftover chuckle slipped out of his lips. Unfiring her seemed to be what he did best. How many times did that make now? Twice? Three times? He imagined the scene with him explaining to the grandmothers why he'd fired her.

"Fine." God help him. He'd bet his right nut this wouldn't be the last time. "You're unfired."

"And you'll double my salary?"

He nodded. It was the least he could do. "But only if—"

"You don't get to add a but. I'm—"

"Hey, you two, I've got work that ain't gonna do itself. If you want my help, shake a leg."

They looked up.

The janitor, leaning over the edge, held out a gloved hand. "You know," he said, his gaze on Max, "there are finer places to meet a woman." And then he glanced at Aggie. "And you...you can do better."

A sharp elbow to his ribs drew a grunt from Max. Aggie smirked at him and then shined a sweet-as-syrup smile up at the janitor. "Aren't you a peach for noticing."

Once again, Aggie Johansson had gotten the last word.

Chapter Twenty-One

Monday at five thirty p.m., Aggie stood at her desk and rubbed her eyes. It had been three nights and three dumpster nightmares since the trash incident. On the bright side, last night's nightmare hadn't been scary. Gross but not scary. She'd dreamt Maxwell Treadwell had kissed her while standing in all those germs.

What kind of girl dreamed of a guy kissing her in a heap of garbage?

A weird one, for sure. Probably suffered from the I'm-not-good-enough syndrome, damn it.

Then again, what kind of girl forgave a guy responsible for her searching through trash for something that's not even in there? And forgive him she had.

A weird one, for sure. Probably suffered from I-can-fix-the-guy syndrome, damn it.

Lucky for Max, she was the revenge and forgive type. Why dwell on what'd been handled? Especially when you knew your own antics set the series of unfortunate incidents into blazing motion.

To his credit, not once all day had he mentioned the incident. Or the pre-incident. Nor had he asked her to clarify if it was her number she'd given Richard. Which pointed to his being the I-deserved-that-and-forgive type.

Instead of rehashing their latest fiasco, he'd been on overdrive working out the details of his bid proposal.

Not that she was complaining about that part. Planning with him made her soul sing, and she didn't use that phrase lightly.

Not only did he ask for her input, he listened to her responses *and* he incorporated her ideas into his proposal.

"Aggie," he said.

She tensed. While she'd be okay with acting like Friday never happened, she knew realistically they would have to eventually talk about it. It was, after all, the adult thing to do. And taking the adult road meant she would admit she gave Richard Meemaw's number so Max would stop thinking the worst of her.

"Yes?" She pretended to be busy with something at her desk because her stomach was suddenly feeling quite twisty and turny.

"Come look at this."

She glided over to him while nonchalantly wiping her sweaty palms on her hips. She didn't stop until she stood close to him. Surely, if he planned on handling this like an adult, as well, he was about to tell her she was worthy of so much more respect than he'd been showing her, and things would change and then he'd kiss her. Okay. The last part wouldn't happen. But, due to last night's dream, she had a fierce craving for his grumpy lips.

He pointed to the blueprint on his desk.

The guy really had nice hands. The kind of hands that enticed her to ruminate about things other than work. She peered at where he pointed. Okay. False alarm. They were not about to adult.

She forced her brain to engage in logic. "Wow." He'd taken her idea and enhanced it like a master artist might a stick figure. "That's perfect." Did he even freaking remember Friday? "You're going to win the bid for sure on this project."

He stepped back and rubbed his neck. "Let's call it a day." His eyes didn't meet hers despite her efforts to catch his gaze.

As a way of masking her disappointment, she yawned. To be fair, it might not have been a mask. Quality sleep didn't occur when scary dreams had you by the throat. "Sounds good. I plan on getting up in the morning and running before work." *Get up early. Run.* Where the hell had her mouth found those words? She didn't run. Not even in her nightmares when being chased by evil and finding refuge in a trash can.

Max gave her a nod of approval. The kind most guys gave a girl when she'd walked out of the bedroom wearing nothing but a smile. "I didn't know you ran." Admiration hugged his words, squeezing them so tight they turned blue.

She silently groaned. She'd been Meemawed. The ornery thing had mentioned in passing this weekend that Aggie should take bagels to work on Monday, because Ms. Grace said Max ran every morning. And runners needed their carbs. And she knew how Aggie tended to take on a guy's hobbies when she liked him.

When Aggie had laughed at Meemaw's suggestion, Meemaw had then mentioned Max's last lady-of-interest ran marathons.

The thing about lies, they're hard to backtrack out of. Especially when they were rewarded with approval. "I love to run. It's great for stress."

He grinned.

Did he know? "What's so funny?" It wasn't like she couldn't run. She probably could run. Probably super-fast.

How fast did he run a mile? If she beat his time, he'd have to respect her. Then again, why did she have to be the one searching for respect? Too bad she didn't have that thought before doubling down on her lie.

He shrugged. "I find it hard imagining you as a runner."

"You should join me sometime. See for yourself."

He reached out and slid a strand of hair out of her face. "How about tomorrow morning?"

His fingers touching her cheekbone stirred her desire to be kissed. "Tomorrow morning, what?" It called upon all of her willpower not to touch where he'd touched.

He cocked his head. There was something in the way he looked at her that hadn't been there before. She had absolutely no idea what it was, but it was new. And unnerving. And it wasn't there before she mentioned her love of running. Was he, too, thinking about kissing?

"How about I join you on your run in the morning?" he asked.

No, no, no. That wasn't going to happen. "Aren't you a peach for trying to bond with your employee, but, to be honest, I don't think running with my boss would relax me. You'd no doubt want to talk business."

A devastating grin stretched his lips upward. "I much prefer when it's me you're calling a peach. How about I promise not to talk business?"

Not having another reason to say no and liking that he liked that she called him a peach, she said the one thing she most didn't want to say. "You have a date. Say seven thirty. Sharpish."

His face lit up. "Where?"

The guy genuinely wanted to run with her. Why? "You pick."

He shut down his computer. "I could meet you at your place. We could run in your neighborhood."

She moved to her desk and turned off her computer. That may not be their safest bet. When people ran in her neighborhood, it was often away from the cops. "I'm tired of running in my hood. Why don't I meet you at your condo, and we can run in yours?"

He nodded. "I'm looking forward to it. And Aggie?"

"Yes?"

"I'm sorry about Friday. I don't know what got into me asking you to do that. It's like…"

"Like what?" she urged.

"Nothing. I just want you to know, despite our differences, I'm impressed with your knowledge and vision. When our contract is over, you should find a job drawing upon those strengths. I'll be happy to write you a reference."

Differences? They were both educated. They were both manipulated by grandmothers.

Was he referring to their different social-economic standings in the community? Damn it. Could the guy not go one day without triggering her insecurities?

Chapter Twenty-Two

At seven thirty-five a.m., Tuesday morning, a brisk knock sounded on Max's door. When he opened it, his breath was wrenched from his lungs. Aggie, makeup free, wearing the tiniest pair of running shorts, the kind elite runners wore in major marathons, a pink sports bra, and what looked to be brand new shoes. No shirt of any kind. The outfit made her painting shorts look like a nun's habit.

The pithy greeting he'd planned failed to launch. Sweat broke out on his brow. "Almost right on time."

"Are you ready to do it?"

He nodded, refused to think *do it* meant *do it*, and headed toward the elevators while mentally flipping through the multiplication's table, starting with nines, to keep his brain off of what it wanted to dwell on. Kissing every inch of her bare skin.

She followed.

In the elevator, they stood along the back wall. He forced his eyes to stay on the door. Tried not to inhale her sweet scent, but it soaked through his nostrils, and the tempting scent all but convinced him it would be okay to fuck her right here, right now.

He dragged a hand down his face. It's not like he hadn't already known she had a killer body—he'd known since the first day they met.

Knowing it and seeing so much of it naked sent him into a tailspin of lust. Now it wouldn't only be her lips he daydreamed of ravaging.

"It's a beautiful morning for a run." Her voice sounded rumbly.

"How far do you want to go?" He glanced at her. Big mistake. *Nine times seven...sixty something.*

She slid her gaze over his body. "How far do you normally go the first time with a new partner?" Her voice husky.

Eight times eight... "Six to ten miles."

"Oh."

With his gaze on the light reflecting the floors going by, he waited for her to expand. She didn't. Twenty hours later, the elevator door slid open, and they exited the building. "Want to stretch first?"

Her eyes gave him another thorough inspection. "I did before I came, but you can. I'll wait and watch."

"I'm good." He turned toward a hill. "I like to get this climb over in the beginning." He fell into a slow jog. "You set the pace. I don't want to go too fast for you."

"Setting the pace is my favorite." She picked up the speed, moving out in front like a true competitor.

He followed, watching in amusement as she maneuvered the hill. Thirty steps in, his insides were bursting with bottled-up laughter. Aggie Johansson's arms were swinging outward like a downhill-careening child, and her knees were pointing awkwardly inward, and her feet came up off the pavement at an angle and...

His laughter faded. Damn it. He was being pranked. For

certain this time.

At the top, she stopped. Bent over and gasped for air.

He wiped all hints of laughter out of his voice. "Are you okay?" She was, of course, pranking him, but maybe he could get the upper hand in this charade if he pretended ignorance.

She looked up at him. Her face was red, and real sweat rolled down her cheeks as she barely nodded.

Maybe this wasn't a prank. "That hill can be a little tough the first time around." A lie. It wasn't over three-tenths of a mile and not that steep. "If it makes you feel better, there aren't any more hills." Of course, if he ran like she ran, he'd be out of breath as well.

She stood. "Your turn to set the pace." Her words came out on little individual gasps. Definitely not pranking him.

He took the lead. She lagged far enough behind he couldn't see her with his peripheral vision. But he could hear her breathing. Pretty sure people in England could hear her breathing. A car honked at them. And as it passed, the passenger shouted, "Go, Phoebe, go!"

What?

"Fuck you," Aggie shouted.

Max stopped running and glanced at her. "What was that about?"

"Assholes being assholes. Phoebe happens to be a kick-ass character from the sitcom *Friends* whose running style is a combination of a toddler and a baby giraffe. Which is a perfectly legit way to run."

He nodded as if he totally agreed. "Shall I chase them down and kick their asses?"

She gave him a squinty-eyed stare, as if measuring his level of sincerity. "I'm done with this. You can finish running on your own."

"Aggie—"

"No." She turned and stumbled back the way they'd

come.

"Where are you going?"

"Home to take a shower and then to work."

Damn it. "But…I thought you enjoyed running."

She turned and glared back at him. "I do. But not with my boss."

Figuring out Aggie the Horrible was like trying to understand Quantum Mechanics as a toddler.

Chapter Twenty-Three

Wednesday, near closing time, when Max returned to his office after spending all of Tuesday with his bankers, and most of Wednesday with clients, he pulled up short.

Nothing was as it had been when he'd left Monday evening. Obviously, he hadn't given Aggie enough to do with her time. When would he learn she could do at least twice as much in one day as his usual assistant?

"Aggie?" The last time he'd seen her, she'd been in those tiny running shorts, striding away from him.

"Oh, hey, boss man." She gave him the smile he was beginning to know as her get-out-of-jail-free smile. The one that made every part of him go tense and yet excited at the same time.

"Oh, hey, assistant lady." He loved how she didn't hold a grudge. He'd been brought up, when someone did you wrong, you cut them out of your life. Like he'd been doing with his father for years. Was her approach better? Get mad. Get even. Get over it.

She moved out from behind her desk, holding a feather

duster. A fantasy starring her and that duster flashed through his brain, escalating the ever-present desire he endured in her presence.

"Before you blow a gasket," she said, "let me explain why I've done what I've done."

He stood at the door and counted to three. He really hated for anyone to touch his things. Always had. Not because he didn't like to share, but because...Mom taught him not to share. When things got shared, things got broken. Broken things had no value. He'd probably been around six at the time.

"I'll hold back my gasket blowing until after you've explained why you've changed the layout of our office without seeking my permission."

She pointed the duster in his direction. "Actually, I'm not in possession of a fabulous reason for not *asking* your permission, other than you'd say no. But I do have a kick-ass reason for the changes."

Aggie Johansson subscribed to the adage it's better to ask forgiveness than seek permission. He, too, believed in the benefits of living by such a rule. It's hard to get mad when someone flipped it on you. "I'm listening."

"Okay then. Have you ever heard of Feng Shui?"

"I remember it being mentioned in one of my college classes. Why don't you give me a brief refresher?"

She floated in front of her desk and leaned against it. "It's an ancient Chinese system of laws. In its basic explanation, Feng Shui says the spatial arrangement of a room affects the flow of energy in the room. And what allows for favorable energy should be taken into consideration when arranging a space, or in your case, when re-imagining new uses for old buildings."

Did the spatial arrangement of his thoughts affect the flow of energy in his life? "How does having my desk facing a door instead of a window-with-a-view affect the energy in the room?"

She crossed her legs at the ankles, drawing his attention to today's death-trap heels. They were black with a lot of straps. "According to lore, when your back is to the door, you're inviting in energy that allows for things at work to be done behind your back."

"Like you rearranging my office without my permission?"

She beamed.

Today her hair flowed down her back, inviting a man's hands. His hands.

"Exactly," she said. "I did, however, place a mirror on your desk so you can see the view out the window."

What would it be like to spend his life with someone as free and easygoing as her? It would be a life of unpredictability. Some unpredictability was good, but he didn't think he could handle a constant barrage of it. He needed more control. More certainty. There'd been enough uncertainty in his life already.

"And the new plants?" He pointed to a tree in the corner.

"This beauty," she said, running her hand lovingly over a branch, "is a lucky bamboo. It's considered a wealth plant."

He'd like her to run her hands over *him* like that.

"A wealth plant?" His voice came out thick, not unlike other parts of him at the moment. Maybe control was overrated. Would it be so terrible to try someone else's approach to life? He could always go back to predictability if he didn't like the change. Just like he could change his office furniture back if this arrangement didn't work.

She braced a hand high on the windowsill, as if posing for a magazine cover. "Having wealth plants helps to anchor your intention for the room. And, correct me if I'm wrong, but your intent is to make money, right?"

It was hard to argue her points when his thoughts were

all over the place. "Father once told me I'd be lucky to earn thirty thousand a year at the top of my game."

"What did you say to him?"

He'd never told this story to anyone. "I bet him I'd accrue my first million by the time I'm thirty-one." Father didn't net his first million until he was thirty-two. He had to do him one better.

"What happens if you lose the bet?"

He rocked back on his heels. "Tell me about your duster."

The look she gave him said she saw right through his diversion attempt. "First, tell me about the bet?"

He eyed the wealth plant and then her legs and then her duster. "If I lose, I sell him my company and go to work for him. The duster?"

She straightened and wiggled the duster at him as if she could read his wicked thoughts. "A clean workplace fosters a clear mind."

He swallowed a whole bucket full of lust and walked to his desk. "And the weird smell?"

As if trying to push every sexual button he possessed, she sauntered over and perched on the edge of his desk. "Weird? I find the scent soothing."

"What is it?"

She slowly crossed her legs. "I'm burning sage to do a space clearing. It will lighten the feeling in here and clear the negative vibes we've had between us."

He forced his gaze to travel upward until it finally met her amused grin. "Aggie..." He said her name because he needed to remind himself who she was. His employee. Not his current lover. "Are you seeing Richard?"

"Not at the moment."

He took her hands in his. "Good."

"Because you want me for yourself?"

Need stroked the flame inside him that had lit the moment

they met. He wanted to lay her on the conference table and strip her naked. "I honestly don't know."

She leaned forward and briefly touched her lips to his. "Let me know when you figure it out."

Fuck. He forced himself to nod and dropped her hands. "We'll leave things as they are…for now."

She hopped off the desk. "Look at you, trying to admit you like me." She threw herself into his arms and full-body hugged him. "Thank you," she whispered against his tie. "I like you, too."

Inhaling her scent, he disengaged himself from her arms. Was he crazy to want to get to know her better? "I think your sage burning is working. Now, get to work."

For a moment, she didn't move. Other than her tongue darting out and licking her perfect lips. "Whatever you say, boss man." She turned and slowly, hypnotically, purposefully sauntered toward her desk. Like she had on so many other occasions in this office.

Shaking off the "Aggie effect," he dropped into his chair. God, he wished he kept whiskey in his desk. He opened the right drawer to put away his phone. The calendar he used to mark off the number of days until his permanent assistant returned caught his attention.

He pulled it out and marked off one more. Twenty-seven business days left. When he started marking the days, he couldn't wait for the end to come. But now…now he found himself liking Aggie's quirkiness. Envied some of her free spirit approach to life. Didn't look forward to the final X. He slid the calendar back in the drawer under a stack of folders. "Aggie…"

She poked her head out from behind her computer. "Yes, boss man?"

"Weren't we supposed to cook dinner tonight before our Bridge practice?"

"Didn't Ms. Grace tell you? Meemaw picked up an extra shift tonight, so it's been postponed."

"Does Ms. Hazel work a lot of extra shifts?"

Aggie worried her bottom lip. "Not as much as she used to. She said something about having an unexpected expense this month, so she wanted some extra income."

"In that case, would you like to have dinner with me?"

"You mean a date?"

"More like a business event."

"Oh. You need me to work late?"

"Just over dinner. Unless you have plans?"

Her lavender-blue eyes sparkled from clear across the room. "I don't have any plans. Can I pick the place for our work...date?"

His breath got stuck in his throat, so he just nodded.

Chapter Twenty-Four

One hour later, Aggie and Max stood outside Pappy's Barbeque, an infamous hole-in-the-wall bar in a seedy part of Kansas City.

"We're here." Aggie stared intently at Max. She wanted to capture his response.

He swallowed, and his Adam's apple moved.

She'd learned over the past few weeks that sexy little bump in his throat always came out to play when a situation left him feeling out of control.

"Have you been here before?" he asked.

"Many times." Just never with a guy like him. She was about to find out if he was the type of guy who would try and fit into her world.

A biker strode by with his helmet under his arm and a skull cap on his head.

"I've been to safer-looking places." He tugged at his ear as he spoke.

"Me too." She tried to look at her surroundings through his eyes. The gravel parking lot consisted of monstrous motorcycles and old pick-up trucks. The windows to the rundown establishment had bars over them.

She heard a soft chuckle and turned her attention back to him. "I'll give you this," he said. "You're never predictable."

Even though the corner of his lips was lifted in a smile, all she had to do was glance into his eyes to see his worry-wart wheels spinning. Strangely enough, she liked that Max didn't try to impress her and act like it was no big deal to walk into a bar like this.

"It's a lot like your posh country club."

"In what way?"

She looped her hands through the crook of his elbow. "Both are picky about who they welcome. But once you're welcomed, you're safe." She waited for his verdict. Would they stay or would they go? She really wanted him to give it a try. Not be turned off by her roots.

"And out of all the places I would have willingly taken you to tonight, this is the place you chose for our business dinner?"

That wasn't a no. But not exactly a yes. "This is my old stomping ground. I hung out here on the weekends as a child while Meemaw served beer. They have the best barbeque in town."

He grinned. "According to whom?"

"The owner. You're not scared, are you?" The ever-constant fear of being rejected whispered in her ear to tell him never mind. Tell him she wanted to go somewhere else. She didn't listen to the voice.

He glanced back at his car then at her. "Let's do this."

"Really?" When it came down to it, she'd expected him to refuse to go inside. To insist they go somewhere with five-star reviews on Yelp. Had he done that, then she would have known for sure she could never fit into his world, because he would never want to honor hers.

She resisted an urge to plaster another impromptu hug

on him. Once per contract was probably enough. "Thank you for trying something from my part of Kansas City."

"Thanks for trusting me enough to bring me here."

How sweet of him. He got it. He knew he was being tested, and he didn't mind.

Like a man who'd been taught manners, Max opened the heavy wooden door. Score one for gentlemen. Inside, a thin crowd occupied the low-lit room, most of them watching a Royal's game on the big television hanging in the corner.

"Aggie, long time no see," the owner, Sally, said. Her voice boomed over the conversations taking place in the one-room establishment.

"Too long."

Three more bikers wearing leather, chains, and skullcaps stood propped in a row against the bar, watching the game. Not sitting, because escapes were quicker if you remained standing.

Sally made the trio lift their elbows and their drinks so she could wipe the counter down with a wet rag. She glanced back at Aggie. "You been in jail?"

The word jail jarred the biker's attention away from their game and onto Aggie and Max.

"Well, I'll be a son-of-a-bitch, if it ain't our lil' Aggie," the biggest of the bunch said. His name was Albert, but everyone called him Bruiser. "Never thought about you having gone to jail. Must have broken Meemaw's heart. What did they get you for?"

"I haven't been in jail," she snapped. Good lord. She did not need that rumor floating around town.

"If not jail," Bill said, "then what?" He eyeballed Max much like a bull does a red cape. "Sniffing richer pastures?"

Fuck. She hadn't expected Bill to be here. "You damn troublemaker. You know better than most I like the pastures on this side of the fence."

Max leaned down and whispered into her ear. "That's

because you haven't tried the grass on the other side." His tone vibrated fifty-shades-of-gray naughty, causing her to want to experience all the things his tone promised he was capable of doing to a woman.

Bill frowned.

"I've not been doing any moonlight grazing," Aggie said.

Like a starving man at a banquet, Bill looked her over. An act meant to piss off Max. "Talk's cheap."

Max draped an arm around her shoulders, causing Bill to stiffen.

"Good thing talk's cheap," Aggie said, drawing Bill's attention back to her, "because unless you've recently won the lottery, all you can afford is cheap." Although she and Bill weren't an item, he could be territorial.

Everyone listening laughed.

Aggie glanced at Max. He fit into her world like a snow cone would in hell. "Shall we find a seat?"

Max turned a devastating smile on her, causing a shiver to flit through her body until it reached the *V* of her legs. There, it hummed over her sex, turning her body into red-hot lust. She nodded and hurried toward the last booth in the corner. A booth as far away from Bill and his biker crew as possible.

"Was it my imagination or does the ugly one want to kick my ass?"

"Not your imagination." She slid into the booth, thankful her legs no longer had to hold her. "Sally, we'll take a pitcher of whatever's on tap."

"You don't want a glass of wine?" Max took a seat next to her instead of across the table.

Not that she minded his closeness, but why? "I'm almost certain they don't serve wine here."

Sally brought the beer and two glasses. "All kidding aside, we've missed you." She poured their beers. "Things are never boring when you're on one of the tables."

"Aw...thanks. I've missed coming around. Unfortunately, I've been busy adulting." Out of habit, she did a full body shudder at the mention of adulting. Funny, but lately, adulting hadn't been so hard.

"We'll need two menus," Max said like the starchy CEO he was.

Sally grimaced and went to wait on another table.

"What did she mean by things are never boring when you're on a table?" Max asked. "You don't get drunk and dance on them, do you?"

"Because you think that's what poor girls do?"

He looked at her as if she'd slugged him. "Has anyone ever told you you have a hell of a chip on your shoulder?"

She shrugged. It's not like he was wrong.

"I was thinking that's what someone who's as fun-loving as you might do," he said.

"I'm sorry. I should stop assuming the worst of you." And start trusting that someone different from her might actually like her.

He placed his mouth next to her ear. "Agreed." His lips brushed her jawline. "I'm simply intrigued at the thought of you on a table. Naked."

Her panties grew wet as her core pulsed with longing. "Who are you, and what did you do with boss man?"

"I have no idea, but I hope you like this guy, because I'm enjoying being him...for tonight."

She turned in her seat and leaned her back against the wall. The action gave her a little breathing room, which helped her think clearer. "Did you ask me out tonight under false pretenses?"

"Remind me again under what pretense I got you here?" He shifted so that he faced her and stretched out an arm to rest atop the back of the bench seat.

"Work."

He lowered his arm, and some of the easiness left his expression. What had she said wrong? She thought they had been joking.

"Right," he said. "I've decided to shorten your hours at work." He glanced at her through hooded lashes.

"I see." The most realistic way to interpret that comment was he wanted to limit the amount of time he was forced to spend around her. The realization felt like a jab to the throat. "What hours did you have in mind?" Then again, she could be wrong. No reason to jump to conclusions. Conclusions that could ruin their evening.

"Grandmother mentioned you're not a morning person, and since you finish every assignment I give you so quickly and you're not willing to make my coffee, I see no reason not to change your hours so you don't have to come in until ten."

Sally brought plates heaped with barbeque sandwiches and seasoned fries to their table.

Aggie beamed up at her. "Thanks. These look divine."

"Did we order this?" Max asked.

"If you come here for dinner," Sally barked, "you're ordering the special."

· · ·

Max waited until Sally left before saying to Aggie, "Is it my imagination, or has she taken an instant dislike to me?"

"She doesn't trust rich guys."

Max took a bite of his sandwich. He instantly knew why it was dubbed the best barbeque in town. And that was saying something in K.C., a town known for world-class barbeque. The cook should enter contests. "Do you trust rich guys?"

"I try not to. Want to shoot a game of pool when we're done eating?" She dipped a fry into a puddle of sauce on her plate.

"I don't know how to play." He watched her lick her

fingertips.

"I'll teach you how." She leaned back.

"Why do you try not to trust rich guys?"

She grabbed another fry and dipped it in the sauce. "Because they tend to not fall for girls like me." He watched as the fry slowly disappeared into her mouth.

He swallowed and had a moment of pure envy over a french fry. "I'll let you teach me, if you tell me what you mean by 'girls like me.'"

She smirked. "You'll *let* me teach you? You'd be damn lucky to have me as a teacher."

He picked up his beer and took a sip. "You're that good, huh?"

She slid another french fry into her mouth with the same sexy slowness and then slowly pulled it out.

He groaned.

Then she bit it in half with a savage chomp. She swallowed. "At pool and other things."

"I'm intrigued."

"You should be. And I mean girls who don't fit into the world of the rich." She picked up her mug and took a sip of her cold beer, but not before he saw a flash of hurt in her eyes.

Who had made her feel less than? Whoever it was, he wanted to kick their ass. "When I think of you, I don't think of a girl who doesn't fit into my world because of her roots. I think of one who doesn't fit into my world because of her personality. You said yourself our temperaments don't mesh."

"Not for the long run. But that doesn't mean we wouldn't be damn good at the short run."

He resisted an urge to say, *Let's get out of here and start the short run now.* "I didn't know you'd be up for a short run. Maybe when you're no longer working for me, we can enjoy a fling."

Her eyes widened. "You misunderstood, while yes we'd

be good for the short run, our having one wouldn't be in my best interest."

"Why is that?" Other than both of their grandmothers would come unhinged if their grandchildren engaged in a casual fling with no commitment.

"Because as much as I like to run, I'm not willing to run with my heart. We all know short runs can turn into long runs, and if that happens, I want to be sure I'm running with someone who won't be embarrassed down the road by the way I run."

He cocked his head. He had the feeling that might be the most honest answer she'd ever given him. It begged for an honest response. "I love the way you run."

She blinked. "Time to change the subject."

"Okay," he said, reluctantly. He'd much prefer they continue with the subject at hand. But a gentleman didn't push a woman to talk about something that made them uncomfortable. "Finish your fries and teach me how to play this game of yours."

Fifteen minutes later, he watched as Aggie chalked her stick and broke the balls.

"Damn, girl, you're hard on them balls," a guy said.

Max glanced over. The bikers now leaned with their backs against the bar and were settled in to watch them.

Aggie never gave them a look as she circled the table with her cue stick. "Looks like I'm solids." She called her next shot and sank it. And the next, and the next, and the next. Then she missed an easy one.

"You missed on purpose, didn't you?" Max took the stick from her.

She shrugged.

Stalling, he roamed around the table, eyed the balls from different angles. She'd made it look easy. Hopefully, it was. When he could stall no longer, he positioned himself closest to the white ball. About to shoot, some guy shouted, "You forgot to call your shot."

The comment startled Max, and the end of his stick hit the fabric of the table.

Laughter rumbled out of those watching.

Max whirled and glowered at him. It was the same guy who'd been all territorial earlier. "Asshole."

The guy's smile vanished, and his hand gripped the neck of a beer bottle. "Aggie, you better teach your man some manners and how to shoot pool before he tears up our table."

Aggie tugged on his arm. He glanced at her, and she motioned for him to lean toward her and then whispered into his ear, "Don't let them ruin our night."

He liked the way her breath slipped underneath his collar. He straightened. "I couldn't agree with you more." He ran a finger down Aggie's jawline. "Want to get out of here?"

"Can't leave a game unfinished." She winked at him. "Follow my lead." She stepped back. "Hot stuff, would you like some help?" She used a voice full of innuendo.

He knew instantly he was going to like what followed. "Honey, if by help, you mean pressing that sweet body of yours against mine, then by all means, please help."

She stood behind him, pressed her body into his, and showed him how to position his fingers on the end of the stick. "Now, look down the stick and gently hit the white ball."

"Aggie, teach me next," the guy shouted. "I don't remember how to play, either."

She ignored him.

Max shot and hit the white ball into a striped ball, and it flew into the corner pocket. Not the ball he'd been aiming at, but thankfully, Aggie said nothing. He moved around the table. She followed. Once again, she pressed into his back and helped him with his stick.

"That fucker knows how to play. He's getting a kick out of your sweet tits being pressed into his back," a guy said.

Max glanced his way. It was the asshole again. "You can trash talk me all you want, but if you talk about, or to, my girl, you better do so with a mouthful of respect. Or you and I will have a problem."

The asshole lurched at Max. "Sissy boy, you got what it takes to make me?"

Max straightened as adrenaline rushed him. "Asshole, the question is do you have the nuts to find out?"

Asshole approached their table, and the two men squared off.

"Winner gets to take Aggie home," the guy said.

"Now, boys." She stepped between them, holding her arms out straight and making them take several steps away from each other. "I'm not the girl who gets a thrill over enticing two men to fight. Bill, go back to your beer. I'm leaving with the guy I came with."

Max narrowed his eyes. Was this asshole *her* Bill?

Bill grunted. "Hey, no foul. Don't get mad. You know how it is. The guys and I don't let just anyone in to drink our beer and date our women."

"I'm nobody's woman, and I sure as hell aren't anyone's reward for a pissing contest." Aggie laid a hand on Max's arm. "I've lost my desire to shoot pool. Shall we get out of here?"

Max threw his stick on the table. "Not before we finish our beer." He'd be damned if he'd run from that idiot.

She grabbed his hand and tugged him toward their table. He took a seat across from her so he could see Bill. She eyeballed Max. Only him. "You okay?"

Moments crawled by before the tension left his shoulders enough he could talk. "Is that *the* Bill? The one you wrote about on your entrance test?"

"Yep."

"The guy's a jackass." Max slammed his beer. "You can do better. Let's get you home."

Chapter Twenty-Five

Thursday at five p.m., the office phone rang. Aggie wanted to ignore the call, but one more task wouldn't kill her.

"Treadwell Properties." She wiggled her toes under her desk. She'd ditched her pantyhose and heels the moment Max left for an afternoon meeting. He'd been due back by three but called and said something had come up. "How may I help you?"

"How did things go in the office today?" Max said on the phone.

Speak of the devil... "Hello to you, too, boss man. Things are just peachy here."

"Did you do anything without first asking permission?"

"Funny you should ask. I actually set up an interview for a new receptionist. Ms. Grace called. She's definitely decided working for you isn't the right fit for her image and has graciously turned down your offer to let her be your receptionist. She said to tell you she's sorry it took her so long to decide."

He chuckled. "It only took her two and half weeks to

make it official. I really thought she might hold out the whole eight weeks you're working for me. You know...to make sure we spent plenty of alone time together."

Did the fact she gave her decision indicated the grandmothers had given up on their matchmaking scheme? "Ms. Grace thought you might get upset when I relayed the news, and I was to tell you not to take it personally. Anyway, now that it's official, I hope it's okay for me to get the ball rolling on the filling of the vacancy. I didn't figure you'd want to be involved in something so mundane as hiring a receptionist. Like I said, I've set up one interview."

"About that. You sound great answering the phone. When my assistant comes back, perhaps you—"

"Don't you dare ask me to be your receptionist." She cleared her throat, hoping he hadn't heard the note of hurt in her voice. "I have better things to do with my life."

"Of course you do, but perhaps you should cancel the interview and we should leave it open just in case you change your mind."

"Not necessary."

He didn't push. "Why do I get the feeling you're mad at me? I thought you did a clearing to get rid of the negative energy between us."

"Sorry. I'm feeling grumpy today."

"Why?"

Good question. "Do you really want to know?" Maybe it was time she took a real risk in life. One that included her heart and not just her life.

"I do, but not right at this moment. I'm in a bit of a rush. I need you to do me a favor."

She'd take that as a big fat no. She smiled so her voice would sound cheerful. "It's your dime."

"Go over to my desk and open the drawer on the right side. I have a stack of business cards there. Find the card from

Jasper, Inc. I need their phone number."

She put the call on hold, walked over to his desk, pulled open the drawer, and found a small stack of cards. A few were stuck between the pages of a calendar. She pulled out the calendar and shook for other hidden ones. Then she thumbed through the cards until she found the one he wanted. Grabbing the phone, she then took the call off hold. "Found it."

"Great. Text me the number."

"Will do. Anything special going on tomorrow?"

"I have another meeting with David Long. It's a critical one."

"Here or his office?"

"His office, but I'll drop by mine before the meeting."

She grimaced. Mr. Long had a lot of...quirks. Which didn't make him bad, but it did make him a challenge to impress. "I'll ask Meemaw to send positive vibes out into the universe tonight for a successful outcome."

"Okay. Tell her thanks in advance." After a moment of dead air, Max said, "Aggie?"

"Still here. It's my understanding that the rules of etiquette when talking to the boss man is that he has to hang up first. Were you testing me to see if I knew that? Surprise. I do."

He laughed. "Never mind. Have a good night."

She hung up and turned to close his desk drawer. Something on the calendar caught her eye. Her name. Written in every square of every workday. She pulled it out and gave it her full attention.

"What the hell?" From the day she'd started working for Max, until the day scheduled to be her last day, he'd written her name and then drawn a big red X through each day that had passed. Even today.

Why? Hurt bombarded her from every direction. She

bit down on her bottom lip to draw her attention away from the ache and refocused it on her mouth. Did Max hate being around her so much he counted down the days until she left?

That would be the obvious don't-kid-yourself conclusion. The other conclusion—the obvious kid-yourself-one—would be Max was counting down the days until he could kiss her because he wouldn't be her boss anymore.

Her go-to, knee-jerk reaction would be to decide it was the first scenario and retaliate. But, as Meemaw liked to say, that would be cutting off her nose to spite her face. And truthfully, that wasn't what she wanted to do.

What do I want? "To not screw things up by jumping to wrong conclusions." In this situation, the adult thing to do would be to pretend she never saw it.

Thirty minutes later, she left the office, locking up tight. Stepping outside into the crisp air, she listened to the rustle of the wind blowing, the sound of a distant siren, and the gentle meow of a cat.

A smile lifted her lips. She adored cats. Aggie followed the mewls. Turning the corner of the building, she stopped short. What she discovered in the alleyway gave her an idea. A brilliant, Max-is-going-to-love-this idea.

Perched on top of the trash bin sat a tiny black kitten, talking to the world. Aggie slowly approached. If it had been sitting anywhere else, she wouldn't have had her idea. But sitting on her and Max's trash bin, it had to be fate. And as such, it had to have been fate that gave her the idea. "When was the last time you ate, precious?" She spoke softly in hopes the kitten wouldn't have a fright and run.

The kitten stopped squawking and eyeballed her. Aggie held out her hand and waited for the kitten to move closer out of curiosity. When it did, she scooped the feline up and placed the bundle of fur inside her jacket pocket. "There you go. Warmer?"

The kitten wiggled.

"I bet you're hungry. Let's go get you some food."

On her way home, she stopped at a pet store. Inside the store was a vet's office. From the veterinarian, she discovered the kitten was a girl. She named her Olivia. Having never owned a pet, she had no idea what all she needed for a cat, so the store clerk helped her pick out food, bedding, litter box, collar, and a cage. Pet ownership was for the rich? Not that it mattered. Olivia would help Aggie pull off her latest plan.

When Aggie and Olivia arrived home, Meemaw shook her head. "You know we can't have pets. It'll cost us a hundred dollars a month more in rent. Cats are expensive."

"Not a problem. This kitten isn't for us. I'm going to take her to work. She'll be our office mascot."

Chapter Twenty-Six

Friday morning, Max's eyes were watering. Had been ever since he got to work. He grabbed a tissue and blew his nose. "Are you burning a new candle?"

Aggie glanced up from a desk drawer she'd been preoccupied with all morning. "No... Why?"

She looked innocent, but her voice...her voice held a hint of a lie. "My eyes are—" The soft sound of a cat's meow cut him off. "What the hell was that?" He prayed he was wrong.

She gave him that smile of hers. The knee-buckler. Her eyes sparkled back at him like sunlight on diamonds. "Ummm." She pulled a tiny bundle of fur out of her desk.

He held out his hand to stop her movement. "Don't come near me. Stay put."

She didn't listen. She walked toward him while rubbing the head of the deathtrap. "Max, meet our mascot, Olivia. Olivia, meet the boss man, Max. He tends to be grumpy when he first meets you but then softens as the days go by." She held the cat out for him to see.

Max sneezed. "What the fuck. You can't bring a damn

cat in our office and declare it a mascot." As he spoke, his eyes were swelling shut and his throat tightening.

"See what I told you," she said to the cat before placing it on his shoulder. And then to him, "Are you okay? You don't look okay."

He pointed to the cat which was now roaming down his arm. "Get it off of me. I'm allergic."

"Allergic?" She nabbed Olivia and carried her back to her desk drawer. "I'm so sorry. I had no idea."

Max scowled in the direction of her voice. His eyes were watering so bad he could only see a blur. "You should have asked. If you'd asked, you'd known." He fumbled until he found the Kleenex box, grabbed a tissue, and wiped at his eyes.

"I never ask. You know that about me."

He loosened his tie and unbuttoned the top buttons of his shirt.

"Do I need to take you to the hospital? You're not going to die on me, are you?"

"Just get Olivia out of here."

"Now?"

"Yes, now."

"But what about the meeting?"

"I'll have to cancel." David Long didn't like change. He demanded things handled in a predetermined way. This would put the man over the edge. He'd advise Richard they should take their business elsewhere. "I'm sorry, but this time, Aggie, you've gone too far." Of all the meetings for her to screw up. This one had the potential of making it all but impossible for him to lose his bet with Father. But, of course, she screwed it up. That's what she did. "I have no choice but to fire you."

"For real fire me?" Her voice came out high-pitched.

"For real fire you." He wiped his eyes again. No boss

worth his title would let this slide.

"We do have a contract, but if that's what you think's best."

He sighed. He could hear tears in her voice. "I'll pay you for the rest of your time. And you'll still get your IRA fund."

"No. No. It's okay. I don't blame you. Firing me is a perfectly fine solution to what I've done." He heard the click of her heels as she walked back to her desk. Rubbing at his eyes again, he managed to see her as she slowly pulled her purse out of her desk drawer. "Although it's not the only solution."

"What's the other?" he wheezed. Why hadn't he ever mentioned to her he was allergic to cats? He normally covered the subject in job interviews.

She set her purse, with the kitten inside it, on her desk. "Perhaps my solution should wait. You look like I need a good criminal lawyer." She stared at him much like a nurse stared at a critical patient. "Are you sure you're not going to die on me? And if you're not sure, could you maybe sign a waiver saying this wasn't my fault?"

"I'm not going to die." It would take hours before he was fine, but he would be fine. He opened his middle drawer and seized his inhaler, sprayed antihistamine in his lungs, and held it there for ten seconds. "What's your other solution?" he asked once he released his breath.

She perched on his desk. "Cancelling a meeting with a difficult client won't help you win him over."

"No...shit." Speaking was becoming more difficult. He reached around her ass and grabbed his bottle of water.

"I *could* take the meeting *for* you..."

"You what?" He slipped his suit jacket off and rolled up his sleeves.

"We've worked on this together, and I know Mr. Long. I know he's unique and grouchy. But then, so are you. I bet I could charm him into a contract the same way I did you."

"You didn't charm me into anything."

"If you say so."

"David will refuse to meet with you. He'll be insulted I sent in my second fiddle."

"Since he's Richard's second fiddle, I'm not sure he has a reason to be offended."

She had a point there. "You may be right."

"If I can talk my way into a few minutes with him," Aggie said, "I'll change his mind. He'll see I know as much about our proposal as you do."

"I doubt you'll get past his secretary."

"But if I do, and if I get the contract, then you have to agree to unfire me and promise to never do it again. It's getting pretty old."

He clenched his hands. How had his well-organized life boiled down to this? To her? To Aggie the Horrible in charge of one of his most sought-after pain-in-the-ass clients? God. Why had he hired her? Her answers on his test should have been all the warning he needed.

"Fine." He drank his water. "Go before my common sense returns and I change my mind." The inhaler had helped. His breathing had eased. But as long as the cat stayed in the room, his eyes would continue to water and swell.

She clapped her hands like a child who'd been told she'd won a trip to Disney World. "Thank you. You won't regret it."

Yeah, right. "No contract. No job. Take that damn cat home and change into something conservative while you're there." The last thing he needed was for Mr. Long to wonder if he'd sent Aggie to seduce him into a contract offer. "He's expecting me at his office in one hour. Don't be late."

• • •

Three hours later, Aggie waltzed back into Max's office,

holding a folder in one hand and a bottle of champagne in the other. "Call me boss lady."

Max glanced up from his desk and gave her a heart-stealing smile. Like she could feel her heart slipping out of her body and floating over to him. *Sweet baby Jesus.* She'd been watching way too many rom-coms with Meemaw.

"He signed?"

Aggie nodded. "He did." Although his eyes were still a little red, Max looked so much better than he had earlier. Thank God.

Max stood. "Wow. When you want to apply yourself, you are something special." He turned and strolled to the couch and sat. "I'm not sure even I could have gotten him to sign the contract."

She followed and held up the bottle of champagne and two flutes. "That's why we're celebrating."

He took the bottle and the glasses from her. "How did you get him to speak to you?"

"He has a coffee press in his office. People serious about their coffee have coffee presses. We talked coffee beans. Where the best ones come from. And about the different cuppas a person can attend around town. I knew of one he hadn't yet been to."

"Cuppa?"

"It's like wine tasting, but for coffee connoisseurs."

He popped the cork on the champagne and poured. He raised his glass in the air. "To Aggie. A woman who has given me more than one gray hair in a short amount of time, but with whom I thoroughly enjoy working with and who is officially unfired."

Her smile faltered. "Seriously?"

"You have far exceeded my expectations. I will actually hate to see you go when our contract is up."

Here was her opening. A chance to make a mature choice.

"Why does our contract have to end? Why not give me a new job title when your assistant comes back?" The immature choice would have been to continue to try and seduce him. Men were a dime a dozen. Fun jobs weren't.

He pulled at his ear. "I'll tell you what. If we can get through the next month with my not wanting to kill you, then we'll talk."

She laughed. "I'm growing on you, aren't I?"

He rolled his eyes. "Like a fungus."

"And to think…a few weeks ago, you thought of me as algae."

"Which is worse? Algae or fungus?"

"I could tell you, but where's the fun in that?" She drained her glass.

Chapter Twenty-Seven

Monday morning, Aggie stood at her desk, and Max sat at his, as she picked his brain about business stuff. "So, you are predicting if you can get Richard and David to pick you for their secret project, then their top three competitors will also want to hire you?" Max surprised her this morning by explaining why he'd been so upset at the possibility of losing David Long's respect.

"Exactly," he said.

"Why?"

"Because, as your friend Bill so eloquently put it, the grass always looks greener on the other side of the fence."

"I'm sure no one has ever referred to Bill as eloquent. Cocky maybe. Eloquent no."

His face contorted. "Are you and Bill lovers?"

"Not anymore."

A quiver ran down his sexy throat as he swallowed. The action set off a quiver inside her own body. One way farther south than her neck.

"Good. You can do better."

That's the second time he'd said that. "Just because Bill rides a motorcycle, has tattoos, and likes to hang out in scary-looking bars doesn't mean he's a loser."

Max raised a brow. "Doesn't mean he's not, either."

"And it doesn't mean you're better than him."

"I didn't say I was better than him. I said you can do better than him."

"Whatever," she huffed.

He sighed. "How's Olivia?"

They were going in circles. "In jeopardy."

Max stopped multitasking and gave her his full attention. "Why?"

"Meemaw says we have to take her to the pound."

"Is she allergic to cats?"

"Our landlord charges extra for pets."

"I see... How much?"

"A hundred freaking dollars a month." How could a tiny cat be a threat to do a hundred dollars' worth of damage to a place a month?

"How about if I—"

She recoiled. "We don't accept charity." Had she sounded like she wanted his money?

He nodded. "I respect that, but hear me out. I'll get allergy shots. If they're successful, I can be in the company of a cat and not implode. What if I pay you to house Olivia until I'm ready to bring her here?"

Had he pulled this idea out of his fine ass? A trick to get her to take the money? "You're making her our office mascot?"

"I read an article over the weekend about how you're right. Office mascots are the in thing to have."

"You should never doubt me." Most of the time, he really wasn't a bad guy. "And thank you for not firing me."

"You're welcome." He rolled his eyes playfully. "I think."

And most of the time, she really liked him. A lot. "You

know what? I think I'll run again. Not with you, but on my own." She'd watched the episode of *Friends* where Phoebe ran in Central Park with Rachel, and if that's what she looked like when she ran, she definitely didn't want Max witnessing her running again until she learned how to run like an adult.

"Why?"

"Because I have a theory."

"Dare I ask?"

"I theorize *you* get your brilliant ideas while running, because running is so boring you have to find things to ponder or you'd go crazy."

He laughed. "You could be right. I do some of my best business plotting during my long runs."

"In that case, I'm going to go for a run after work and plot against you."

· · ·

Max was enjoying his and Aggie's morning talk. It was like they'd finally settled in with each other and could let their walls partially down. "As long as you're not plotting yet another way to make me want to fire you." He'd been in business for years, and she's the only employee he'd ever fired.

"I've never purposefully plotted a way to get myself fired where you're concerned."

The slight rise in her voice told him he'd hit a nerve. "Have you plotted to get other employers to fire you?"

"Oh. Well." She grinned, kicking his heart into his throat. "That's the result of strategic long-term thinking."

"Getting fired is part of your long-term plan?"

"It's complicated," she said.

"I'm capable of complicated."

After a long sigh, she continued. "Growing up, I watched Meemaw work a series of jobs she hated. I vowed I would never settle for a career I didn't like. When I get into a new job, as soon as I know it's not my forever job, I start sabotaging. Doing what it takes to get fired."

"Why not quit?"

"Short answer. Where's the fun in that?"

Her answer amused and worried him. The last thing he needed to do was fall for a woman who based life decisions on the level of fun they provided. "And the long answer?"

"My maturity level could use a boost. I enjoy plotting a little too much."

How long would it take her to reach the level of maturity needed to soothe his worries that she'd blow up his life if they ever got involved? "While you're plotting against me, could you plot a way for me to get more of the young upstart business?"

"Now that you mentioned it, I've been thinking. Treadwell Properties needs more of a social media presence. We can start with an Instagram account. There, we could share photos of your projects and mock-ups of your ideas for future projects. All the hip generation uses the app for promotion."

"Is that something my assistant can do, or does that require a new position?"

"In the beginning, your assistant could handle the extra work. But eventually, you'd want to grow into a company with a hired social media specialist."

"What is a social media specialist?"

"Someone who knows all the social media influencers and can network to get your company mentioned in their posts and videos."

"I like that idea. What else?"

"You should come up with a manifesto for your company."

"A manifesto?"

"It's a shout out to what your company stands for. Apple has one. Google it. It's great. I could help you come up with one for Treadwell Properties."

She spent another forty-five minutes giving him a detailed plan of how her ideas would work.

When she finished, he stood. Drifted to the windows. Back to his desk. Over to where she now stood.

"What are you thinking?" She twirled a strand of hair while waiting for him to respond.

He grabbed both of her hands and squeezed. "Why in the world did you graduate bottom of your class?"

She frowned. "I—"

"Don't answer. It doesn't matter." At this moment, he really didn't care about her grades. Actions and ideas spoke louder than transcripts. "Your idea is exceedingly brilliant."

She squealed, grabbed his cheeks, and kissed him.

He froze. He'd been envisioning kissing her. But in his visions, it hadn't been when standing in his office while still her boss. It had been at the end of their eight weeks, in a romantic setting.

She dropped her hands and stepped back. "Oh God. I'm so sorry. I don't know what came over me. I—"

He wrapped a hand around her nape and pulled her back into his arms. "You've effectively blown the 'will we or won't we' landmine between us; we might as well get the most from the explosion."

"I have?"

"You have." He brushed his lips against her cheek. Her body shivered against him. His body reacted in ways he couldn't put into words. "If you don't want me to kiss you, say no."

She moaned but didn't shake her head no nor say the word he most didn't want to hear.

His lips glided over to the freckle he'd noticed on the first day that sat all alone right beneath her earlobe. "How about now?"

Another groan. This one louder.

He moved his lips to the outer corner of her mouth. "Last—"

She wrapped her arms around his neck and moved her head so that their lips centered nicely upon each other and his words were lost in a moment that made absolutely no sense on paper.

They were as different as assets and liabilities. Yet the kiss kicked him in the back of the knees. Caused him to nearly tumble them both to the floor. For the first time in his life, Max knew true temptation. Knew it as clearly as he knew his social security number. Aggie Johansson should come with a label that said: WARNING—ADDICTIVE AS FUCK.

Moving one hand down to rest on her delicious ass, he pulled her harder against him. First kisses were meant to be gentle, exploratory, lingering. But that's not what he gave her. This kiss delivered what he lacked in their battle of the words. This kiss branded, and scolded, and delighted him hard enough to rock his world with thoughts of possibilities.

In return, she gyrated and gasped and groaned, igniting him beyond the point of reasoning.

When they parted for a quick breath, she placed her hands on his biceps, squeezed as if testing them for size, and then leaned slightly back. "Did you compliment me so you could kiss me?"

Her breathing was as hard as his, and the hunger in her eyes matched the hunger eating at him, yet, once again, even in his daze he realized she was schooling him with her wit. "If I was capable of thinking straight, I would have fired you so I could kiss you without potential consequences."

Her eyes widened as if in horror. "I'm glad you're not thinking straight. I don't want to be fired. I like my job. A woman should never willy-nilly choose a man over a job."

Which, in the emotionless truth of life, meant there should be no more kissing. She'd just vocally chosen a job over him. The irony of that didn't escape him. The woman who went through jobs like children went through candy chose the job. "Aggie—"

"Max—"

He jammed his fingers through his hair. "Ladies first."

"That kiss was nothing more than my getting carried away with you singing my praises. When we first met, you branded me a joke. A bad joke."

"More like an undetonated stick of dynamite."

Her lips twitched. "And, of course, you kissed me back. I'm very kissable."

"Very," he husked. There was something he wasn't remembering. Something on the tip of his memory.

"And, in case you're wondering, I promise I'm not secretly pining for you. And we've established you're not my type, nor I yours. We still need to make sure our grandmothers aren't harboring any lingering longings for us to be together. Meemaw's had her heart broken by one rich guy. I couldn't stand it if it happened again."

"How would I break Ms. Hazel's heart?"

"By my offering you mine, and you saying no thanks."

He froze. "I thought I wasn't your type?"

"Relax. You're not. But sometimes when you play with fire, you get burned. While I would recover if you broke my heart, I have to remember mine wouldn't be the only one you broke. Thus, reluctantly, I choose the job over a dalliance." The more she spoke, the higher her voice pitched, and her cheeks glowed with a soft flush, and her neck developed splotches of red.

He knew the correct response. But it was so seldom he had the last word. "You started it."

"Touché," she said, giving him a smile that scrambled his brain.

Chapter Twenty-Eight

Ten minutes later, Aggie met Meemaw at Vinos and Pinots for a happy-hour dinner before Meemaw went to work.

"I had a nice little chinwag with Officer Bobby and lost track of the time," Meemaw said.

Aggie sighed. "Were you speeding again?" Officer Bobby had pulled Meemaw over at least once a week ever since she won a convertible at a poker game, and so far, Meemaw had been able to talk herself out of every ticket. The guy never gave her anything but a warning.

"Just a smidge. Anyway, I hope you don't mind, but he and his lovely fiancée will be Grace's and my new bridge partners."

"You guys are firing your grandchildren?" Surprise but not relief swept through Aggie. She hadn't hated being Max's Bridge partner. "Why?" Did this mean the grandmothers had given up on matchmaking the two of them?

Meemaw leaned across the table and gazed intently at Aggie.

Oh God, could she see Aggie's happiness?

"Sugar, Officer Bobby practically invited himself."

Aggie laughed. She very much doubted it happened that way. Poor Officer Bobby was probably still wondering how he'd come to agree to learning the game of Bridge.

"Why are you so darn happy?" Meemaw asked.

Aggie startled. She could lie and say she was just super relieved she didn't have to play Bridge anymore. Or she could tell Meemaw the truth. At least part of it. The part that didn't include her kissing her boss. "Max complimented me today."

"Really. On what? Leg compliments don't count."

"It wasn't on my legs. It was on an idea I had to help him bring in more of the younger crowd's business." Just saying it made her grin like a Mega Millions lotto winner.

"I knew you had it in you to impress him. What else happened?"

Damn, she was sharp. "Nothing else. Isn't that enough?"

"I don't know. I don't have my glasses on to properly analyze your smile. My gut's telling me it's more than an I-made-the-boss-proud smile."

Aggie picked up the menu and held it in front of her face. "That's all it is. Now, what do you want to order?"

"Something easy to digest. Grace's country club is voting on my becoming a member tomorrow morning, and I'm already too nervous to keep food down."

Aggie dropped the menu. "What? Why is this the first you've spoken of it?" She had heard her right...right? "My meemaw is up for membership at a swanky country club?"

"I am, and I didn't tell you because I may not get in. I'm sure Grace bullied her way into getting my name on the list, but that doesn't mean she can bully anyone to vote for me, especially since the votes are secret."

"Even if you don't, just getting recommended is a big deal. Let's go out tomorrow night and celebrate both our good news."

Hazel shook her head. "I don't want to count my chickens before they hatch. There's a fine chance I won't be invited. Not that I care a lick if they say no."

"There's a finer chance you will be invited." Aggie believed in putting out into the universe what you wanted. And she very much wanted this for Meemaw. It might be just the thing to heal her low self-esteem. "There's a saying, if you plan to celebrate it, it will happen."

"I don't think that's a saying, but if it makes you happy, we'll boldly plan a celebration for tomorrow night. And we'll invite Grace and Max to join us because that's what we'd do if we knew for certain I was going to get the elusive invite."

"Exactly." Surely if the grandmothers had uninvited their grandchildren to play Bridge, that meant they'd give up on their matchmaking idea. She and Max would just have to be careful not to rekindle that hope over dinner.

Her phone vibrated in her pocket. She pulled it out and read the message.

I have a solid lead on your mom.

Her heart rate jacked up, and her stomach clenched. The message was from the private investigator Richard Harris had loaned her. She dropped her phone back in her purse. This could be it. She could finally reunite with Mom.

What if Mom hates me?

If that happened, she would deal.

Nothing could be worse than the not-knowing hole inside of her.

Once she talked to Mom, the hole would heal. Her heart might not mend, but the hole would be gone, because she would have answers.

Then again, how foolish was it to chase after a woman

who didn't want you in her life?

"Everything okay?" Meemaw asked. "Was that Max telling you to get back to work and impress him again with your brain?"

Aggie tried to give her a smile, but gravity made an example of its optimism. She couldn't tell Meemaw. If Meemaw found out, she'd fret her love for Aggie hadn't been enough. And that wasn't true. And never in a thousand years would she hurt Meemaw.

"You nailed it. Max wants my ass back at work." Luckily, Meemaw would leave for work from here and would never know she went straight home afterward. "He said when he hired me, our hours would sometimes be untraditional." She pulled her phone out and sent a text.

Keep me informed. Night or day.

Chapter Twenty-Nine

Max had been delighted when Grandmother called and asked if he'd like to go to dinner with her, Ms. Hazel, and Aggie. A celebration of sorts in anticipation that Ms. Hazel would be accepted into Grandmother's country club.

Now he sat next to Aggie in a booth at a small restaurant he'd never been to but found charming. It was an Italian place Aggie recommended for the four of them. And they were indeed celebrating Hazel's membership. The committee had voted this morning.

Grandmother lifted her glass of wine. "Here's to Hazel being the newest member of Martinis and Cigars."

Hazel's face lit up brighter than it had been all night. Something he wouldn't have thought possible considering how much she'd already been glowing. It was as if she viewed becoming a member of the club as equivalent to winning a gazillion-dollar lottery. He had no regrets spending the weekend cashing in so many favors to get the votes to go her way.

"Thank you for nominating me." Ms. Hazel's cheeks were

a rosy red. "I promise to do my best not to embarrass you."

Grandmother waved the comment off with a flick of her wrist. "Nonsense. You won't embarrass me. You will do me proud."

"Enough about me." Ms. Hazel raised her glass. "Here's to Aggie dragging a compliment out of Max. To you guys finally hitting it off."

Aggie stiffened next to him.

They had hoped the matchmaking had ended but had come prepared in case it hadn't. He reached out and squeezed her hand. His signal for her to throw the first dart.

She squeezed back.

"Oh, I wouldn't put too much emphasis on his compliment." She paused and took a sip of her drink. "It came right after I relayed a message to him from someone whose name I can't remember. The message was, and I quote, *last night was puuuuuurfect*."

Both grandmothers set their drinks down, their expressions comical.

"Max, dear, do you have a girlfriend?" Grandmother asked. "I had no idea."

"I hope not because I have a date with a different woman Saturday night."

He felt Aggie's gaze.

"Anyone I know?" Grandmother asked.

"I don't believe so. Did you guys know Aggie has an actual boyfriend?"

She swatted at his arm. "Don't throw me under the grandmother bus just because you stepped out in front of it."

"Felt more like I got there by a shove, not a voluntary step." He sipped his wine to keep the ladies from seeing the laughter in his smile.

"Aggie Johansson," Ms. Hazel snapped, "do you have a boyfriend, and if so, why didn't you tell me?"

She sat up straighter. "I planned to tell you as soon as I figured out if he liked-me, liked-me."

Ms. Hazel pursed her lips like Aggie's words were blasphemous. "You shouldn't worry about if he likes-you, likes-you. He should worry about if you like-him, like-him. I don't care who he is, you're the catch, not him."

Max couldn't agree more.

Aggie smiled. "I love you."

Ms. Hazel harrumphed. "And does he?"

"And does he what?"

"Like-you, like-you?"

Aggie glanced down at her hands. It was as if she couldn't lie straight to Ms. Hazel's face. "I will find out soon."

He resisted an urge to whisper in her ear that he liked-her, liked-her.

Ms. Hazel's lips pinched. "And do you like-him, like-him?"

Her head came up. "Absolutely." That came out sounding quite sincere.

"Why?" Ms. Hazel demanded.

"Well, for starters, he has a Harley that's paid for and a job."

Max clenched his jaws to keep from saying something he'd regret and reminded himself this was an act. A planned act. Not things being said to rile each other up.

"That does mark all your boxes where men are concerned," Ms. Hazel said.

Max watched Aggie as she spun her story for her grandmother. Someone as free-spirited as her would definitely find riding on the back of a Harley exhilarating.

Had she ever dated someone like him? Someone who drove a Porsche. And had more than a job. Maybe if she did, her standards for what's great in a man would change. Fuck. What a pompous-ass thought.

He'd learned today his real assistant didn't plan on returning. He should definitely offer the position to Aggie. If he did, though, he wouldn't be able to ask her out on a proper date. Ever. While he'd never envisioned himself with someone like Aggie, now that he'd met someone like her, he kind of wanted someone like her in his life. Someone who would remind him to slow down and laugh. Have fun. And run like a child.

If he gave her the job long term, he'd never find another like her to date. Someone capable of filling this sudden need he had in his heart. A need that wasn't there before he met her.

"In fact, we have a date tomorrow night," Aggie said.

Max snapped his attention to her and willed her to look at him. He wanted her eyes to tell him she'd concocted the date as part of their ruse. That she didn't really have one. He felt another work night coming on. Despite the fact, she had to feel his gaze on her, she didn't glance his way, so he cleared his throat to get her attention.

"I hate to do this to you," he said when she glanced at him. "But I have a business dinner with a new client tomorrow night, and I planned on taking you. You've worked so hard this week, I thought dinner at a fancy restaurant would be something you would enjoy."

She gave him a bemused smile. "Aren't you a peach? I don't know how a girl like me could say no to an invitation like that."

His shoulders relaxed. When their contract ended, he was going to tell her he wanted to date. Or maybe as soon as the dinner ended. "Great. And, because it's a business function, I'll give you my credit card and let you go shopping on company time tomorrow for something new to wear."

"And a blowout and a mani-pedi?" she asked, her smile staying one notch below the one he liked best.

"I don't know what any of those are, but sure."

Her smile completely disappeared, and the color of her eyes turned frosty morning blue. No lavender in sight. "You really know how to make a girl an offer she can't refuse."

She was really playing this up for the grandmothers. "Then you'll cancel your date?"

"Oh, you misunderstood where I was going with my sarcasm."

He tugged at his tie. Grandmother insisted he dressed up for tonight's dinner. "Excuse me?"

"Tomorrow night is me and my guy's third date." Aggie stared at him wide-eyed. "A girl doesn't cancel on the third date."

Time for him to step up his game and pull his weight in this pretend dislike of one another. The grandmothers hadn't bought into it at card night, so they really needed to go all in tonight. "Cancel. Tomorrow night, you're working late. As per our contract, you're available to work twenty-four hours a day. Tomorrow night is a working dinner."

Her eyes narrowed. "You know how to spoil a girl's fun, don't you?"

• • •

An hour later, Aggie drove Meemaw and her home in Meemaw's poker bounty, Sweet Sally. After she and Max had gone into their pretend boyfriend-girlfriend spiel, things had changed. Their fun evening of celebration became one of more silence than laughter. She deeply regretted taking the pleasure out of Meemaw's night of triumph. "You okay?"

Meemaw didn't answer right away. "To tell you the truth, I'm a little sad you and Max aren't mooning over each other by now. I thought for sure the two of you would be a perfect match. I guess Grace and I aren't as good at picking out two people meant to be together as we'd hoped."

Aggie's conscience flicked her with a taut rubber band. But it was for the best. It really was. "Meemaw, he's my boss. Nowadays, bosses don't have office affairs."

"If he weren't your boss, would things have turned out differently?"

Aggie stalled. Meemaw and she always told each other the truth. Lying gashed at her heart, leaving painful lacerations.

And frankly, tonight she realized she saw Max as boyfriend material.

More than boyfriend material.

Future material. He was smart, almost funny, caring, dependable, a great kisser, solid. His solid made her liquid less sloshy. Made her a better person. Wasn't that so much more important in a guy than how fast his Harley went?

The realization had scared the sweet tea out of her. No way would he ever see her in the same relationship light. And that wasn't her thinking with a chip on her shoulder. It was just a cold, hard statistic. The mere fact he wanted to buy her an outfit for tomorrow night's business dinner said as much—he didn't trust her to have anything to wear to a fancy restaurant. He was afraid she'd show up in something cheap and embarrass him.

Meemaw might think things had changed and people from the opposite sides of the track could fall in love and make things work, but Aggie didn't. Sure, they could fall in love. But "make things work" was a whole different story.

"I do like him," she admitted. "I mean, don't get me wrong, he's an uptight, pompous ass, but he has an adventurous side. The other night he went to Pappys with me and hardly complained."

Aggie received the full-force of Meemaw's smile. "Do you like-him, like-him?"

"I like that he has his head screwed on straight. It inspires me to want to get mine screwed on straighter."

She laid a hand on Aggie's arm. "I don't see a darn thing wrong with how your head is screwed."

"Because you love me, warts and all."

Meemaw shifted in her seat. "So, what are you going to do about this like you have for him?"

She rolled to a stop at a red light. "I don't know. But I do know you're going to stop trying to manipulate my relationships. Okay? I told you the truth. Liking someone is an ocean away from loving someone. Let me take it from here." The light turned green. They proceeded several blocks with no conversation. What was Meemaw thinking?

"You're such a peach for confiding in me," Meemaw said. "I promise to not meddle any further. The last thing I want is for you to disappear out of my life because I was too bossy or too interfering."

Her words gave Aggie's heart a papercut. She pulled over to the side of the road. "Meemaw—"

"Tarnation. Is Officer Bobby pulling you over, too?" Meemaw twisted in her seat to look out the back window. "I don't see his lights. You don't have to pull over unless he turns on his lights. You know that, right?"

Aggie took off her seat belt and smiled. "Meemaw, I love you. I would never disappear out of your life. You're the perfect amount of bossy and interfering."

"Aren't you a peach for allowing me the right to do a little interfering? Now. Let's talk about what you're going to wear. No way on my watch will you let a man buy your clothes. I don't care if it is for work."

Aggie nodded. Her reaction hadn't been an overreaction. The gesture had been a bullshit stab at her upbringing.

Chapter Thirty

For about two strides, the next evening, Aggie tried not to embarrass Max as they were led through a restaurant inside a private club to their private dining room. Then she gave up her attempt at blasé sophistication. The statues, brass, and dark woods inside the lush restaurant were too much not to gawk at like a child at the circus.

Max pulled out her chair. They were in the Boardroom, a room with a round table and a widescreen for those conducting business after dinner. Their potential customer had yet to arrive. "You look lovely," Max said, taking a seat next to her.

Heat warmed her cheeks. "It's hard to look bad in this lighting." Truth be told, minus the tiara, she felt like a damn fine damsel. Using the money she'd set aside to find her mother, since thanks to Richard, her new private detective didn't cost a dime, she'd purchased a black cocktail dress off the sales rack at White House Black Market. The detective was actually the man she was supposed to have had a date with tonight. No, not a date. A meeting. They'd rescheduled.

She'd called it a date for the sake of the grandmothers.

"You'll be happy to know none of this cost you a cent." Tonight, she wore her lucky pink stilettos. No cost. Manipulated her hair into a French twist all by herself. No cost. Painted her own nails. No cost.

He grimaced. "I would have been fine with you buying the moon with my credit card."

The vibe of sincerity in his tone evaporated her snark. "Thank you. You're looking rather handsome yourself." He wore a dark suit, crisp white shirt, and a lovely lavender tie with a matching pocket handkerchief. Rather fanciful for him. "Is the tie new? How about the suit? Did you, too, have to go out and buy something suitable for dinner?" And, just like that, her snark returned.

Before he could reply, the potential client entered the room.

Max and Aggie stood.

The men greeted one another. Then Max said, "Mr. Smith, I'd like to introduce you to my assistant, Ms. Johansson."

Mr. Smith held out a hand and shook Aggie's. She'd expected him to say *call me* and offer her his first name, because that's what would have happened in her circle of acquaintances. He didn't. *Toto, we're not in Kansas anymore.*

As soon as they sat, a waiter handed them cocktail menus.

Max ordered a bottle of wine. Aggie didn't recognize the name, but their guest nodded in approval.

"I take it you've been here before, Max." Mr. Smith wiped his utensils with his napkin.

"Many times. Their food is divine and their service impeccable."

Mr. Smith placed his napkin back on his lap and smiled. "In that case, order for me. I trust your judgment."

A silent sigh of relief flittered through Aggie. The menu had dishes she couldn't pronounce. She had no idea what they were. Thank God she at least knew which fork went with which portion of the meal. "A brilliant idea," she said to Mr. Smith. "Be a peach, Max, and order for myself." Had she used the word "myself" correctly? Should she have said "me" instead? Ugh. Grammar rules were her jam, why was she second guessing? And did saying "be a peach" make her sound less intelligent? Not at all. Southern women were charming and smart and, if the two gentlemen she was having dinner with didn't know that, they could just kick it.

The meal came in stages. The appetizers were a meal all by themselves. Her favorite was the pan-fried calamari with hot cherry peppers and the lobster bisque.

"Ms. Johansson, tell me about yourself," Mr. Smith said.

"I graduated from Kansas State with a liberal arts degree."

"How did you come to work for Max?"

"We are both blessed with meddling grandmothers."

His smile lost its starchiness. "My grandmother is an accomplished busybody as well. She holds a special spot in my heart."

For the entrée, Max chose for them the bone-in kona-crusted, dry aged KC strip with shallot butter. Accompanying the entrée were dishes of lobster mac 'n' cheese, roasted wild mushrooms, grilled asparagus with lemon mosto, and creamed spinach.

"How about you?" she said to their client. "Tell me an interesting fact about yourself."

"The most interesting thing I'm involved in at the moment is overseeing a trivia night fundraiser for charity."

Aggie took a bite of the lobster mac 'n' cheese. A groan of pleasure erupted from her lips.

She didn't realize how orgasmic it came across until both men paused in what they were doing and gaped. *Fuck. Fuck. Fuck.* Filling the awkward silence, she said, "Speaking of trivia, did you know, for men, sex burns about one hundred to two hundred calories on average? On the other hand, for women, it only burns approximately sixty-nine calories."

More silence.

"I speculate this finding must be based on the woman lying on her back and the man doing most of the work. Now, if the couple were actually doing the position sixty-nine, then surely a woman would burn more calories."

If possible, the silence grew even more silent. Like outer space silent.

Her attempt to lighten the moment had backfired. She resisted the urge to crawl under the table. Her ticking bomb of a mouth had just exploded all over their nice dinner.

As if coming out of a coma, Max coughed. "Aggie—"

Laughter burst from Mr. Smith's lips. When it subsided, he said, "Max, I will have to hire your grandmother to bring someone like Aggie into my life, too. Aggie, what other trivia do you know that might come in handy for trivia night?"

"About sex?"

• • •

Max waited for an emotion to come that didn't. Instead of being upset at Aggie for her ability to say the most inappropriate things, he wanted to laugh. God help him, but he liked that about her. Didn't want her to change.

"Um, let's go with not about sex," Max said to her. Thank God, Mr. Smith had a sense of humor.

Aggie beamed at Mr. Smith. "One more, and then I promise I'll move on to trivia about vegetables." She glanced at Max as if asking for approval.

Making him squirm appeared to be her superpower. He nodded. If he lost the contract, he lost the contract.

"Did you know there's enough sperm in just one male to

impregnate every fertile woman on the planet?"

The waiter brought their dessert to the table, a flourless chocolate espresso cake.

"Ms. Johansson, you are a treasure. I hope Max is smart enough to know what he has in you."

"He isn't, but that hasn't stopped me from trying to educate him."

"I'm sitting right here, you know," Max said.

"Indeed, you are," Mr. Smith said. "Max, this has been the most fun business dinner I've ever attended, and I've attended a lot. Most of them were a sleeping pill in the form of a gathering."

"I'm glad to hear that, sir. If you like, I've prepared some slides to share with you with my ideas on a new location for your next business endeavor."

Max spent twenty minutes showing Mr. Smith three different locations, each with his plan as to how the properties could be re-imagined offering a unique atmosphere for a bookstore slash bar business venture. "What do you think?"

Aggie hadn't helped him on this proposal. He glanced at her to see what she thought. She gave him that smile. The one he loved so much.

"Max, I like your ideas. I like them a lot. Number three is the one I'm drawn to the most."

He brought his attention back to his client. "Fantastic. Shall I have a contract drawn up?"

"Not so fast. I have an equally appealing proposal from one of your competitors."

"What's it going to take to tip your decision in my direction?"

Mr. Smith glanced at Aggie. "Your assistant reminds me a lot of myself at her age."

She dropped her fork. It hit the table with a resounding clank. "Did you grow up poor, too?" Her words weren't loud, but they shouted hurt feelings.

Mr. Smith tilted his head toward her. "That's not what I meant, but I know what it feels like to have to prove yourself to everyone you meet. What zip code did you grow up in?"

"64133. You?"

"64134."

Aggie's posture relaxed. "My grandmother moved into 64134 after she left home. I forget the one she grew up in, but it was worse."

Mr. Smith nodded as if the two of them were now bonded in the same way soldiers of war bonded. "What I meant about being like me is I would wager to guess you were raised to place high importance on a well-rounded education. As was I. Not just one you find in the books."

Her cheeks flushed. "I'm sorry. I shouldn't have assumed you were judging me. I'm just so used to people looking down their nose at me."

Max's heart splintered. Had he ever made her feel less? Probably. Hell. No wonder she branded him a pompous ass. He deserved the title.

"It wasn't until I earned my first million that I figured out there wasn't a damn thing wrong with me." Mr. Smith tugged at his shirt sleeves revealing his gold cuff links.

"Thank you," she said. "I tell anyone who wants to listen there's not a damn thing wrong with me, but...well...some insults stay with you long past their use-by date."

"You'll get there." He glanced at Max. "Ms. Johansson's knowledge impresses me. I want the two of you to be on my team at trivia night. If we win, the contract's yours."

"You're such a peach. Contract or not, I'd love to be on your team," Aggie said. "My meemaw has been filling my head with trivia since before I could speak."

Chapter Thirty-One

Max and Aggie stayed behind to discuss the dinner after Mr. Smith left. Now, coming up with no other reason to linger, Max said, "Give me your keys, and I'll have our cars brought to the front."

"I came in an Uber. Betsy wouldn't start."

"Betsy?"

"My car."

"You named your car?"

"You didn't name yours?"

"Never crossed my mind," he said.

"Tell me what kind you drive, and we can come up with a name for him or her."

"A black Porsche."

"Definitely a him. What else can you tell me?"

"Why don't I give you a lift home, and you can discover more for yourself?"

She eyed him like a banana she couldn't wait to eat.

The slight ache he'd had all night while sitting next to her amplified, causing his breaths to become hot and heavy as they left his body.

"Can we put the top down?" Her words were emphasized with a captivating flick of her tongue over her ruby-red lips.

"I'm always up for a topless ride."

Her eyes widened, and the slight tilt of her head told him she caught his play on words. Always beautiful, tonight she stunned him in a little black dress held together with a single button at the left-side of her curvy waist.

"Me, too," she responded, her voice husky.

In his car, she picked the radio station. Classic country.

"I would have pegged you for a rocker."

She stared straight ahead. "I am a rocker, when I'm in the mood for what rock brings out in me."

He turned the car out onto the road. Realized his palms were sweating. "What kind of mood brings out the classic country girl in you?"

"You'll see." His cock picked up on the promise in her voice and jumped to attention.

"I'm intrigued." He'd always been comfortable around women. Not so with Aggie. She morphed him into a self-conscious teenager.

She laid her head on the headrest of the leather seat and smiled as the wind blew in her face. "Do you know where I live?"

"I do. I drove—"

"Oh, I love this song." She leaned forward and turned up the sound, making conversation impossible. Which left him with nothing to do but think about the part of the evening behind them. Tonight was... An adjective for tonight evaded him. His inability to string words together had started the moment she waltzed into the restaurant, her eyes wide like Cinderella meeting her fairy godmother for the first time.

His first glimpse of Aggie, dressed to impress, blew several fuses of his internal wiring. From the distance, her fire engine red lipstick beckoned him, and every other man in the room, to sample her lips. Her hair pulled back in some sexy updo had his fingers itching to remove the bobby pins holding her tresses in place.

Her dress, a short black number, made him want to cancel the meeting and get a room. She must have decided their agreed-upon office length didn't apply to business dinners. Her long legs wore glimmery hose, and, as usual, a pair of ridiculously high heels adorned her feet. Pink.

The only jewelry she wore were tiny stud diamond earrings. He'd had an instant craving to buy her a locket she could wear with those earrings. One long enough to snuggle between her ample breasts.

A red light brought him out of his reverie, and he rolled to a stop. If he didn't distract himself, things were about to get awkward. He lowered the volume.

"Hey." She tossed him a scowl. "It wasn't over. Don't you like country music?"

"I love it." Grant made fun of his country music–loving side. One of the few things he and his best friend didn't agree on. "Would you like to come back to my place and celebrate our first successful business dinner together with a drink?" The invitation wasn't spur of the moment. He'd been contemplating asking her ever since inviting her to dinner.

And now, as the question hung between them, he told himself the invite had nothing to do with him making sure she didn't call the guy she was supposed to have had a date with tonight. Had nothing to do with Max not wanting them to hook up. Because if that were the case, it would mean he was jealous of the other guy, and he had no right to be jealous of any man in her life.

Aggie shrugged in a way that knocked a guy's self-esteem down a hundred flights of stairs. "Sure." Then she turned the radio back up and sang. A little off-key…which didn't appear to bother her in the least. "Join me," she shouted.

The ease of her demand captivated him. It was as if tonight she didn't see him as her boss. The knot he'd been feeling all evening loosened. "Okay."

Together they belted out "I've Got Friends in Low Places." At some point, he realized they were holding hands. Not sure when that happened, pretty sure he initiated the move, certainly sure he didn't want to let go of her hand.

He turned in the opposite direction of his condo and drove the long way home.

When he finally pulled into his parking spot, he angled to her. "What would you say if I told you I like-you, like-you?" *Hell.*

Her smile slipped all over her face before settling into a straight line. "I'd say you're a little drunk, and tomorrow at work, you won't be able to make eye contact with me. You might even call in and say you're working from home in an effort to avoid the girl you like-like when you're drunk on success and smooth liquor and Garth Brooks."

The insult stabbed him in places having nothing to do with ego. "I'm not drunk. I know exactly what I'm saying." He didn't go around declaring his like-like for someone haphazardly.

She rolled her eyes and then grasped the door handle. "Are we going to sit here all night, or are we going to go up to that fancy-ass condo of yours and have a drink?" She opened her car door and slipped out, denying him the opportunity to do so.

They rode the elevator in silence. Unless you count the saucy taunts her perfume whispered in his ears. Which were probably embarrassment red. He was the guy who declared like and didn't have the words immediately reciprocated.

Inside his home, he turned the light on dim and headed to the kitchen for a bottle of wine and breathing space. What he needed was a shot of whiskey to put out the flames of humiliation.

As if understanding his need to regroup, Aggie followed at a slow pace, her heels making a rhythmic click on the wood floors.

Looking like she didn't have a care in the world, she leaned against the counter within his line of sight. Obviously, having men tell her they liked-her, liked-her was par for the course. "How old were you when they gave you your trust fund?"

Her question surprised him. He didn't turn around. "I don't have a trust fund." Actually, he had one, but he didn't use it. He picked out a wine he hoped she would appreciate. Bold with hints of sweetness. He grabbed the opener and turned to face her.

"Then you can afford this place on the income of a guy still trying to build his business?" She sounded skeptical. "I mean, I know you're successful, but this place spits on average incomes. You have to be kick-ass successful to afford a condo in this zip code."

"Grandmother gave me this place when I graduated from college. Her parents gave it to her when she graduated." He sounded liked a privileged prick.

She let out a sharp laugh and rolled her eyes. "Meemaw gave me a cup with the year I graduated on it, and we went to Red Lobster for dinner. And used a coupon."

He poured them wine and led them to his living room. He sat on the couch and patted the cushion.

She chose a chair across from him. Further sign he'd fucked up with his declaration of like. The odds of him getting her out of her dress later tonight weren't in his favor. "Is that why you have a chip on your shoulder where I'm concerned?" His words weren't meant to be harsh, just his damn pride trying to rebuild lost ground.

"What do you mean?" She curled her feet up under her, being careful to drape her dress ladylike around her legs.

He jerked at his tie, loosening it around the knot in his throat. He had bought it new for tonight. The lavender silk matched her eyes. "You resent my being born into money." She wouldn't be the first person he'd met in life who didn't like him because he'd come from wealth. There were plenty of people in the business world who thought less of those who didn't have to pull themselves up by their bootstraps. People like Mr. Smith.

She played with the earring in her right ear. "I don't resent it. I just don't trust it."

He sipped his wine, savored the flavors while telling himself to relax, and then swallowed. "Any particular reason why?"

She mimicked his action. "Not that it's any of your business, but my grandfather came from money. When he discovered Meemaw was pregnant with my mom, he bailed. But not before telling Meemaw a lot of hurtful shit."

His insides coiled. "What do you mean?"

"He told her she was dumber than dirt if she ever thought a man like him would settle for a woman like her."

"Bastard," Max said under his breath. Her comment the other day about Meemaw having her heart broken by one rich man suddenly took on a whole other light. He'd have to tread lightly so he didn't hurt either of them.

"My mom grew up knowing her father considered her trash," Aggie continued.

"I'm sorry." An instinct to track down and harm the asshole who'd hurt Ms. Hazel gnawed at his gut like a hungry dog trying to gnaw through a leash. "Not all Silver Spooners look down on those not so fortunate. If anything, I admire you more because you made something out of nothing." It had taken tonight to realize, but it was true.

Her eyes narrowed, and she leaned forward. "At which point do you think I went from being a *nothing* to a *something*?" The words were clipped and as tense as her posture.

His heart stuttered. God no. "I didn't mean I thought there was a point when you were a nothing. I meant there was probably a point when you had little-to-nothing."

She leaned back, her eyes frosty.

"Let me be clear. You're really quite something."

"Whatever." One by one, she removed bobby pins from her hair then ran her fingers through the strands. "I'm the girl you like-like." Pride kept her words from sounding as offhand as she probably would have liked.

He nodded. "Exactly."

She glanced away. "This wine is fabulous. Perhaps you could send a couple bottles of it home with me, seeing as you now know how poor I am?"

He laughed. "Give it up. I refuse to think of you as anything but my equal."

As if his laughter took her out of her head, she laughed as well. "And you're saying that because the like-you, like-you line didn't work. You're just tossing out words to see which one I bite, so you can reel me in for sex."

He stood and walked toward her. "And how do you feel about having sex with a guy on the first date who is about as smooth as a cactus?"

With her normal frankness, she looked him square in the eyes. "Tonight was a business meeting in which we ate. Not a first date."

"Fair enough." He held out his hands. She placed hers in his, and he led her back to the couch where they had a seat next to each other and propped their feet on the ottoman. He dropped an arm around her shoulder. "What's your stance on having pre-dating sex with a guy?"

She laid her head on his shoulder. "I am your employee. Aren't you afraid I'll accuse you of harassment?"

He pulled back. "Do you feel harassed? If so, I'll stop." He withdrew his arm. Unintended pressure was still pressure.

She sat up straight and laughed. "Unlike the day you interviewed me, this isn't harassment. But, as a business owner, you should be much more concerned with the idea of sleeping with an employee than you appear to be."

He relaxed. "You did your fair share of harassing on the day of the interview." He ran a finger down the curve of her neck. She sounded so mature and sincere. And damn it to hell, she had a point. "But you're right. What kind of movies do you like? I can microwave some popcorn, and we can watch one. I'll even agree to one of those lovey-dovey girl-night movies."

She exhaled. "Didn't anyone ever teach you where there's a will there's a woman ready to make it happen?"

"Ummm." When she sat so close and stared so hard into his eyes, his brain had serious glitches. Not that it worked well when she sat across the room from him.

She held out her slender hand. "Give me your phone."

He didn't ask why, just did as she demanded.

She glanced at it and shook her head like he was quite dense. "Unlock it."

He did.

She opened his setting's app and opened the recording app. Holding the phone toward her mouth, she said, "This is Aggie Johansson. I'm about to have sex with my boss, Max Treadwell. I'm not in any way being coerced. If I say no now, or say no tomorrow, I will still maintain my position with his corporation. If, after tonight, we both decide to end my employment early, he agrees to pay out my contract." She handed him his phone back, dug hers out of a pocket he didn't know she had in her dress, opened her recording app, and stuck the phone in his face.

"What do you want me to say?" How sweet and sexy—she wanted to save him from himself. And what else did she carry in her pockets? Knowing her, a hammer.

"That you don't plan on using our sex to force me to keep working for you when our contract is up. And that you won't use it against me in a future letter of reference. And you are under no illusion that this is the start of something that involves our hearts. Etcetera."

"I agree to all of those things," he said into her phone.

She placed her phone back in her pocket. "Now, where were we?"

"Does this mean we're having sex?"

"It means sex is still on the table. But, unless you step up your game, I'm doubtful it will happen tonight."

• • •

Aggie homed in on Max's face to catch his real reaction before he masked it with indifference or arrogance. Thank God, the dark prevented him the same opportunity in the car to zoom in on her face when he admitted to liking her. And thank God, he hadn't been able to see how her belly did a twisty-twirly rollercoaster thing.

He scowled like she'd accused him of wearing lacy lingerie, followed almost instantly by an arrogant lift of the brow. "A lady has never told me to step up my game."

Messing with him rated right up there with going a hundred down a deserted road on the back of a Harley. "Then, most likely," she purred, "the ladies you've been with were after your money and didn't care if you had actual game." This might rate higher than a careening Harley. That realization washed the starch out of her smugness.

Why the high excitement? As far as danger went, teasing

him was as close to a big fat zero on the risk scale as would be eating a banana while standing. Sex with him wouldn't be dangerous. Fabulous but not dangerous. And she'd make damn sure she kept her heart intact, so no peril there.

A man who offered her no sense of jeopardy normally translated into Mr. Boresville. Made her itchy to move on to another man.

Which meant tonight's excitement laid in something entirely other than danger. Was she changing? Had her taste in men gone from bad, bad boys to rich, good boys? Gah. Next, she'd be wearing granny panties and drinking tea with her pinky extended.

He raked his fingers through his hair, causing his shoulder to bunch and hidden muscles to flex, completely scrambling her brain waves. Her lips parted. Just how magnificent were his shoulders when stripped of a shirt? Did he have any scars or other tats or bullet holes?

"Has anyone ever told you, you are hard on a guy's ego?" His voice held both humor and frustration.

"If you find that's harsh, here's something else I've been thinking."

His thick black lashes suddenly hooded his eyes. Why did men always have great lashes? "I'm listening?"

Her plan had been to say something flippant about his never-ending boring choice of ties. But since he appeared to sit on the edge of calm, cool, and freaking collected despite her hard ego pokes, she was obliged to step up her game and push him over the edge. "I've been thinking, and I'm not trying to be rude, you should pull out of the trivia game night."

He grunted.

"Mr. Smith wants to win, and though you are a peach of a boss man, you won't make a strong trivia team member."

The guy didn't even blink.

She went for the all-out shove. "You are what organized teams like to call the weakest link." She'd first heard the term weakest link being applied to children from poverty by a group of teachers talking about standardized test scores. They hadn't realized she attended the school on a scholarship.

His eyes widened, and astonishment splashed puddles of gray in their irises. "I beg your pardon."

"Don't sound so startled. It's not like I told you there'd be no more NFL football. I only mentioned your weakness as a trivia team member."

"I'll have you know," he paused as if picking his words carefully, "I seldom miss the final *Jeopardy!* question. And I have been known to run some categories."

"Hmm. For the sake of your male, aka fragile, ego, let's pretend I believe you." Max didn't know Aggie knew he had a Harvard-educated brain in his pretty little head.

His tongue poked at the inside of his cheek, running along it in a sexy gesture of frustration. "My ego doesn't need soothing. It's comfortable in its knowledge which of us is right in this conversation."

"And you're okay with my being the one who's right?"

He laughed, a warm, masculine rumble zinging her in places a guy's laugh had never reached before. Her heart. It was okay if her heart fell in love with his laugh, just as long as it didn't fall in love with him.

"I'd wager a bet," he drawled, sounding centerfold-sexy, "that I know more than you when it comes to trivia."

As she measured her next words for weight, she slowly ran her tongue up and down the crease of the right side of her lips. Two could play the sexy game. "We do live in the Show Me State. Are you willing to prove your brain isn't the size of my little toe?"

He dragged a finger down her cheek, bringing the pad across her bottom lip. "What did you have in mind?"

"How about a game of trivia? The first to stump the other wins."

He leaned back and laced his fingers behind his head. "Or…"

She stilled. His "or" promised naughty things to come. "Already afraid you'll lose?"

"Or we could play striptease trivia."

Yep. Naughty times ahead. Heat plunged through her going straight to the *V* of her legs where it settled into a pulsing throb. "I'm listening." And ready to say yes.

His gaze swept her body and lingered where she currently throbbed. Could he hear the pulse of her need? "The rules are easy. If you stump your opponent with your question, they have to remove an article of clothing."

She fought like hell to rein in her desires. Battles must be fought with clarity of mind. "And what will be your handicap?" She managed to sound sincere.

He grumbled. "I don't need a handicap."

She stood. Not to get away from him, but because… Her skin was hot and tight. She turned to watch his face. "So, your plan is to play this like…we're equals?"

He nodded.

She raised a brow, gave him a rakish once-over. Also lingering where she hoped like hell he throbbed. "You must be really proud of your manhood, seeing as it will be on display while I'm still fully clothed."

He stood. Squared his body toward her. A warrior preparing for battle. "I am." Nothing about his posture showed fear. If one looked close enough, and she did, a little about his posture said hard-on. "But that's not how this game will play out."

Despite her attempt to remain poker-faced, she grinned. Who would have guessed a battle of wits could be more exhilarating than a ride on a death-trap? "You do have on more clothes than I do." By her calculation, he had twelve to thirteen items to play with, depending if he wore an undershirt. "I guess that's a built-in handicap without us having to actually call it such." Her words came out husky, and she cleared her throat. "Who gets to start?"

"Ladies first."

Aggie did a quick calculation of what she wore. Two earrings. One dress. New panties and bra. Not new, because she'd planned on having sex when she got dressed tonight, but new because she was a strong proponent one simply did not wear the same pair of panties out with two different men.

There was a certain yuck factor, if things progressed to sex, in having two men remove the same pair of panties.

Moving on. Two shoes. Two stockings. One garter belt.

Ten items in all. "Do we have categories like in *Jeopardy!*?" Why the stall? It's not like she'd lose. She'd been training for this moment her whole life.

"Anything goes. There are no rules."

Why did she get the feeling no rules would play against her odds of winning? She shrugged away the kernel of concern. "Okay. First question. How much time does the average person spend kissing in their lifetime?" She could do this all night. She'd been collecting fun facts since kindergarten.

He focused in on her lips. "To answer that question, I will need to kiss you."

Her lips parted, and she had no control over the fact her tongue came out and licked her lips as if in preparation. "That sounds like cheating." *But please do convince me I'm wrong.*

He winked. "It's only cheating if you placed in the rules ahead of time a directive against such a thing, and you didn't."

She smiled. "I see. Then you may kiss me."

He hooked his thumbs in his pant pockets. "So you're one of those women?"

She resisted an urge to play with a strand of her hair.

"One of what women?"

• • •

Max stepped closer. Close enough he could see the creamy, rounded curves of Aggie's breasts. "A woman who expects the guy to do all the work." He wouldn't mind working on her all night.

She made a buzzer noise. "Wrong." Her palms settled on his face, and she pressed her curvaceous body against him. Her high heels raised her to the perfect height for kissing. Her eyes sparkled as she pressed her mouth to his.

As her lips moved against his in a slow dance, robbing him of breath and sending a jolt of desire through him, he fisted his hands to keep from grabbing her ass. Her hands slid down to his chest, and her lips moved over to his jaw. Much to his delight, her tongue darted out and licked him.

He groaned. Thoughts about inviting her to lick other parts of his body consumed him.

Another kiss danced across his lips, this one firmer. When her tongue brushed against his bottom lip, his control snapped. Ready to take over the pace, he tilted his head down to deepen the wine-flavored kiss. God. He wanted to skip the game. Take her to his bed. Fuck her until the sun rose and set on tomorrow.

She made a funny little noise in the back of her throat. The kind that drove him mad.

He slowed their kiss and sucked her bottom lip.

She trembled and pulled slightly away. "Is that enough research?"

He stepped back and raked his fingers through his hair. "I would say the average person spends less than a year of their lifetime kissing. On the other hand, a person lucky enough to be kissing you could quite easily spend twenty-five years of their life standing in one place and kissing you the way you deserve to be kissed. Slowly and thoroughly."

"Ummmm. According to Fox News, the correct answer is three hundred thirty-six hours. About twenty-five percent of a year."

"Then I got it right? I said less than a year."

She shook a finger at him. "That's not how trivia works. Close enough doesn't count. Lose the tie."

He slowly undid the knot. "Later, when we go to my bedroom"—he loved the way her eyes were watching his every move with the tie—"let's take this with us. It might come in handy with what I want to do to you."

She exhaled a soft breath, and her cheeks glowed a rosy hue as she gave him a slight nod. Then she turned and picked up their wineglasses. "I'll pour us more while you Google a trivia question."

"I don't need to Google a question."

She hurried away and came back with their glasses filled above the classical fill line for wine. She enjoyed a long sip of hers. "What's your question?"

He sat their glasses down. "What percentage of people like to talk dirty during sex?"

"Sounds like a piece of trivia you might have picked up from *Cosmopolitan* magazine. Are you a closet *Cosmo* quiz taker?"

"Answer the question."

"Forty-four percent." She stated her answer with the conviction of someone who didn't get trivia wrong.

Which made it all the sweeter for him to say, "Wrong." Ten thousand dirty words popped into his brain to say to her as soon as he got her naked.

"What's the correct answer? And what is your source?"

"Fifty-eight percent. I don't have to tell you my source. Take off an earring."

Her mouth opened and closed and then opened again. "How about I leave it on and instead I'll tell you if I like to talk dirty during sex?"

If he didn't remove his pants soon, he would bust the zipper. "Do you?"

She ran a finger down his chest, stopping at his belt buckle. "That's one of the many things I like during sex."

He reached down and adjusted himself. Time to end this game. "Next question." He wasn't too proud to lose if it meant taking her to bed.

"Which college has self-reported over one-fifth of its graduating seniors are still virgins?" she asked.

Did someone really conduct a study on this? "Duke?"

"Harvard. Take off your jacket."

He did. "How old am I?"

She blinked. "That's not a trivia question."

"Sure, it is."

"I don't know, like, fifty."

He grimaced. "Thirty. And because you were so far off, take off two things."

"Fine." She bent over, giving him a prime view of her ass as she undid the straps and slid off both of her high heels. From her bent-over position, she glanced up at him. "My turn." She didn't straighten until he took his eyes off her ass.

He nodded. "Your turn."

"What device was invented in the nineteenth century to prevent female hysteria?"

He didn't take time to come up with an educated guess. The quicker he was wrong, the quicker he could get her naked. "Mascara."

She rolled her eyes. "Weakest link for sure."

The dig dug at his pride, but pride didn't stand a chance against his lust. "And the answer is?"

"The vibrator. Take off two items."

"I thought you'd never ask." He removed his cufflinks. "In Ireland, it is believed if a woman eats this while thinking of a man, he will fall in love with her. What is it?"

She smirked like he'd asked her the answer to two plus two. "Easy. A four-leaf clover."

Her smirk had been justified. "I'm impressed."

"Why, thank you. How many times does the average person fall in love before getting married?" She leaned in slightly, her gaze sharp on his face. As if she were suddenly an FBI agent questioning a suspect.

Why did the question sound intentional instead of whimsical? "Three."

Their gazes remained locked several seconds before she shook her head. "Wrong. Seven. Remove two items."

"How many times have you been in love?" he asked as he removed his shirt and undershirt. She'd started this line of questions; a follow-up was appropriate.

She held up her left hand and started lowering one finger at a time. When all five fingers were down, she raised her right hand and lowered one finger. "Six."

He wanted to ask her about every single one of them and why they didn't work out. But that might sound like he wanted to be the next, and that's not what he wanted. Was it? "What is the height of the tallest building in the world?" Keep it light and easy.

"Really? That's the best you've got? You really must want me to remain fully clothed."

Give him a break. He could barely remember his own name at this point. "Okay. What's my middle name?"

She twisted her lips as if she knew she knew the answer but couldn't quite recall the correct response. Then a look of relief lifted her lips. "Andrew."

Damn. She was good. "Wrong. Donovan," he lied. "Two items."

She removed her remaining earring and then undid the single glorious button holding her dress together, but her hand did what the button had been doing.

"You don't get to artificially hold it in place."

She leisurely removed her hand, and the dress fell open like a curtain revealing what's behind *Let's Make a Deal*'s door number three.

He inhaled harshly, like a man who'd been suffocating and suddenly found air. Her body...fuck. Deal of the day.

She shimmied out of the dress. To the beat of his thudding heart, it fell to the floor.

"You're staring," she said, her voice sounding husky to his clogged ears.

He brought his gaze up, over her shimmery legs, lingering on the garter belt holding her hose by black snaps, the tiny thong panty, its matching black bra, and finally to Aggie's face. "As would any man when presented with a fucking masterpiece."

"You don't think I'm..." She grimaced.

"What?" Surely, she wasn't insecure. She had the kind of curves men drove over a cliff to see.

"Never mind. Thank you," she said in a haughty tone. "Prepare to lose your pants."

God, he loved her personality. Loved her spirit of adventure. Loved... "Yes, please, ask me a question." Could you love something that would surely drive you crazy in the long run? Maybe even ruin you?

"What's your name?" Amusement lifted her lips.

"Goner."

She chuckled. "Remove the pants."

"Thank you." Like a fumbling virgin, he did. "What day of the week did I arrive into the world?"

She tapped her cheek with a single finger, narrowed her eyes, and appeared to be doing the calculation to figure it out.

A century later, she said, "Saturday."

Hell. Once he fucked her like crazy, he should take her to the casinos. Her luck, and it had to be luck because why would she know that, was scary. "Wrong. Sunday. Remove your bra."

She did.

"Fuck. Those are the perfect amount of perfection."

"Thank you. What day of the week did my mom drop me off at Meemaw's?"

The question tortured his heart, made him want to reach out and hug her. Made him want to make sure she never felt abandoned again. Did she ask the question to remind herself to be leery of him? "Sunday."

She exhaled a long breath as if fighting a demon. "Saturday. Remove your Ellen boxers."

He kicked out of his shoes, his socks, and then his Ellen's. His erection, standing proud and ready for action, sprung free. He scooped her up in his arms and took a step toward his bedroom.

"Wait," she said.

"Why?"

"I have a condom in my dress pocket."

Chapter Thirty-Two

Aggie laid on her back in the middle of Max's enormous bed and tried not to stare too openly at his massive erection. She bombed. As in, an utter fail. Was it possible to fall in love while playing a game of strip trivia? Asking for a friend.

Loving someone's laugh and his cock are not the same as falling in love. This is just sex.

"I'm glad to see the size of your erection matches the size of your ego." She sighed lustily. "It's rare the two run parallel."

He chuckled, the warm sound caressing her skin, sending tiny tingles down her spine. "I'm glad you're glad."

Through her peripheral vision, she watched him dig the condom out of her dress pocket.

"Do you make it a habit to carry a condom in your pocket?" He had the kind of voice that always caught a woman's attention, but when layered with a tone of arousal, it became a wonderful sex toy. One far better than the preeminent of vibrators.

"A girl never knows when she'll lose track of the

whereabouts of her purse during an amorous moment." If he couldn't handle the truth, he couldn't handle her.

"I see." He tore the package open, gently tugged it out, and handed it to her. "I've been fantasizing longer than I care to admit about watching you roll a glow-in-the-dark, neon-pink condom down my length."

"I'd love to do the honors." She took it and sat up on the edge of the bed. He nudged her legs apart and moved between them. Up close, as if a magnifier stood between her eyes and him, his cock amplified. The sight burned a path of desire to the core of her own sex, which pulsated in expectancy. As she slowly positioned the condom on his tip where precum shone, her fingers grazed him.

He hissed, and she basked in the fact she affected his breathing as much as he affected her whole freaking body. "Hurry the hell up. I fucking want to fuck you right now."

She paused. Was he among the 90 percent of men who found women who take sexual initiative sexy? God, she hoped so. "How exactly are you going to go about fucking me?"

His hands fisted at his sides. Anticipation evident in every taunt inch of his body.

"I will start by touching you here." He unfisted a hand and ran a finger down her slit.

The contact of his warm finger against her wet center intensified the ache she'd been feeling all night. "Did you know the clitoris has eight thousand nerve endings?"

A sexy smile lit up his gray eyes. "I hope I'm engaging all of them right now." He slowly dragged his finger in an upward motion.

She groaned. Nodded. "What else?"

"What else what?" he asked.

The demand in his voice left her craving something she'd never craved before: to relinquish control during sex. There were so many things in her life she had no control over, but sex had always been one she did. "What else are you going to do to show me who's in charge while you're fucking me?" She would have never guessed tonight's fancy dinner would bloom into this moment between Max and her. A moment so monumental and yet so inevitable. Sparks had been flying between them since day one. Oh hell. Who was she kidding? She'd bought new panties for tonight.

"I'll enter you."

Erotic, yet… "Without foreplay?"

He arched a sexy eyebrow, and lust ricocheted through her like stray bullets at a shootout. "All of tonight has been about foreplay." The more he spoke, the raspier his voice.

Excitement danced in her belly. "Did you know in California there's a law making it illegal for either partner to climax before the other during foreplay?"

His pecs flexed.

A small feminine sound came out of her throat, making him smile.

"I will definitely make you climax first."

Her hips gyrated against the mattress and his finger. "Talk is cheap. Action is much more impressive."

He removed his finger from where it played its delicious stroking game.

She moaned in protest.

He straightened and clasped his hands behind his back. "After I've penetrated you, I will force myself to withdraw."

She stopped wiggling. "But why?"

"To give you the foreplay that will have you screaming my name."

"I've never had foreplay so good I screamed a guy's name." Is that because she'd never handed over control? Only one way to find out. Surrender and see.

Something flickered on his face. "Excellent."

That was not love on his face. That was something else. *Just because my thoughts are a blender of lust and love doesn't mean his are.* "Did you know sex toys are banned in some states, like Alabama?" Trivia grounded her when her attention span spun out of control.

"Do you have sex toys?" He looked amused.

She blinked. *Holy fuck.* Were they going there? "Since we're at your place, the better question is do you?"

"I've never needed them to please a woman."

She tried to lift one brow; they both went up. "What happens after you penetrate me and then withdraw?"

"I will lick or nibble or caress every delectable inch of you."

She closed her eyes on the image of his tongue going where his finger had been. "Starting where?"

"The arch of your foot."

She gripped the sheets tighter. "That's a long way away from the part I'm thinking your tongue should lick."

"My leisurely exploration will encompass all the highlights of your naked body. I'll let you know which places taste the best with love nips."

She knew the proper response if she wanted to match him dirty-talk for dirty-talk. But knowing and executing were on two different levels. "I bet you like the taste of my sweet spot best." The frank words coming off her tongue turned her on. "Are you going to nip me there?"

She'd lied when she said she liked to talk dirty. Not really lied. She just hadn't yet found a man she wanted to talk dirty to. Until this moment, sex had been about the release, not the foreplay.

Did talking sexy to Max equal some sort of commitment on her part?

His eyes closed. "Now that your hands have done what I needed them to do, I want to bind them to my bedframe with my tie. Scoot up there and center yourself."

Bondage! Her stomach tightened, her breathing quickened, and a quake of anticipation-shivers collided with red-hot desire. Control was so overrated. She raised her arms above her head and spread her legs so he could settle between them while he bound her wrists.

The sensation of the cool silk against her warm skin was its own form of foreplay.

"Your tits make me want to start there with my licks." His words were crude as if he needed a minute to downplay the emotions she could see in his eyes. He needn't have worried. Reading a guy's eyes was not a Johansson strong suit.

She might not be the type of woman he normally bedded, but damn it, she had every intention of being the best sex he ever had. "My nipples are on board with your plan."

He glanced down, lingered, smiled, and then glanced back at her eyes. "Honey, my tongue isn't coming near your tits until we're both panting wildly." As he spoke, he centered himself.

She wiggled against him. "Be a peach. Slide that in. Let's see how it fits."

As if he'd been there a hundred times before, surprisingly, he did just that.

Sweet baby Jesus. He'd said he would do that first, but she hadn't believed him.

They both gasped.

He started to pull out, and she squeezed her muscles around him. "Not yet."

He unleashed a smile on her, rocking her foundation. "Did I ever tell you I like to read the last page of a book before I read the book?"

That damn smile should be a registered weapon. Why did he want to talk books? Probably the same reason she wanted to talk trivia. They each had their own walls. Walls that, if they weren't careful, would tumble during sex. "You've never told me that," she managed to say.

"I do, because I want to know the ending is good before I commit my time to the book."

Another way they were different? She lived for surprises and new adventures. "And what does that have to do with what we're doing?"

"I just read your last page. The ending is everything I want and so much more. Now, I will read your other pages. Savor every word. Linger over every chapter."

Maybe he was on to something. And maybe, once you found a book you loved, you could be happy reading it over and over. She tried to move her hands, wanting to trap him in place. Her hands didn't budge. "Why don't you reread the last page? Make sure you didn't miss any of the good parts."

His gaze locked with hers, and the heat doubled in her body. "I plan on rereading that page many times. Just not at this moment. Now, I will read your acknowledgments page." He withdrew.

Acknowledgments? She didn't have acknowledgments. *I'd like to thank the man who knocked up Meemaw and helped to create Mom. And the man who knocked up Mom to help create me.* "I'd prefer you skip to the good parts. The sex scenes."

He raised his left hand to her face and gently cupped her cheek. "I plan to attend to all of those pages as soon as I've tasted all of you."

She wiggled against him. "Do you have a licking fetish?" Never would have pegged Max Treadwell as a kinky-on-the-sheets kind of guy.

He groaned. "I have an Aggie fetish."

The tone in which he spoke the words sent a river of need storming through her. She struggled to maintain her side of the conversation and failed.

He, too, failed.

Instead of voice, he spoke with his fingertips, erotically brushing them downward. Over her chin, down her throat, over the swell of her breast, navigating the indentation of her waist, pausing momentarily to cup the side of her hip, before delightfully detouring its downward motion to cut across to the *V* of her legs.

A sheen of sweat broke out over her body. She mentally encouraged him to take his caress fest toward her center.

As if reading her mind, the tip of his finger settled in the perfect spot. The spot with eight thousand nerve endings.

She sucked in a quick gasp, anticipation paralyzing the rest of her. Man, that statistic told the truth. "I bet you can't make me come with your finger." She threw out the taunt in hopes he'd linger there and prove he could.

In an act of cruelty, he slid his hand back to its original path and continued the downward journey until he made it to her feet. "You're probably right." Only then did his tongue flick out and touch her skin. "But I bet I can with my tongue." His tongue dragged across the sole of her foot.

"Sweet baby Jesus." Her back arched in a silent plea for him to hurry his journey upward.

He simultaneously massaged the inside of her foot at the base of her big toe and at the center of the pad of her foot. "Did you know both of these points are directly and intimately connected to both the male and female reproductive organs?"

She shook her head back and forth.

"By rubbing them, you increase the blood flow to the core of the body. Is your blood all moving toward the center of your body, Aggie?"

She raised her hips in response.

"I'll take that as a yes." He replaced his fingers with his tongue at the pad of her foot.

The sensation did everything but make her explode.

"Who taught you this?" Her voice sounded like she had orgasmed. She might have.

"I've been researching trivia ever since I met you."

His words travelled to her brain like molasses going uphill, but when they arrived, her heart melted. "You have? Why?"

"To someday impress the girl."

Holy fuck. What a charming thing to say. And it came from Max the Pompous Ass. Had a spell been cast upon him and neither of them were aware? "What other trivia have you learned that will come in handy right now?"

He ran his tongue over her ankle, stopping at a place toward the back of her leg about an inch above her ankle. He poked his tongue there. "Attention to this area promotes the yang. It sends a warming energy through the body." He dragged his tongue up and down.

"If I get any hotter, I may burst into flames."

He moved higher. His erection rubbing against her in the sensuous upward journey.

He stopped at her hip bone.

"You missed a spot. Remember, I mentioned the location earlier?"

He looked in her eyes and then, using his tongue, put pressure on the skin right above her bikini line where her hip hinged. "Not yet. Not before I teach you about this zone." As he held and released every few seconds, a sense of calm floated through her.

Which, weirdly enough, amped up her sensitivity.

• • •

Wearing a pink condom should have eased Max's need to explode inside of her. It didn't. Taking the time to offer her foreplay demanded every fucking ounce of self-control he possessed and a ton he'd never had to call upon.

After a delightful amount of attention to her breasts, he journeyed to her throat. "Did you know the entire area between the jawline and the shoulder is an erogenous zone?"

She gave him a heavy-lidded smile. "I knew that. I'm impressed you do."

"I also know that this small indention"—he poked his tongue where the neck and collarbone met—"is particularly sensitive."

Her body pushed up and enticed him to cease with the foreplay and get down to the business of giving her an orgasm.

Having her tied to his bed and completely at his mercy wound him up in ways he'd never been. "Are you ready for me?"

"For a century now." She ground her hips into his.

He reached between and touched her with two fingers. He rubbed.

"Holy shit."

And rubbed.

"Oh hell."

And rubbed.

"Max!" Aggie screamed.

Hearing his name, feeling her convulse, he guided his cock to her center. She was so fucking wet. He struggled not to lose his control as she enjoyed tonight's first orgasm.

He planned on pushing in slowly. Inch by delightful inch. She had other plans. As soon as he entered her, she raised her hips and took the slow dance into her own hands. Figuratively speaking, because her hands were very much still tied to his bedframe.

She quickly taught him she didn't need her hands to tango.

She slid her legs around his waist and squeezed.

"You can't expect a man to maintain when you do that,"

he warned.

"We can do slow next time. Right now, I need another orgasm."

He laughed but obliged. Their movements easily synchronized. As if they'd been forever lovers. He lowered himself enough to rub her tits with his chest as they danced their way toward the frenzied finale.

The most seductive thing of all was the way her eyes stayed opened, and she locked gazes with him the entire time. As if freely, knowingly, giving him a glimpse into her every thought and reaction to their first sexual encounter.

It was only as she came again, they closed, her noise of enjoyment sending him on his own eye-closing journey of pleasure. When they were spent, he captured her lips in a kiss he hoped she could read for what he couldn't yet say with words.

His heart was still his, but this was the closest he'd ever come to giving it away. All it would take would be for her to say she wanted it. That he could be number seven.

The realization both scared and excited him. He could name far worse things than to fall in love with Aggie Johansson. She'd always keep him on his toes. She'd never bore him. She'd be a wonderful mother to their children.

Son of a fucking bitch. What in the hell was he thinking? She wouldn't stop at love number seven. That was an average number. There was nothing average about her. If he gave her his heart, she'd turn around and hand it back in a matter of months.

Which should be perfect, because he didn't want to do love. At least not until he'd scored his first million and didn't have a dumb-ass bet hanging over his head. But unlike the average person who fell in and out of love seven times in their life, he'd never even fallen once. Which meant he was the outlier in the number game. He knew as well as he knew the color of Aggie's eyes, he'd be the one who skewed the statistics by only falling in love once.

He untied her hands, rolled off of her, and stared up at the ceiling. He should say something but didn't trust his mouth to say something neutral. Something he'd said a hundred other times to women after sex. Like…that was fun. Shall I take you home?

She rolled onto her side and leaned up on one arm.

He turned his head to stare into her eyes. Her orgasm turned them to the color of ripe plums.

"That was—"

Suddenly needing to stop whatever she meant to say, he sat up quickly. Afraid her next word would be "fun." The most vanilla of all vanilla things one could say after sex. And for him, it hadn't been fun. It had been spectacular. It had been mind-blowing. It had been life-changing. Not plain old "fun."

"Let me go dispose of the condom, and then we can indulge in pillow talk." He shot out of bed and headed toward the bathroom, desperately needing a moment to regain his senses. Understandably, she'd want to go home. She didn't have an overnight bag with her. He'd take her. But he didn't want her to say the word "fun."

Behind the door, he heard mooing. His shoulders bunched, and his gut tightened.

Who in the fuck just texted her?

Chapter Thirty-Three

Fog clouded Aggie's brain like someone had stuffed it into the center of a cotton-filled pillow. Tonight met every fantasy expectation she'd ever had about having sex with a man. And not just any man. A man she could spend her future with. Yes, call her a sap, but she'd spent more than one minute over the years dreaming about *that* man.

You know...*that* unrealistic list of everything a man would say and do before you gave them your heart. The very list you created to protect yourself from ever falling in love, because no one, absolutely no one, could ever live up to the expectations on *that* list.

The sound of mooing had her scrambling off the bed and into the living room to recover her phone, happy for the reprieve from thoughts of *that* man, and read the text. It was from the P.I.

As promised, I'm giving you an update. Discovered your mom is an addict and a felon. She's currently on parole and not living at the address listed with her parole officer. Should know more soon.

She fumbled the phone but caught it before it hit the floor. *Mom's a felon. I'm the daughter of a felon. Not just a bastard child, but the bastard of a felon.*

"Everything okay?" Max wrapped his arms around her middle and pulled her into him so her bottom nestled nicely into his magical hips.

She quickly lowered her phone so he couldn't read the screen. Heat, the crazy overwhelming, non-sexy kind, flanked her on all sides. She stepped out of his arms. "Fine. Fine. Everything's fine. I'm fine." Where was an air conditioner vent when she needed one?

"You don't sound fine."

She twisted and glanced at him. "My ride will be here in a few minutes. I need to get dressed."

The joking left his gaze. "Stay."

She wanted to smile and tell him to stop being so perfect, but she couldn't. Her fear of eventual rejection still sitting front and center in her brain right next to the bold black word "felon." "Don't be silly. Meemaw knows an Uber took me to the dinner. She'll expect one to bring me home. Anything less and she'll fantasize we've fallen in love."

He pulled her into his arms and nuzzled a kiss into her neck. "And we didn't…right?"

Now, his voice had all kinds of weird nuances that, under different circumstances, she would have loved to analyze. Or…her ears were still stuck in a cotton cloud and the nuances didn't exist. "Neither of us do love. That's why tonight was doable. We can still work together, and it's not a big deal. Besides, remember, I'm an Enthusiast and you're a Reformer. Keep me around long enough, and I will cause your world to implode."

"Not if I don't give you means to light the dynamite."

The minute he let her into his life, he'd given her the match to do the job. But she wasn't going to stand here and argue her point. "At the very least, you'd eventually find me an embarrassment to be around."

"I don't give a fuck that you came from poverty."

He said that now, but in the cold light of day, everything always looked different. "Not because of my economic status, but because I'm an Enthusiast and you're a Reformer. Read up on them. You'll see in black and white where it clearly says Reformers eventually find it embarrassing to be around Enthusiasts." Especially when they discovered their Enthusiast came from felon blood.

"Not if the Reformer learns to chill and enjoy the idiosyncrasies of the Enthusiast."

Her phone mooed.

"Who keeps texting you?"

"Relax. It's just my ride." She stepped out of his arms, grabbed her dress, and slipped it on. Max handed her shoes to her, and she wiggled her feet into them. "Be a doll and bring the rest of my items to work on Monday."

"Why not tomorrow?"

"I'm taking tomorrow off. Compensation for dumpster diving for my boss." She needed time to wrap her head around this latest news of Mom. Before he could respond, she hurried out the door and into an open elevator.

It was best if their relationship never moved past a one-night stand. She'd use the long weekend to get her shit together, and then on Monday she'd play it calm, cool, and uninterested. Better to be the pusher than the one pushed.

Her phone mooed. She glanced at the screen.

Max: *I wanted your last moo of the night to be from me.*

...

Max fixed himself a scotch on the rocks and strode onto his balcony. The sky sparkled as if it were hosting a grand ball for all of heaven's angels. Hell, he was in such a great mood, if he saw a shooting star, he'd for sure act like a kid and wish upon it.

He sat down on a chaise lounge and Googled love between an Enthusiast and a Reformer on his phone.

Tonight gave him an inkling of how sweet it would be to give his heart to another. Spending time with Aggie made him question his five-year plan. Would having a woman in his life really upset his professional goals to grow his business? It's not like loving her would prevent him from hustling business.

Or would it?

He chose the first article listed that also included the word Enneagram and read all about the potential trouble spots between the two.

...Enthusiasts deeply resist feeling trapped by Reformers.

Was that why she'd been through so many jobs? Fallen in and out of love so many times? If so, he should give her space. Treat her like a spooked animal. When animals were spooked, they ran. He didn't want her to bolt.

When he saw her on Monday, he'd act like nothing happened between them. He'd let her make the next move, wait for her to nudge him, before he initiated an I-might-be-falling-for-you conversation.

Chapter Thirty-Four

Between sex with Max and discovering her mother was a felon, too many emotions were crowding Aggie's brain to go home, so she had the driver drop her at an all-night diner. She had to get her shit together before letting Meemaw see her. Under no circumstances could she let her know the truth about Mom. Or that she and Max had sex. Or that…

Over a cup of coffee, she did what she always did when unsure of her next step: write an updated life plan.

She dug her lucky pen and a tattered notepad out of her purse. At the top, she wrote Aggie Johansson's start-over, reinvent-herself-as-the-daughter-of-a-felon, life plan. Number one: possibly move to New York City.

Hell, the only reason she'd stayed in Kansas City this long was so Mom would be able to find her. But if her parole got revoked, Mom didn't have to find her; she could find Mom in the state penitentiary.

Back in the day, when Aggie first mentioned wanting to live in the big city, Meemaw confessed that she, too, had always dreamed of living there. They could go there on a grand adventure. Start a new chapter in their this-is-my-life books.

Gah. Max and his damn tendency to read the last page first. Once he learned her last page included felon blood, he'd for sure not want to read any more of her chapters.

And by going to New York, she wouldn't be tempted to stay around and try to have a sex-only relationship with him. Leaving would result in a clean, clinical cut.

Her phone mooed. She glanced at the screen.

Meemaw: *Everything okay? Expected you home by now.*

Aggie glanced at the clock on the wall. Two a.m. What possible reason could she give Meemaw for being out this late?

Aggie: *Spending some time with my boyfriend.*

Meemaw: *Max? Is he your new boyfriend?*

Aggie: *No. He's my boss. The law frowns when those lines are blurred.*

Silence followed.

Pulling her thoughts back to her life plan, she took out another piece of paper and along the top wrote the word "Manifesto." If a company could have one, so could she. Closing her eyes, she thought about what she believed.

What she stood for.

She opened her eyes and placed her pen onto the paper.

The words flowed from her fingertips as if they'd been bottled inside of her, waiting for a chance to escape like a genie does from a bottle.

Stilettos are the devil's playground. Stilettos are a

*wink from God. Crocs have no deity. Secrets seldom
stay under a rock. Never settle. People will come and
go from your life, trust none of them. Except one.*

Love. Doesn't. Survive. Between. Opposites.

Your parents will love you only if you're lovable.

Always sing in the shower. Never in the tub.

Always do the one thing that most scares you.

*Search until you find but hope for less than your soul
desires.*

Knowledge slays.

Felon.

When the words stopped pouring, she lowered her pen
and analyzed each bit of her manifesto.

Shoes. There were worse things in the world than being
an out-of-the-closet shoe snob.

Secrets. Would Meemaw discover Mom's secret? Aggie
hoped not.

Trust. Did she have trust issues? That would be a big fat
yes. Were there times when secrecy had a place in a trust
relationship?

Loveable. She squeezed her eyes shut. She'd known
forever she wasn't particularly loveable. A mom didn't
abandon a loveable child. Not after four years of getting to
know her.

Singing. People who couldn't sing learn early; the
acoustics were horrible in a bathtub. If you wanted a decent
shot at sounding like Beyoncé, take a shower.

Scare yourself. Tonight, she'd done that. She let herself
momentarily consider love with Max.

Hope. She would keep searching for Mom, but her soul

would be braced to receive less than it hoped for. It hoped for a motherly declaration of love and heartfelt apologies.

Knowledge. While it made her sad to realize she and Max should never be anything more than a one-night stand, knowledge did slay false hopes.

Knowledge kept her from careening down a pathway to heartache. Knowledge told her it was time to make another career change.

Felon. The word that would cause any man like Max to run.

Aggie rubbed at the spot over her chest. The spot where her heart lay beneath. Who knew writing a manifesto could cause simultaneous pain and comfort?

All in all, not bad for her first one.

She closed her eyes again.

I had sex with Max, and I liked it.

Chapter Thirty-Five

On Monday morning, Aggie caught the city bus to work. Ever so slightly late, when she hurried into the reception area, she discovered the door to Max's office was closed. His signal to stay out. She breathed a sigh of relief. She now had time to catch her breath and get her game face on.

This would be the first time they'd seen each other since their sexy times on Thursday night. Under no circumstances could she allow any little part of herself to hope the sex meant more than it did. Because it didn't. It was just a great fuck.

If you didn't learn from history, you were doomed to repeat it. And Meemaw's history taught her not to give a rich guy an opening to crush you with their rejection. They might like sex with the woman from the other side of the tracks, but that did not spill over into happily-ever-afters.

Their relationship had to be shoved back into the box marked boss/employee. And on her lunch hour she was going to laminate her new life plan. "I am the pusher, not the pushed," she reminded herself.

As she busied herself with the coffeemaker, his thick,

rich voice carried easily through the closed door. Maybe she should make some noise to let him know she'd arrived.

"Trust me, I know. The apple never falls far from the tree. I'm not stupid. I will proceed with absolute caution."

She jumped and dropped her empty cup. It landed with a clanking thud on the counter. That sounded very much like a man who thought he had the upper hand in shutting down a woman in danger of liking him too much. If he thought he was going to be the pusher in this equation, he had another thought coming.

"Aggie? Is that you?" Max called out. He sounded cheerful. A man so relaxed he initiated a conversation between walls. Was she not the bad apple he'd been referring to?

She picked up her cup and smoothed a hand over her hair. Not that it mattered, but to be fair to him, even if she was the bad apple, in a lot of ways, the description fit. You don't live the life she'd lived without gathering a few bruises in the process. "Sorry I'm late. I'm fixing a cup of coffee. Would you like a cup?" Why in the hell did she offer to bring him a cup? She wasn't that sort of assistant. He was going to think she thought they were a possible thing.

"I'm good."

Whistling floated through the walls to her ears. She'd never heard him whistle. Not even when he got a contract.

While she waited for the coffee to brew, she refused to allow herself to read anything into his good mood. It probably had nothing to do with him still liking-her liking-her. She forced herself to send a text to her college friend, the one now living in Brooklyn, and asked her if the open-couch invitation still stood.

"Aggie, anytime you're ready to get to work, we've got a lot to accomplish today." A wall no longer between their voices.

She turned to give him an I've-already-forgotten-we-had-sex smile, but it never reached her lips.

Max stood in the doorway looking at her the same way he'd looked at her the day they met. Like she was a pain in his ass not fit to breathe the same air as him. She was most definitely not his reason for being in a good mood.

The investigator must have told Richard Mom was a felon, and Richard told Max, and now he was shutting her down exactly like she'd feared he would if he knew? Asshole.

Knowing he'd want nothing to do with her when he found out, and actually seeing it on his face, were two different beasts. She turned to add sugar to her coffee. "I'm just about ready." She hated sugar in her coffee, but she'd be damned if she let him see her hurt. How dare he judge her for Mom's baggage.

Max wanted to yell at someone. Instead, all morning he'd been whistling the opening bars of "You've Lost That Lovin' Feelin'" by the Righteous Brothers. He'd learned the distraction technique when his parents divorced, and his dad refused to let his son be sad about Mom no longer living with them.

Calling Grant hadn't eased the tension causing his headache. Grant had concerns that Max's view of Aggie was skewed by his lust. He had reminded Max that he was, after all, his father's son—a man who'd always been able to justify sex with an employee—and that apples never fell far from the tree. A ridiculous saying even if it did hold more than an ounce of truth. Then to compound the headache he'd given Max, he went on to vehemently spout the same shit advice Max had given him back in high school: don't reveal love if it might not be reciprocated.

At the time Max gave the advice, it felt solid. Now, the pithy words gave him heartburn on top of his headache.

According to Grant's parting remarks, nobody would win if Max told Aggie about his throbbing, scared-shitless heart.

Hell, maybe Grant was right. Maybe it wasn't love that had him in knots and, instead, was a hangover from excellent sex. Maybe it was the pulse in his cock throbbing in his heart.

He stood still as she studied him, her brows squished together and lips pursed. He could practically see her walls. The ones he'd briefly gotten around Thursday night. "You look lovely."

When she bent her head and returned her attention to stirring sugar into her coffee, he watched. This wasn't just her normal walls. Something wasn't right.

"Go on. I'll be right there," she said breezily.

Fuck Grant's advice. They weren't eighteen anymore. Adults handled love differently than high-schoolers. He wasn't going to act like Thursday night never happened. It did, and it affected him. In a good way. "Actually, I wanted to talk to you about something."

"I hope it's about work." Her voice was louder than normal. "I have an idea for something to add to your proposal for the bid project."

Hell. That sounded very much like something a woman would say who wanted a man to know that what happened between them was a one-and-done type of event.

Which left him with only one option. Call her bluff. "Work with me after your contract ends?" If she got excited and said yes, she wasn't interested in a personal relationship but, instead, a business one. If she said no, there was hope.

"You have an assistant." The breezy tone now contained a frost warning. "One who will return in a month."

"She's not coming back."

"She's not?" The two words snapped at him like an angry turtle.

"Would you like her job or not?"

She took the cream out of the refrigerator and poured it into her coffee.

Since when did she take cream in her coffee? Or sugar?

"Let me get this straight. You can't have your real assistant back, so I'll do?"

"Damn it, Aggie—"

"*Damn it, Aggie*," she mimicked.

He clamped his mouth shut on what he wanted to say. Telling a woman to grow up never went over well in any situation, let alone when they were in a mood.

"Cat got your tongue?"

"I'd be happy to have you continue to work for me." Not thrilled. "Is your answer yes?"

"Sorry to burst your happy bubble of hope." She picked up her coffee cup and purse. "I'm not available."

Relief surged through him and his headache disappeared. She wanted what he wanted.

"I'm moving to Brooklyn." She marched past him and into his office. To her desk.

Confused, he followed. A no was supposed to have been a positive sign. But hell, he'd prefer a yes than a no with this caveat. Anger whipped through him. Mostly at himself, but also at her. "Of course you are. This is par for the course with you, flitting from one thing to another."

She plopped her purse on her desk. It landed with an ominous thud. "I don't flit. I drift."

"Why Brooklyn?"

Her nostrils flared. "It's part of my life plan."

"*You* have a life plan?" This ought to be good fodder for his next drinks with Grant.

"You *don't*?"

He stuffed his hands in his pockets. "As a matter of fact, I do. It doesn't include *you* taking off to New York City."

She opened her mammoth purse. "Don't worry. I'm going to work out my contract. I've grown up since you met me." She pulled out a tape measure, a condom, and a crumpled sheet of paper.

Why was that damn condom always on top of whatever she was looking for? A man couldn't think when it came out to play. He scratched his head and tried to focus. "What about Ms. Hazel? Are you really going to take off and leave her behind?"

"She's going to come and live with me. Once I'm settled."

"Grandmother will hate that. It's been a long time since I've seen her so happy."

Aggie's eyes clouded.

Hell. He'd rained on her parade. If this was what she wanted, who was he to be an ass about it? "Ms. Hazel will love living in Brooklyn. She will charm the hell out of the locals, and it's not like Grandmother doesn't have plenty of other friends."

His words brought a smile to Aggie's lips and a crinkle to her eyes. That was all the proof he needed to know this was something she really wanted to do. It wasn't one of her fly-by-night ideas. Like an office mascot. "Meemaw has never been out of the state. It will be an exciting adventure that I can give her."

"She's lucky to have you as her granddaughter." He remembered reading a poem in high school that spouted some bullshit about loving someone, letting them go, waiting for a full moon and then they come back, and everybody got laid. Or did they come back and a bird shit on your head for good luck? Whichever it was, he'd see if it held true.

He waited for her to say more. She didn't. Instead, she turned her attention back to reloading her purse.

"I guess, given that you're leaving town, there's no need for us to talk about Thursday night." It was a Hail Mary. One last attempt to see if there was any doubt in her mind about what she wanted.

She removed a stick of gum from her purse and unwrapped it. "We had fun, but I'm sure you agree it was a one-time judgment lapse." She stuck the gum in her mouth.

"Or—" A knock at the door interrupted him. Whoever it was, they'd have to come back. He jerked his head that direction. The door stood open. And in it stood Tabitha from high school.

Fuck. He and Grant had bumped into her once again Friday night at Ties and Stilettos Cocktail Lounge.

She gave him a bright smile. "Max, darling, I know you weren't expecting me, but since I was on this side of town, I thought I'd offer to take you to lunch. I had so much fun Friday night, and I thought why not stop by and tell you that in person. Too much is said over texts these days, and sometimes the message just doesn't come through clearly enough." Tabitha turned to Aggie. "Isn't that right?"

"Absolutely. Did you say Friday night?" Aggie sounded nothing like Aggie.

"I did."

"You must be the reason Max has been whistling this morning." Aggie tossed Max a heated glare.

Of course, she'd come to that conclusion. He'd not given her any reason to come to another.

"Is that true?" Tabitha asked. "Are you whistling because of me?"

Max and Aggie's gazes were laser locked. He could see the hurt in her eyes.

"Trust me." Aggie jerked her head toward Tabitha. "I've never heard him whistle at work."

Tabitha beamed at Aggie. "He's kind of hard to read

sometimes. Thank you for telling me."

Max went to his desk and sat.

Tabitha followed. She sat on the edge of his desk and crossed one leg over the other. "Remember that idea I mentioned?"

He nodded.

"I've improved upon it. Hint. Just imagine me in a bikini, holding a martini. Take me to lunch, and I'll tell you more."

Aggie knocked a mirror off her desk, and it broke. The noise drew their attention. "Damn it. Seven years bad luck." She quickly picked up the pieces and dumped them in her trash bin. Straightening, she said, "I'll give you two some privacy. I'm going to go buy office supplies and then do lunch." She grabbed her purse and rushed to the door. "I promised Bill this morning I'd meet him for an early lunch. If you and Tabitha leave for your lunch date before I get back, be sure and lock up." She was out the door before he could stop her. Probably because his brain got hung up on the word "Bill."

That asshole was undoubtedly the reason she'd decided to move to New York City. There was doubtless some damn biker gang there he wanted to join. Or he was running from the law.

Three minutes later, Tabitha left. Alone. The last thing he wanted was to help her plan a tropical class reunion.

Which left him with nothing to do but sit and wonder about Aggie and Bill. And her errands. And if sex with Bill was one of her errands.

Two hours later, his phone rang. He snatched it up, needing something, anything, to take his mind off Aggie. "Treadwell Properties."

"Is this Max?"

"It is." Max rubbed his left temple with his free hand.

"This is Ruby from the Club."

He sighed. Hell. Had she somehow discovered about the favors he'd cashed in to get Ms. Hazel admitted? "How may I help you?"

"Do you remember my great niece, Jodi? You met her at our Christmas social last year."

"Of course, she's quite lovely and entertaining." And bored him silly.

"She's run into a bit of a bad patch with the men in her life lately. I'd like for her to find a nice young man who can see her potential."

"I'm not sure where you're headed with this?"

"I'd like for you to take her out. And I can even help you make a good impression. You see, I have two tickets to *The Lion King*. Her favorite. Why don't I give you those? You can take her out to a nice dinner and then the theater."

Max frowned. "Thank you for calling. And thank you for the offer. But—"

"What do you know about Johnny John?"

"Who?" He pinched the bridge of his nose.

"He's a man who could stir quite the embarrassment for Grace should he come back to town."

Max straightened and lowered his hand to his desk. "That sounds very much like a threat." Of course, he knew a little about the man. The little that Grandmother had told him when he'd questioned her on why she married someone she didn't love.

"You have good ears. Did I mention I have a dear friend who writes for *The Society Page*?"

The pencil he held in his hand snapped. Max couldn't care less what Ruby did to hurt him, but he couldn't be callous where Grandmother was concerned. "If I take Jodi to the musical, are you going to drop this whole Johnny John threat?" Caving to blackmail tasted like cheap, sweet wine, but he would swallow a whole bottle of it if it meant protecting Grandmother's pride.

"For now."

He flung one half of the pencil across the room. "Not good enough. You either have to drop it forever or we're not closing this deal."

Ruby harrumphed. "Call Jodi, as soon as we hang up."

"What night are the tickets for?"

"Wednesday night."

Max hung up and called Jodi. Right as he pushed dial, Aggie cruised in. He placed his hand over the receiver. "Would you mind waiting in the reception area and shutting the door? This is a private call."

Jodi answered the phone. "Hello."

"Hi. Could you hold one second?" Damn it. He hadn't wanted Aggie to hear him call her. Then again, she'd been out to lunch with Bill.

Aggie's eyes narrowed. "Fine. But if you're about to plan another date with Tabitha, don't forget Wednesday night we agreed to cook dinner for the grandmothers. Their big tournament starts on Thursday."

He nodded. Shit. Now what? "Sorry about that," he said to Jodi. "This is Max, from the country club."

"Hello, Max. How may I help you?" Jodi sounded formal.

Here goes nothing. "I wanted to call and let you know your aunt Ruby is trying to blackmail me into asking you out. I thought about caving, but I'm certain that is the last thing you'd want. So I decided to call and clue you in on what's going down."

"For the love of God," Jodi snapped. "Thank you for the heads up and not taking me out on a fake date. I'm absolutely mortified she tried to blackmail you into the act. What is it with that generation that they think they can interfere in everyone's life?"

"Got me. Grandmother has been the queen of meddling

as of late." Remembering Ruby's concern about Jodi's bad run of luck with men, he added, "I want you to know, it's not that I don't want to take you out, but I am seeing someone right now."

"You're sweet for saying that. I'm not even going to ask you what it is Aunt Ruby tried to blackmail you with, but if she asks, what shall I say we did?" Her shaky voice told him she wasn't taking the news as breezily as she would have him believe.

Laughter erupted from the outer office. He had a pretty good idea who Aggie was talking to.

"*The Lion King* and dinner, Wednesday night."

"Got it. Thanks."

He hung up. If Ruby discovered he'd called her bluff, he'd deal with the fallout when it happened. Right now he wanted to know who in the hell Aggie was laughing with.

Treading like a cat-burglar, he reached the door and opened it in a grand caught-you fashion.

Aggie glanced his way. "I hope my laughter didn't disturb you. I was watching bad boss videos to drown out your voice. I didn't want to eavesdrop on you and your new girlfriend." Her tone was perfectly neutral.

"I wasn't talking to my new girlfriend."

"But you admit you are thinking of Tabitha in that terminology?"

"Does Bill know about Thursday night?"

She cocked her head and studied him. "He's not the territorial type. Thank God. I can't stand guys who get all *you're mine* just because I had sex with them."

Score one for Aggie. "Does that mean you're not interested in hearing an explanation of how I came to hook up with Tabitha Friday night?" Fuck. That came out sounding wrong.

Her could-care-less expression wavered. "I would

assume it was for the same reason I hooked up with Bill? If I'm wrong, then please do explain."

The admission suckered punched him, and he turned toward his office door to keep her from seeing the shock on his face. "Let's pick this conversation back up when your contract is over."

"Yes. Let's."

He casually stepped into his office, quietly shut the door, and then stomped to where the broken pencil laid and chucked it at the trash can. When had his life gotten so fucking complicated?

. . .

Aggie stared at the closed door. The asshole had actually gone out on a date one night after they had sex. Why in the hell had she let any inch of her brain hope she was wrong about his character? Let herself believe he wasn't the sort to judge her based on her past? That he found her special as-is and didn't give a damn about roots she had no control over?

Johanssons weren't lovable. They sucked at love. They were the loveable losers of love.

No more schooling necessary. Lesson branded on this gal's brain.

She walked to the window and glanced out. A robin sat on the sill. Was it a sign from the Universe she should let her dreams take flight, move to NYC? The bird turned its little body around so that they were staring at one another. Its little head cocked to one side as if saying, *Do you want to talk about it?*

Aggie nodded. She did want to talk about it. "It's like this: a guy who takes another woman out twenty-four hours after having sex with you is serious when he says he doesn't do love. A guy is a guy is a guy. They all think with their dick.

Don't you agree?"

The bird flew away.

Aggie sighed. If only she could fly as easily.

At least she didn't embarrass herself and tell him how gooey on the inside he'd turned her. It would be a cold sensation on the tongue of a guy in the midst of a ghost pepper–eating contest before she told him she hadn't really gone out with Bill. This weekend. This morning. Or this afternoon.

One month left on their contract. She could do this.

Chapter Thirty-Six

Wednesday evening at four twenty p.m., Aggie's cell rang. She didn't have to glance at the caller I.D. to know who it was. Max. The guy she couldn't stop thinking about but wanted to stop thinking about. Thank God he hadn't been in the office much this week. Or at least part of her thanked God for that. Another part of her missed Max's ugly mug and average conversation skills.

"I'm on my way," she said instead of hello. She glanced out the bus's dirty window and watched the street signs tic by one...block...at...a...time. It's funny how when you're running late, time moved so much faster than moving vehicles.

"What's taking you so long?" Max asked in his signature pompous tone.

She rolled her eyes. "If you must know, I missed the bus." Tonight, they were fixing dinner for their grandmothers.

"Why didn't you drive?"

"My car still won't start."

"Why haven't you had Betsy fixed? You can afford it, can't you?"

The fact he remembered her car's name softened her heart, which pissed her off. "What's with the fifty freaking questions?"

"If you'd taken an Uber, you could have been here on time."

"I happen to prefer public transport." She didn't plan on fixing Betsy. This freed her to save up enough to pay Meemaw's rent and utilities two months ahead. No way would she leave for New York and cause her to have to work extra shifts to cover the expenses Aggie normally covered.

"I happen to prefer people who are dependable."

"I'll tell you what, you take a bus to work tomorrow morning, and if you get there on time, then you can be pissed at me. Otherwise, stop acting like a privileged asshole."

There was a short pause. "I deserve that. Do you have the ingredients for the cookies?"

She shifted her grocery sack off the seat next to her so a woman just getting on the bus could sit down. Her contribution to tonight's dinner—no-bake cookies. "Just because I'm late doesn't mean I'm not responsible."

"That's exactly what it means."

"Do you have the steaks lying out? They need to come to room temperature before you cook them."

"Is that some piece of trivia Ms. Hazel stuck in your brain when you were a child?"

The mention of trivia tripped her thoughts down paths better left untripped. "I like my steaks medium. Meemaw likes hers medium rare. If you get hers too done, she'll forever think less of you."

"I know how to grill steaks."

"Trying to be helpful. By the way, I got a Hallmark card for us to give them tonight, wishing them luck at the Bridge tournament. That is, if you want to sign the card with me." She could have bought a cheaper one, but…well…the girl was still trying to impress the boy. If only in a small way.

He didn't reply immediately. "Thank you. That was very thoughtful."

"Just doing my job. A good assistant knows when the boss needs to give gifts and cards. By the way, do I need to pick up a trinket for Tabitha? Have you enjoyed third-date sex yet?"

"I would never ask you to buy trinkets for one of my women."

Just hearing him say *my women* made her want to gag. "This coming from a man who asked me to buy his toilet paper."

• • •

Max glanced at his watch. That had to have been the quickest dinner party ever. Both of the grandmothers were on their best behavior, and they left as soon as the meal ended. They said they needed their beauty rest for the tournament. Which left him with Aggie. A woman who'd been perfectly charming each time he'd called the office over the last two days and perfectly charming during dinner tonight, but that didn't stop him from feeling the iciness coming off her every time she had to respond to something he had said.

He walked back into the kitchen and found her loading the dishwasher. "I told you to leave them."

Instead of arguing or calling him privileged, she shrugged. "Fine, you load them while I drink. My bus doesn't come for an hour."

"It's dangerous taking a bus home after dark. I'll take you."

She picked up the wine bottle and poured herself another glass. "Not going straight home."

Jealousy punched him in the throat. Instead of acting on

it, he busied himself putting the dishes in the dishwasher. He'd missed her energy yesterday while he'd been presenting at a conference. Sure, he could have stopped by the office during the lunch break, but he wanted to give her some space to work through what had her so cranky. Obviously, that hadn't been enough time. He pushed the dish rack in so he could close the door, and it went about three inches and stopped. Pulling it back out, he glanced to see what the problem was.

"You need to put the meat fork at an angle. It's hitting the twirly thing. That's why it won't shut."

"Thanks." He adjusted the meat fork and put a pod in the detergent spot.

"You're not going to run it now, are you?"

"What's wrong with now?"

She laid her phone down. "It's not full. You're wasting water. Or don't you care about the environment?" She spoke as one would when scolding a child.

"Got it." Taking a breath, he eased to the table and sat down next to her. "If we're going to fight, clue me in on why."

Her lips twisted. "I couldn't begin to explain."

"Then you're forcing me to draw my own conclusion. My conclusion is that you're after some make-up sex."

She picked up a cookie. "You are an egotistical ass. Of course I don't want make-up sex. You're seeing another woman." She popped the whole cookie in her mouth.

"As usual, you're wrong."

She swallowed. "There's nothing usual about my being wrong. And I'm not this time. You went out with Tabitha."

"I take it by your attitude my going out with Tabitha has made you jealous, and you don't like the taste of that emotion." If he could get her mad enough, maybe they'd get past the wall between them.

She laughed. A fuck-you laugh. "You and I were a casual hookup. Now, we're boss and employee again. I can't populate one reason why I should be jealous of Tabitha." She picked up her phone and tapped an icon.

"Put your phone away. We're talking." Damn it. This was not going the way he wanted it to go. He'd hoped getting her alone and away from the office would give them time to clear the air.

"Earth to Max. Work hours are over. You're not my boss right now. You can't tell me to put my phone away."

"Then tell me who you're texting?"

"I'm ordering an Uber. You know, since you don't want me to take a bus after dark."

He slammed his fist on the table, and she jerked back, causing her wine to spill. He froze. God. He'd become his father. "I'm sorry. I don't want you to leave." He grabbed the washcloth and cleaned the spill.

She picked up her wineglass, downed the rest of it, and stood. "I have no desire to continue to be your casual fuck-pal. Once was fun. Anything more than that will just muddy the waters between us."

He paused mid-wipe. "I don't consider you a casual fuck. That's what I've been trying to tell you since Thursday night."

She turned her foot toward the door. "And how about Tabitha? Did you consider her a casual fuck?"

He left the dishrag where it was and walked to her and put his hands on her shoulders. "We didn't. I didn't. No."

A tight smile lifted her lips. "That explains your grumpiness. Don't give up. I've been told well-bred females are a bit trickier to bed."

He wasn't sure how to respond to that statement, so he ignored it. "Please stay, and we can talk about Thursday night."

The spark in her eyes went dim, and she shook her head. "I've recently discovered some things are best left in your past."

"Like what?"

She opened her mouth and then shut it.

"What?"

"My ride's here." She grabbed her purse where it hung on the coatrack and walked to the door. "See you later, boss," were her parting words.

"Fuck." For now, he had no choice but to let her leave. She'd made it abundantly clear over and over again they were officially back to employer and employee status. But when their contract ended, all bets were off. No way in hell would he watch her get on a plane to New York without telling her how he felt.

Chapter Thirty-Seven

Friday afternoon, Aggie sat at her desk and listened to Max as he carried on a phone conversation. Now and then, her brain went from listening to chastising herself for not having *make-up* sex with him Wednesday night when she had the chance then praising herself for having the backbone to say not interested.

If she tried to have a casual relationship with him, her heart wouldn't stay out of the equation. Hell, it had done everything but bare its ass to the world after only one romantic night with him. His heart, on the other hand, would stay clothed and uninvolved. Any guy who could have sex with a woman one night and then take another out the next had a well-behaved heart. A heart that knew no meant no. A heart that never bucked the rules set out for it to obey. A heart, no doubt, holding out for a society lady.

"I don't care what it costs. I want the land." Max leaned back in his chair, his feet up on his desk and his tie hanging loose around his neck. Even on Fridays, the guy came to work dressed to impress. "I agree. It's two hundred thirty-five acres of awesome potential."

She'd shown up to work on Thursday worried about his reaction to her walking out on him Wednesday night. There hadn't been any need to worry. From the moment she walked through the door three minutes late, he had acted like nothing went down between them. That they were back to being boss and employee with an easygoing relationship that allowed smiles and laughter. She'd stepped up to the plate and played along.

He chuckled. "Okay. You've got me there. I do care how much it costs."

Max caught her staring and threw her a wink.

Her stomach did a flip-flop. Okay, the occasional wink was new. This was the third time in two days he'd winked at her. The wink annoyed her. Because she liked it, and it made her have thoughts like: what would life be like if she could change her destiny? If a Johansson could capture the heart of an upper-crust winker and not only his lust?

She shook the pity party off. She didn't need a man to be happy. Her happiness was all on her. It wasn't anyone else's responsibility to make it happen.

"Hopefully, it won't go over my top number. If it does, call me." Max clicked an ink pen open and closed as he talked.

Invitations to this particular auction went out this morning. The owners would hold the auction this afternoon. The whole thing cloak and dagger, hush-hush.

The landowners didn't want to deal with the public sentimental outcry over their decision to sell the amusement park.

He ended the call and swiveled his chair around to face the windows.

After about ten minutes of silence, she asked him, "Want to brainstorm ideas of what you could do with the theme park should you win the bid?" Her brain had been buzzing with ideas ever since learning of the auction.

He glanced at his watch. "Sure. I've got a few minutes."

A few minutes? Did he have plans with Tabitha? It was a Friday night. She pushed the thought away as she slipped on her heels, picked up her ink pen and a pad of paper, and walked to the conference table.

He pulled up an image of a map of the theme park and projected it onto a large screen. "My initial idea is to turn these quirky buildings into offices for start-up businesses," he said. "Whoever buys the renovated property could offer five-year leases. The rent would be cheap, but in return, the owner would get a percentage of the tenant's gross income starting year six and lasting until year ten."

"You could rent to clothing designers, specialty boutiques," she offered. "There could be a gourmet coffee shop. A beer and wine shop. And beauticians building their clientele could open a small one-chair salon. Oh, and you could offer food trucks a permanent home on the parking lot." If she wasn't leaving town, she might even want to rent a building and start her own business.

He sat back, crossed his arms over his chest. "What other ideas do you have for the property?"

"You could turn all the buildings into a series of little houses that a hotel would buy and rent to travelers." She liked that idea. If advertised correctly, it would become a destination hotel.

"You're a natural visionary. It's a shame you turned down my offer to stay on as my assistant."

"Do you want to work late and come up with more ideas?" she asked.

"Can't. I have plans."

"With Tabitha?" The words skidded out of her opened mouth.

"Does the fact you're asking about my dating life mean

you've reconsidered your position on us?" He'd asked the question nonchalantly, but it felt like being examined by a hot-shot defense attorney.

"Us?" She forced herself to laugh. "You didn't offer an us. Just more sex." Why had she said that? It sounded like she wanted an us. Which gave him the perfect opening to say there'd never be an us.

He stood and moved to her side and leaned a hip against the table. "Considering you plan to move to Brooklyn, I was under the impression you don't want an us, either? Am I wrong?"

Either. So he admits it. He doesn't want an us. "No, you're not wrong. I have big plans for Meemaw."

He ran a finger up her arm. "That's what I thought. Aggie, my decency is what kept me from offering you an us. Just say the word, and I'll happily become indecent and offer you an us."

She forced herself to think. He had a date tonight, and here he stood flirting with her. And he had said "either." "How long does an *us* usually last with you and a woman?"

His hand cupped the back of her neck. "With you, I'm thinking it might be a very long time."

That wasn't forever, and that wasn't a declaration of love. That was just a rich man saying, *I want to fuck you until I get tired of you.* "I'm not prepared to give you an answer. I need to think about it. I haven't even given the topic of us any consideration."

With his free hand, he grabbed her wrists and pulled her up so that they stood toe to toe. "Do you have some salve to go with that scathing burn?" The words were humorous, but it wasn't humor she saw in his eyes. It was lust.

"I'm not a nurse."

"And I'm not a saint." He yanked her into him. "You have exactly one second to tell me not to kiss you." His thumb meandered over her jaw and up to scrape across her bottom lip.

"What does *us* mean to you?"

"I don't know. I've never offered an us. Right now, what I know is that I can't look at you without wanting to tear off your clothes. To cruise my hands over your lush curves. To kneel between your thighs and stroke you with my tongue until you wake up the dead crying my name over and over. And then I want to fuck you."

Again. Not a declaration of love. She rolled her eyes, and the movement caused all of her intelligence to evaporate. "Kiss me already. We'll figure out the details later."

• • •

Max didn't wait for a second invitation.

He took her mouth in a kiss of ownership—hell, he wanted to own every part of her. A kiss that said the words he couldn't yet wrap his brain around—*I'm falling in love with you, Aggie the Horrible*. His good intentions of keeping it just a kiss evaporated. He lowered his hand to her skirt and tugged it up until it was bunched between them. He slipped his hand inside her panties and palmed her. "You're so fucking wet."

"That's what happens when you talk about tonguing me."

His fingers found her clit, and he rubbed, enjoying the feel of her hips bucking against him. "Next time we do this, my tongue is going inside your sweet pussy."

"Why next time?" she asked, her hard breathing making her words almost unintelligible.

He didn't answer but instead slid two fingers inside of her and continued to rub with his thumb.

When she begun to mewl incoherently, he bit her earlobe.

"Oh fuck. Max." She clutched his shoulders. "I'm—"

He took her mouth and branded her with a kiss while

he kept his hand in place, and she rode out the waves of an orgasm. Only when she loosened her grip on his shirt did he remove his hand and take a step back, allowing her skirt to fall into place. "I have to leave. Come over later tonight and bring an overnight bag. We'll finish this."

She pushed her hair out of her face, and her heavy-lidded stare melted the last remaining barrier protecting his heart. "Cancel your plans and take me home with you right now."

He jammed his hands in his pockets. A man could lose himself forever in this woman. "I can't." Damn Ruby and her blackmail. She'd discovered he hadn't taken Jodi to see *The Lion King* and now had switched from vague threats of revealing information about a guy from Grandmother's past to a very real threat of exposing the hand he'd played in getting Ms. Hazel admitted into the club. And he couldn't explain it to Aggie, because then she'd know Ms. Hazel didn't get into Grandmother's club without major strings being pulled.

Her eyes narrowed. "Do your plans include a woman?"

He nodded. He wasn't going to lie. "It's complicated, and I'm not at liberty to explain the complication to you. But I'll cut it short and be home before it even gets dark outside."

"And you think I'm the inappropriate type of girl you can ask to come over for a fuck after you have a date with someone society deems appropriate?"

"Damn it. That's not it at all. Where did you get such a ridiculous notion that society finds you inappropriate?"

"Meemaw's taught me a lot of things, but the most important thing is that actions speak louder than words. Your actions do not match your words."

He sighed. "Aggie, would you do me the honor of going out with me tomorrow night? Give me a chance to prove you wrong?" He couldn't just declare love. If he did, she'd be like Grant and think he'd fallen in love with sex and not her. All of her.

She smoothed her skirt with her hands. "Thanks for the orgasm, sorry I didn't get to give you one in return, but it's best if we just keep things strictly business until our contract ends."

He stabbed his fingers through his hair. And that's why his walls should have stayed up. To save him from how this felt. "That's not what I want. My plans with—"

"It's what I need. I suggest you spend the time getting your complications figured out."

Chapter Thirty-Eight

Friday afternoon, one week after he gave her an orgasm in his office, Aggie spoke to Max on the phone.

"Do you have questions about the bid project?" Max asked. He'd won the bid on the defunct amusement park, and he'd given her a ton of tasks to complete.

"Not a single one," she said. "My to-do list is complete." The project had kept him out of the office all week. Either that or what happened between them last Friday afternoon at closing time did. "Did you call to have me mark a week's worth of days off your I'm-almost-rid-of-Aggie calendar?" After today, there were only ten more working days to X out. That last X couldn't come soon enough. Or at least, that's what she kept telling herself.

Silence greeted her question, followed by a muffled curse. "I didn't know you knew about that calendar."

"It's hard to keep secrets from your assistant."

"I admit it did start out as a way to mark down the days until I was rid of you, but now it's my way of counting down the hours until you're not my employee and I can be with you."

She forced a laugh. A laugh meant to imply *you don't impress me much*. "Isn't that sweet. You want to send me off to New York with your lips the last ones I came into contact with while in Kansas City." Like he wanted his moo to be her last moo the night they played striptease trivia. It must be a territorial thing.

"Or the lips that enticed you to stay a little longer."

"A little longer, you say?" *And yet again, not forever.* "Why on earth would I stay when a grand adventure awaits?" Of course, he wanted her. He wanted to have sex again. But sexual desires weren't enough. Sexual desire would wear off after *a little longer.*

He sighed. "You wouldn't."

"Did you call just to see if I was still in the office at four thirty?" She was kind of surprised she was still there. Then again, who was she kidding? She'd stuck around in the hopes he'd drop by the office before calling it a week.

"Damn it, stop trying to pick a fight."

Was that what she was doing? Picking a fight to make it easier to leave when the time came? "How may I help you, boss man?"

He sighed. "I called to remind you not to forget to file our bid by eleven tomorrow. But not a minute before that."

This wasn't just any bid. It was *the* bid. The one he had so much riding on. "Why not after work today?" She'd planned on dropping it off on her way home then drink a bottle of wine and take a sleeping pill, all in the hopes of sleeping twelve hours. Between learning of Mom's criminal record and Max's continued dates with Tabitha, she'd been having nightmares. When she woke from the dreams, she had no one to talk to because Meemaw wasn't home. One of the families she cleaned for had asked her to house-sit while they were on vacation.

"I don't trust blind bids. Where there's a will, there's a way for the unscrupulous to sneak a glance at early bids and adjust theirs accordingly."

"Really? I didn't take the O'Reilly group as the type who allowed shenanigans."

"They have an assistant collecting the bids. Money makes a bastard out of all of us at one time or another. Can I count on you?"

What a pompous thing to ask. "I don't forget deadlines. I'm a professional. Have I let you down once since I've started working with you?"

"Call Mr. Smith and double check the location and time of trivia night."

"Saturday night at eight at the Country Club Plaza. Trivia teams are to arrive an hour early. All the money raised will go to Safehome. We should, and by we I mean you," she said, "donate to the cause."

"Excellent idea. Write them a company check for five thousand dollars. Bring it with you."

Once she arrived home, Aggie limited herself to only two glasses of wine before taking a sleeping pill and crashing. The combination would leave her groggy in the morning, but not too groggy to take care of the bid on time.

Chapter Thirty-Nine

Saturday morning around ten, Aggie's phone rang. Struggling out of the cobwebs of a nightmare, she answered. "Hello."

"Is this Agnes?" The woman's voice was harsh and yet quiet, as if she didn't want anyone to hear her.

Aggie's brain woke with a jolt, and she sat up. "It is?" Had something happened to Meemaw? Was this the police? God, had she been speeding again? "Who is this?"

No one responded. Glasses clinked in the background.

"Hello? Are you there?" Aggie glanced at her screen to see if she'd accidentally hung up on the person. She hadn't. "Helloooooooooooooo." She glanced at the clock. Hell. It was a good thing her phone rang.

She had less than an hour to drop off the bid. She pulled on a pair of jeans while she waited for whoever was on the other line to answer. Ten more seconds and she would hang up.

"This is Darlene."

Goose bumps exploded on her arms and her legs stopped working and she crumbled to the floor in an unceremonious heap. "Mom? Is this...you?"

"I wouldn't say it was if it wasn't. I'm going to be at The Cat and the Fiddle until five. If you're not there by then... well, whatever."

Happiness choked her airways as she used the side of the bed to pull herself to a standing position. *Mom wants to meet me.* "Is that in Kansas City?"

"Springfield." Mom disconnected.

She ran to the bathroom, stripping out of her clothes as she did, showered quickly, and then picked out an outfit to meet Mom in. Not too dressy, but something special. Why hadn't she bought a just-in-case outfit for this moment—she couldn't show up in jeans and a T-shirt as if it were no big deal to meet Mom for the first time as an adult.

Halfway through putting on her makeup, it hit her. She didn't have a car, and she had to drop off Max's bid. And tonight was the charity event. "Shit." *Think. Breathe. You can figure this out.*

She grabbed her phone and called Meemaw. "What time are you going to be home?" She crossed her fingers.

"Good morning to you, too. Trying to get a boyfriend out of the house before I show up?"

A laugh, sounding like a strangled alley cat, left Aggie's throat. "I need you to do me a huge favor."

"What's that?"

"I'm supposed to drop a bid off today by eleven. Could you do that for me?" Every moment she spent doing something else right now cost her time with Mom.

"Why?"

"I can't tell you right now, but I promise I will when I get back. The drop off is at Great Southern. Ten minutes from us. Can you do that?"

"Are pickles green?"

"You're the best." She hung up and called Bill. He liked

adventure. "I need a huge favor," she said the moment he answered.

"Aggie, this you?"

She relaxed. He sounded sober. "I need a ride to Springfield."

"When?"

"Now."

There was a pause. She could hear him peeing.

Guys could be so gross.

"You still live at the same address?"

"I do."

"On my way."

She did the math. If he got to her house by ten thirty, the way he drove, they'd be in Springfield by one fifteen p.m. They would need only another thirty minutes to find The Cat and the Fiddle.

She should be in Mom's presence no later than one forty-five. She'd get to spend almost three hours with her. If Bill and she left Springfield, by four thirty, she'd be back in time for the charity event. Barely. Not as early as she was supposed to be, but she'd make it before the actual event started.

She went into the bathroom to finish getting ready. Making the trip on the back of a Harley meant wearing her favorite Wrangler jeans, her lucky bomber jacket, and boots. She put lotion on her hands and sprayed perfume in the air and then danced through it. She stuffed clothes to wear to the charity event in a backpack. She'd have Bill drop her at the hotel. She could change in the restroom.

Ready to go, she grabbed her phone.

Unfortunately, her lotioned-up hands fumbled the sucker. Her heart sank as it hit the counter before bouncing once and landing in the toilet.

"Son of a bitch." She fished it out, ran with it to the kitchen, and placed it in a bowl with dry white rice. The honking of a horn startled her. Bill. She washed her hands, grabbed her jacket, ran out the door, and hopped on behind Bill. They could use his phone.

Turning the corner at the end of their street, Meemaw's Mustang sat at the stoplight. Aggie waved. Damn it. She should have left a note asking her to cover for her at the trivia event if she didn't get back in time.

She'd just have to make sure she got back. Maybe Mom would come with her.

Chapter Forty

As directed, Max arrived Saturday night at the fundraiser an hour early. No sighting of Aggie. Damn it. Did she miss the bus? He should have picked her up. He called. Straight to voicemail.

"Max, so glad to see you. Where's our ringer?"

Max pivoted. *Mr. Smith*. "You know how women are. They never run exactly on time."

"Our table is the first one." He pointed toward a group of tables all with microphones. "I can't wait to clean house with my competition. I've a few side wagers going."

Max chuckled. "This should be fun."

Thirty minutes later, Aggie still hadn't shown. Max called Ms. Hazel.

"Hi, honey. Are you calling to see if I got the bid turned in on time?"

"Bid?" He tensed, waiting for the response although his gut already told him what the answer would be.

"Aggie asked me to do it for her."

"I see." His grip tightened on the phone. "Thank you. I'll

have to buy you dinner. I'm actually calling because I need to reach her. Do you know how late she's running?"

"Late for what?"

"We're on a trivia team for a charity auction."

"Oh dear."

Fuck. "What does that mean?"

"Earlier, I saw Aggie on the back of a Harley. She had a backpack on, like she does when she's going on overnight trips."

"Damn it." This shouldn't surprise him. She wasn't responsible. She'd told him she wasn't responsible. Why did he think for even one moment she'd actually stay responsible for her entire eight-week contract?

"I'm so sorry, Max. It's not like her to not be where she's supposed to be when she's supposed to be there. Well, actually it is, but she's been doing so well working for you. I thought she'd turned over a new leaf."

"I guess some leaves just don't stay turned."

"This explains why she sounded strange on the phone," Meemaw said. "She was pulling an Aggie and didn't want me to know."

"An Aggie?"

"Anytime there's a new boyfriend in her life, she gets all fidgety and flighty."

Max cursed.

What in the hell had he been thinking to hope he could have a future with Aggie when her contract ended? She was irresponsible at best, unreliable at worst.

"Tell you what," Ms. Hazel said. "I'm free tonight. Why don't I fill in for her? I taught her everything she knows."

"I would be forever grateful." He gave her the address and hung up. A voice cleared behind him.

"Please tell me Aggie's here." Mr. Smith had a vein pulsing in his forehead.

Max sighed. This wasn't going to go over well. "I'm afraid there's been a change of plans. She can't attend, but her grandmother will fill in. Trust me, she will do just as well, if not better."

Mr. Smith's face turned red.

"I'm so sorry. I know it looks bad—"

"It does indeed look bad. I want to do business with a company who stands behind their word. I don't have time to worry if I can trust those I hire to do a job."

Max couldn't argue. Monday, he'd fire Aggie, and this time, there'd be no unfiring. She'd done irreparable damage to his business reputation this evening. And for what? A ride on the back of a fucking Harley.

Chapter Forty-One

Aggie hopped off the back of Bill's bike and stared at a bar sitting in the middle of a shopping center. "The Cat and the Fiddle."

The vehicles sitting outside weren't junkers, weren't Harleys, weren't Bentleys. A place for average Joes looking for a beer without a fight.

Her stomach churned as if it had decided to make a vat of butter.

"I'll be back by two thirty." Bill revved his bike.

She gave him a thumbs-up and turned to stare at the door leading to Mom. The thought spun the thick butter up her throat, causing her to gag. She bent over until the sensation passed. *Mom.*

Standing upright, she squared her shoulders and pulled open the heavy wooden door. The lights were dim, trapping her in darkness until her eyes could adjust. Few glanced her way. Those who did were indifferent.

She bit her lip to keep it from trembling the way her knees were. No bouncer available to point out Darlene. She made her way to the bar at a gait meant to show no fear.

"What can I get you?" the woman tending asked. She looked hard. Twelve-kids-and-counting hard.

"Bitch, where's my beer? I asked for it ten minutes ago." This came from a customer whose head and neck were covered in tattoos.

Aggie shivered. She'd completely misdiagnosed the type of bar this place was. No average Joes in sight. Lots of scary Joes.

She'd been in her share of forbidding bars. But never alone. She'd always been with hot male muscle packing heat.

"Shut up, George. You'll get it when you damn well get it," the woman barked. She snapped her attention back on Aggie. "I ain't got all day."

"I'll take what's on draft." Aggie glanced around for a woman sitting alone. She found none. Everyone had someone. As they should in a place like this. Why did Mom choose here? Couldn't they have met at a mellow lunch joint?

"A buck fifty."

Cheap drinks. Would that be the only rainbow she found tonight or the beginning of multiple rainbows? She paid and enjoyed a fortifying sip. Had Mom changed her mind? Decided not to come? Or was she here with others? Were they watching her right now and laughing, because she didn't know which was Mom?

The bartender served three more beers. A man spilled his, and it flowed downhill toward hers.

"Damn it." The bartender grabbed a rag and mopped up the mess. She paused with her rag in front of Aggie.

Aggie picked up her beer.

"What's got a girl like you in a place like this?" she asked as she cleaned the counter under her drink.

Part of her was happy she didn't appear to belong in a place like this. The other part wished she blended in more.

Shadows don't get jumped by hoodlums. "I'm supposed to meet a woman named Darlene. Do you know her?"

The bartender gave her a more thorough glance. "I might." Her voice had notes of protection and wariness. "Why?"

"Umm." Darlene might not want people to know she had a grown child. "She's got something I'm buying. Craigslist."

The bartender's lips tightened. "I've told her a hundred times not to be selling that shit in my bar."

She startled. "Oh. No. I didn't mean drugs." Was that what got her busted on a felony charge?

"Sure you didn't. She's over there. Slumped in the last booth."

She glanced in that direction. There was a woman collapsed over the table as if passed out. "Is she okay?"

The bartender shrugged. "Don't she look all right?"

Aggie trudged to the booth. Gazes followed her. She was glad she wore sturdy boots meant for ass kicking and not notice-my-ass stilettos that would be a handicap in a fistfight. She sat on the opposite side and waited for the woman to notice. She didn't.

"Mom?" How weird to say that word out loud. She reached over and shook her shoulder.

The woman roused. Grumbled.

"Mom?" Aggie said again, a little louder. She liked saying the word. It felt comforting.

The woman sat up in a half-assed sort of way. Like if her hands were to move, she'd face-plant at once. Her hair resembled a dyslexic rat's nest, her makeup a five-year-old playing dress up. She struggled to get both of her eyes open. What few lashes she had were matted together by cheap mascara. "Who the hell are you?"

The butter thickened in her throat. "Your daughter." The words came out dry and brittle. God. How could this be

Mom?

"Ain't got one of those. Threw the one I had away a long time ago."

The fist of slurred words landed squarely in Aggie's unsuspecting gut, and she flinched. Her eyes watered. She had to open and close her mouth several times before words fell out. "You didn't throw me away. You asked Meemaw to raise me."

Mom scratched her head. Squinted her eyes. "Beth?"

Aggie placed a hand on her stomach. Thank God she hadn't ate today. Did Mom have more than one daughter? Or did she forget the name of the one she had? "Not Beth. Aggie. Do you remember me?"

"I remember you. Fucking bane of my body. Lowered my going cost by half."

This time the fist of words caught her in the jugular, and she gasped for air. Waves of bile washed through her and threatened to spew. "Why's that?"

Mom cackled like a person in an old dilapidated insane asylum. The kind where you couldn't tell the real patients from the ghost patients. "You look smart. Figure it out."

"But if you didn't want to have a baby, why didn't you take precautions?" She'd wondered this so many times over the years. If there was one thing Meemaw preached, it was birth control.

"You got any money?"

Aggie twisted her lips. Another answer, not to the question she'd asked but to the one she'd been flipping over and over since receiving Mom's call. "Is that why you asked to see me?"

Mom grabbed Aggie's beer, drained it, and belched. "It sure as hell wasn't to see you." She wiped her hand across her mouth, belched again, and slammed the mug on the table, causing Aggie to jump.

"It wasn't?"

"Hell no. You went and got me in trouble with my man. Got home from work and he wanted to know who in the hell whatever your name is, and why you'd hired some guy to find me. Only thing I could figure to say was ya owed me and needed to pay it up as part of your sobriety shit."

Aggie wrapped her arms around her middle and held herself. "So you didn't want to see grown-up me?" Why did this hurt so much? Why would Mom want to see her grown-up daughter when the only thing that accomplished was reminding her how much of her life had been screwed up because of her?

The bartender brought over a pot of coffee and two cups. "This might help get her brain clear. She's not half bad when she's sober."

Aggie nodded in thanks but couldn't muster a polite smile to go with the gesture.

Mom tasted the coffee. She glanced at Aggie. Rolled her eyes. "Listen, Barb. It's nothing personal."

"It's Agnes. You named me Agnes. And it's very fucking personal to me." *Why can't she remember my name?*

"Well, it shouldn't be. I ain't nobody but the broken-down body who carried you." Another hoot. This one louder than the last and more ominous. If that was even possible.

They sat in silence until Aggie poured the last of the coffee from the pot. Mom's eyes fixated on the porcelain cup in her hands. She wasn't sure if Mom realized she still sat across from her.

"Who's my father?" She hadn't planned on asking that particular question. Meemaw's experience taught her the answer could be painful.

Mom's eyes momentarily cleared. "Some asshole who thought wearing a condom was torture."

"Torture?"

"That's what he said. So I said fine. One time, we'd do it without a condom."

Aggie ground her teeth. The number of torture items a woman wears to impress a man: four. Spanx, stilettos, underwire bras, and thongs. The number of torture items a man wears to impress a woman: one. A condom. A fucking condom. Meant to tell the lady he cared enough not to pass on a disease or a baby. And they fucking couldn't be bothered with doing even that much to impress a woman with how copiously they cared. Fuck. Fuck. Fuck.

Except Max hadn't complained. He wore a hot-pink one for her. She wished he were here.

Aggie inhaled a calming breath and unlocked her jaw. "Do you remember his name?" Silly question. Mom didn't remember his name. She didn't remember her own daughter's name.

Mom pulled a cigarette out of her purse and lit it. "Can't remember something I never knew." She stuck it in her mouth and inhaled.

Aggie sighed. "Are you sure?"

Mom exhaled a ring of smoke toward her. "Your daddy was some John who paid me twenty bucks to pull down my panties and bend over. Gave me an extra five for the no-condom thing. Offered me twenty more to spend the night with him in some fancy hotel. Told him I wasn't Julia Roberts and he wasn't Richard Gere." She laughed at her joke.

Aggie didn't laugh. "I see." *I'm the product of a hooker's work. My mom's a hooker.*

"Don't be using that hoity tone with me." Her cigarette dangled from her lip as she spoke. "I'll have you know your daddy drove a Mase...Mase-ratty and wore cufflinks. I got you a daddy with bucks. Lot more than my mom did for me. She did it for fucking free. I at least got twenty-five and a pair of gold cufflinks."

Aggie winced at her grammar. Meemaw said Mom had made straight As all the way through school then dropped out one week before graduation. That's when she dummied down her appearance and started talking like someone who'd had no schooling.

Meemaw thought she'd done it all to get back at her for not allowing her to go on the unofficial senior trip. "Do you still have the cufflinks?" Maybe there were fingerprints on them that would lead her to her father. Not that she wanted to meet him. Or maybe they'd been reported stolen, and she could find out the name of her father that way.

Darlene sobered. "Sold 'em for crack. You got any money for your ol' momma? I asked that bitch who raised you, and she said she'd paid my bail, and there'd be no more coming."

A new wave of tension snapped Aggie's shoulders back. How long ago had that happened? Surely, not recently. If it had been recently, Meemaw would have told her. Wouldn't she have? "No, Momma, I do not."

Mom burst into tears. "If I don't go back with some money, my dealer will cut me off."

Aggie resisted the urge to touch her. Afraid if she did, Mom would recoil, and she didn't know if she could handle the rejection. "Maybe that's a good thing."

If Mom heard her, it didn't register in her expression. "He's nice-looking. We'd have pretty babies. Except I can't have any. Got fixed right after my first child. Never met her. Gave her up. Bitch gave me stretch marks."

Aggie turned her head and wiped at an escaped tear. She'd lived with Mom for four years. How could she forget that? When the tears were dried, she refocused on Mom. "Come home with me. You can start over."

Mom's smeared lips twisted into a snarl. "Why would I leave a fine man like the one I've got to live with you and that old hag I got stuck with growing up?"

Aggie jumped to her feet and doubled her fists. "Meemaw is warm and kind and generous. Don't you dare say something bad about her." The room grew quiet, the smell of a pending fight drawing the attention of the scavengers. Aggie didn't care if they were all on Darlene's side.

She would fight till her death before she let someone badmouth Meemaw. "She chose to be my mom when you chose not to. She worked three jobs to put food on the table, so I didn't have to crawl through trash bins in search of our next meal. She held me at night when I had nightmares."

Mom shook her finger at her. "Every child has nightmares. That one's not on me."

Her mouth fell open. Darlene didn't have a maternal bone in her body. "My night terrors were about you coming back to get me, and I would have to leave with you."

Darlene snarled. Without warning, she tossed a cup of lukewarm coffee at her. "You're nothing but an ingrate."

Aggie picked up a napkin and slowly wiped at the mess on her jacket. "And you're nothing but..." She wanted to say whore but couldn't. Two means didn't make a nice. Darlene was her biological mother. A broken woman. "You're a person in need of help. Let me help you. I can take you to a drug rehab. They'll see to it you get the help you need. It's not too late for you to find your own happiness."

"Fuck you," Mom said.

The smell of rotted dreams filled her nostrils. "Please come home with me." Why had she thought meeting Mom would be like living out a scene in a Hallmark movie?

"Rita, I'm happy as piss."

Being called Rita threw gasoline on her dreams, and they exploded into blue flames. Flames that licked at Aggie's soul with the two-pronged tongue of hell's blazes.

I shouldn't have come.

She told herself to leave. To stop trying for something

unobtainable. "Momma, may I have a hug?" A hug. That should be obtainable. That didn't require Mom to remember her name. That didn't require Mom to love her. That just required an ounce of decency.

Mom smiled, fumbled her way out of the booth, and stood. She held out her scrawny arms.

Stunned she agreed, Aggie stepped into them. Mom smelled like cigarettes and vomit. Aggie didn't care. She was being hugged by Mom. "Thank you." Tears burned the back of her eyes.

"Anything for my little girl." Mom patted Aggie on the back with one hand and with the other lifted Aggie's wallet out of her jacket pocket. "Don't say I never gave you anything."

One of the tears dropped. And then another. What did you do when your own mom stole from you? Act like you didn't know? Or confront?

She wanted to act like she didn't notice but couldn't. She held out her hand. The check for tonight's charity was in there. "Give it back." The hug had been a scam.

Mom's face screwed up like a wad of used toilet paper. "Bitch." She threw the wallet at her. When Aggie bent to pick it up, Mom spit, the drool landing on the back of her hand.

Aggie straightened and brushed away the tears. "I wanted to love you. I wanted you to love me."

Mom sunk back into the booth. "Love is for losers. You chase that bitch, she'll break you and then hide the glue so you can't fix yourself."

Aggie turned and fled outside where she waited for Bill. Her heart ached, but she didn't shed any more tears. Sitting on a curb, she vowed to let no one break her heart and then steal her glue.

Vowed never to give her heart until the other had given theirs first. When Johanssons fell in love first, it led to failed love.

Failed love made one decide life wasn't worth the effort to keep your daughter.

Two thirty came and went, but still no Bill. She closed her eyes. When she awoke, it was dark outside. She asked one man for the time. He didn't respond but pulled out his phone and turned it so she could read the screen. Two a.m.

"Fuck." Aggie paced and fought for breath. She'd missed the trivia night event. "Oh, hell. This is bad. This is really bad." She should have insisted Bill wait on her. She knew better than to count on him to come back. He was unreliable. Which was how Max would now view her.

She spun in circles, trying to solve the issue. She came to a stop when she realized there was no solution. She'd have to explain to Max. Or…she could just send him a text. Only she didn't have her phone. When she got back to town, she could leave him a note telling him what happened and say she quit to save him the trouble of firing her.

Yes. That's what she'd do.

Only, that's not what she'd do. She couldn't run away. She had to face him. He deserved the satisfaction of firing her. She owed him that much.

What time did the next bus leave for Kansas City?

Chapter Forty-Two

Max pretended to be busy behind his desk when Aggie walked through the door Monday morning. He didn't want to say something he'd regret. But that didn't mean he didn't have plenty he planned to say.

She'd screwed up. He had every right to be mad and to rip into her. Even if in the end they had won trivia night, that didn't let her off the hook. Mr. Smith said Aggie's no-show didn't leave him with a favorable view of his company.

"You're here early." She sounded nervous.

He took his time looking her way. Hell. She looked like roadkill. Was that his fault?

She'd called him yesterday, asking if they could meet. He'd declined. He wanted her to sweat over facing him and the music of not showing up. He'd asked Ms. Hazel not to mention she'd come to his aid.

From the looks of her, she'd sweated plenty. He almost... almost...no. Not true. He didn't feel sorry for her. Not even a little.

"Nice weekend?" He purposefully held all hints of anger

from his voice. He'd promised Ms. Hazel he'd hear Aggie out. He strode to the window and stared without actually seeing anything.

Grandmothers were always the last to see fatal flaws in their grandchildren.

"I went to Springfield Saturday with a friend and didn't get back until yesterday afternoon late. And then Meemaw was in a mood, and we fought about nothing."

His gut soured. She'd actually spent the night in Springfield. "Were you with Bill?"

She came and stood beside him.

He held his breath and waited for her response.

"How did you know?"

The air whooshed from him. "Lucky guess." Game over. She'd jeopardized an important contract for Max just so she could spend the weekend with a loser. The asshole from the bar. "What was in Springfield? A concert? A motorcycle rally?"

She cocked her head as if trying to decipher his mood. Like, she'd expected a full-on dressing-down by him but not calm questions. "Nothing special. A...night club." She walked over to her desk. Her office phone rang. She answered it, turned her back to him, and mumbled words he couldn't understand. When she turned his way, she looked even worse than two minutes earlier. "I need to tell you something. Perhaps you should sit."

He twisted back around and stared out the window and at the buildings. Buildings full of businesses. Full of business owners who hired employees to work for them. Did they have employees like Aggie? "I'm fine. You can say what you want to say while I'm standing here." He waited for her apology. Surprised she hadn't blurted it out the moment she arrived at work.

"Please sit." Something in her voice compelled him to do

so.

"What?"

She walked in front of her desk and faced him. "I know you're mad because I didn't make it to trivia night."

"Mad isn't the word I'd use to describe how I'm feeling." Trivia night was the least of what ailed him. She'd spent the night with Bill. That wasn't the action of a woman who'd fallen in love.

"Well, when I tell you what else I need to say, it will be the right word."

"I can't believe you fucking stood me up for the charity event. Of all the selfish, unreliable—"

She picked the stapler up off her desk. "Your bid didn't get turned in."

His gut clenched. Was this some type of sick game? How many times could she kick him in the balls before he cried uncle and showed his cards? "Ms. Hazel said she did it for you."

Aggie walked behind her desk and sat. "She dropped it at the wrong bank. Not her fault. I gave her erroneous information. That's who just called. They said they had the packet there and didn't know what they were supposed to do with it?"

He gripped the arms of his chair to keep himself from lunging. "The wrong bank?"

"I'm sorry. I don't know how Meemaw and I got our wires crossed." She opened a desk drawer.

He jumped to his feet causing his chair to roll away. "Don't you dare blame this on Ms. Hazel. She's not at fault. You're at fault for being a fucking flake." With his heart and with his business.

She slammed the drawer shut. "You're right. I am. I'm sorry."

Realization that this wasn't some big damn joke on her

part that could be solved with a conversation slammed him like he was the first car in a ten-car pile-up on the highway where everyone was going ninety-five in a seventy-five zone. "Sorry! You think sorry will fix any of this?"

She blinked.

"Well?" He stepped out from behind his desk.

She stood and walked to the side of her desk as if ready to make a run for the door. She looked him in the eyes, and tears formed.

He jerked his gaze away and glanced down at her feet, expecting her signature heels. She had them on. But they didn't match. One pink. One black. "Tell me this is some horrible joke on your part." He looked up at her, hoping like hell he'd see a got-you smile.

"It's not. I'm a total fuckup." She swiped at her face where a tear dropped. "It's just...I've been...I'm so sorry. I've been distracted by—"

"Distracted. Your leaving town on the back of some hoodlum's bike and missing the fundraiser is distracted." He didn't care how devastated she looked or that she shed a damn tear over the incident. "This—"

"Unforgivable. I know."

He snorted. This explained all of her jobs since graduating from college. All of the men sending mooing messages to her phone. It wasn't because she kept changing them until she found the perfect fit. It was because she was a fuckup and no doubt fucked up every job, every relationship she'd ever had. "How? How do you screw up a guy's life in the space of two months?"

She stood very still. "It's what I do."

Not enough. He fucking deserved a real answer. "Was Bill that great of a fuck?"

She jerked. "You have no right—"

His head exploded. "You're right. I don't. But you know

what I do have the right to do? Fire you. You're fired. Take your things and get out. Get out of my office. Get out of my sight. Get out of my fucking life."

Her irresponsibility cost him the deal. The deal that would finally make his father sit up and take notice. The deal that would prove he could run with the big dogs. The deal that would make him his first million. Now, his dad would continue to see him as a joke. And his heart was fucking collateral damage.

Aggie didn't move. "You haven't even asked me what happened. I'll have you know—"

"I don't give a fuck what your side of the story is. You could have run into Jesus himself, and that wouldn't excuse your screw up or your night with—"

"Really? Jesus himself wouldn't get me out of this?"

"I should have never hired you. My original opinion of you was spot on."

"I'll have you know—"

"Shut up. Just shut up. You're a fucking screwup and the bane of my existence."

All of the color drained from her face. "Your what?"

"My gut told me not to hire you. I should have listened. My gut has never led me wrong. My dick, on the other hand, has. Obviously." She spent the fucking night with Bill.

"That's not fair." Indignation whipped across her face. "I've done a great job—"

"A great job? Is that what you call screwing up the best deal I've ever had a chance at making? I don't call that a great job. I call that a fuckup. My friend told me apples—"

"Don't fall far from the tree. I know. I heard. Mom's a felon, therefore, that's in—"

"You're fired. Take your things and get out of my sight."

She moved around her desk and sat down in her chair. "I'm not going anywhere. We have a contract."

"Then you're on permanent vacation."

A sob tore out of her throat, but he didn't give a rat's ass.

"Fuck you. I quit. I'm tired of working for a stick-in-the-mud prick. My life didn't suck bowling balls before I met you. Being around you day in and day out is like living in a...a drab factory. One where a person isn't even allowed to defend themselves."

He ran a hand through his hair. Compared to Bill, she found him boring. Well, they could fucking have each other. "Why are you still here?"

She stood. "Bite me, you insufferable, pompous ass."

• • •

Aggie sank down on the tile in the hallway and gulped for oxygen. He hadn't seen reason. Or given her a chance to explain about Mom. She fumbled through her purse until she found a wad of tissues. Tissues left over from the day she'd interviewed. She blew her nose.

How could she have screwed up so royally twice in one weekend? How had they done at trivia night? Had they lost? Won? What must Mr. Smith think of her? Why didn't Max let her explain?

She blew her nose again. And how could he have been so nasty? So hateful?

Bottom line: two people found her the bane of their existence. What were the odds Mom and Max would both use the same word to describe her? A word that meant a curse, a blight, a misery. A word that offered no room for returned love.

Good thing she didn't love him. Wouldn't that be the melted icing on the flopped cake?

Except. Nope. No excepts allowed. Excepts were for losers who turned to drugs to forget.

She'd be damned if she let herself turn out like Mom. Fucking wasn't happening.

Pain drew her gaze to her hands. Her nails had brought blood to her palms. She relaxed her grip and did several deep belly breaths. Max had every right to be furious and unforgiving.

She wouldn't plead for forgiveness, she didn't deserve that, but maybe she could fix her bid mistake before she disappeared from his life. She'd go pick the packet up and take it directly to O'Reilly's today. Beg them to accept it late. Explain what happened. Beg them not to punish Max for her mistake.

If needed, she'd tell them about her search for Mom and how that played into her dropping the ball on the project. Yes. That's what she'd do.

Then, she'd get the hell out of K.C.

New York City, I'm coming.

She waited for an adrenaline rush. She always got an adrenaline rush when venturing into a new job or dating a new guy or buying a new pair of heels. Nothing happened. Unless she counted the gush of sadness leaking from her eyeballs.

Fuck. She'd fallen in love first. With a guy who hated her to eternity.

Chapter Forty-Three

Meemaw stood at the kitchen sink and scowled.

Aggie squirmed where she sat at the kitchen table with her knees drawn up under her chin and her arms wrapped around her legs. She wasn't used to Meemaw being hopping mad at her. "Meemaw, please don't be annoyed. I hate when you are."

"Do you think I want to be? You're better than this. I can't believe you lost another job. It's not like they grow on trees."

Knowing she'd let Meemaw down pierced her heart. "I didn't mean to lose this one. I really didn't. And it was almost over anyway. Plus, he's going to pay me for the last two weeks. We have a contract saying he has to."

"He sure as heck is not paying you for the last two weeks," Meemaw snapped. "Johanssons don't take money they didn't earn." Meemaw rubbed her neck. The bags under her eyes told Aggie she hadn't been sleeping much, either.

"Yes, ma'am."

Her contrite tone didn't lessen the fervor in Meemaw's

glare. If anything, it seemed to make her madder. "You're like your mom when it comes to quitting. Darlene quit school when I wouldn't let her go on a boy-girl trip. She quit me when I told her to give you up for adoption. She quit you when a guy came around who didn't want you." She picked up the dishrag laying over the faucet, wetted it, and walked to the kitchen table and wiped its already clean surface.

"You told Mom to give me up for adoption?" Why had she never heard about this?

Meemaw walked back to the sink and rinsed out the rag. "It's not as bad as it sounds. I first begged her to give you to me to raise."

"How is that better?"

Meemaw turned and leaned against the sink. "Honey, Darlene wasn't fit to raise you. After your father dumped her when she told him she was pregnant, she was never the same. She got it in her head that all of the female Johanssons were cursed, that you were cursed, and it was her fault you'd face what we'd faced with our hearts. She took to drugs to forget her pain."

"Mom knew my father? He wasn't some John she turned a trick for?"

"Where in tarnation did you get that idea? Never mind. I don't want to hear it right now. That'll just get me off track of what needs saying."

"Tell me what needs to be said."

Meemaw pointed a finger at Aggie. "I can't believe you've turned into a quitter. I tried so hard to teach you follow through. When you wanted to play on the boy's football team, I went to the school and forced them to say you could. Then, when you wanted to quit, I wouldn't let you. When you failed your driving test the first time and wanted to never do it again, I sent you back the next day to try again. When you didn't get into the first college of your choice, you wanted to quit. Not go. I wouldn't let you do that. And now, you've lost every job you've ever had. Why? What did I do wrong that turned you out a quitter? And don't say it's because of some damn curse. I don't believe in that nonsense."

Aggie lowered her feet to the ground and wiped at the tears streaming down her face. "Meemaw, I love you," she said passionately. "You did nothing wrong. My failures are not on you."

"Then why?" Meemaw wiped at her own tears. "Why are you a quitter?"

Aggie searched for the right words to make Meemaw understand. "I'm not a quitter because things are too hard. I'm a thoughtful quitter." The moment she said them, she knew she'd chosen the wrong ones.

Meemaw threw her hands in the air. "Well, as long as you have given it some thought, then I guess it's now okay to be a quitter."

Aggie's chin jerked up. It wasn't like Meemaw to be sarcastic. "That's not what I mean."

"It's what you said."

"I quit my jobs because they don't fulfill me."

Meemaw laughed. "Do you think cleaning offices overnight fulfills me? Cleaning the toilets of the rich fulfills me?"

Aggie stood, walked to her, grabbed Meemaw's hands and, when she went to pull away, held them tight. "Not in this lifetime. And that's why I leave. I've spent my life watching you work jobs you don't like, but you do them because you had me to raise, and a sure dollar was better than a maybe dollar."

"You're not making a lick of sense."

"I want to do better in life. I want for the next generation of Johanssons to have nothing to hang their heads about. I want them to come from a family name no one turns their nose up at. And I want them to know they deserve happiness."

"Am I supposed to understand what you're saying amid all that pretty talk? Because I don't."

Aggie let go of her hands and leaned against the sink with her. Shoulder to shoulder. "I need to believe there's something greater than a nine-to-five crap job. That there's more meant for me and you. That our lives have real meaning."

"Our lives have plenty of meaning. We have love, and that's enough."

"It's not enough. The world is ugly. I feel ugly because Mom threw me away. I quit my jobs because I'm tired of feeling ugly."

"You don't lose a job because you feel ugly. What a bunch of poppycock."

Aggie turned toward her. "I want a job beautiful people have. One that fulfills me for thirty years and then sends me into retirement with a fat pension."

A washtub of tears slid down Meemaw's cheeks. She pulled Aggie into a hug. "What have I done? While I've been hanging my head in shame my whole life because my parents thought me worthless, and Darlene's father thought her worthless, I've turned around and taught you to do the same. I am so sorry you've ever felt ugly. You're beautiful and perfect."

Aggie shook her head against Meemaw's neck. "None of this is your fault."

"Don't be a ninny. If I say it's my fault, it's my fault." Meemaw pulled away and wiped at the tears. "The last time I felt this ashamed of myself was that moment when Darlene's father told me I was dumber than dirt."

Aggie hated the man who'd done so much damage to Meemaw's self-esteem. "Someday I'll be able to take care of you. To prove to you, you did a great job raising me."

Meemaw glanced out the window. So did Aggie. The

eyesore view of the railroad tracks stared back at her. They were a constant reminder to the Johansson women of their station in life.

"I've been taking care of myself since I was thirteen," Meemaw said. "Don't need no help now."

A knot formed in Aggie's throat. She put an arm around Meemaw's shoulders. "I know that. You're the smartest, kindest, strongest woman I know. But someday, I want to be in a position where I can whisk you away from your job and let you live with me, where you're free to only do those things you like. Let someone take care of you for a change. God knows you deserve a happy retirement free of financial worry."

As if suddenly too tired to stand, Meemaw moved away and sat down at the table. "I thought you enjoyed working for Max. That was a beautiful person job. Why did you get yourself canned?"

Aggie hopped up on the counter. It was time she told Meemaw everything. "I've been searching for Mom. Until I met Max, I had had no luck. But then I hit it off with one of his clients who happened to have a detective on retainer. He loaned me his detective. That guy found Mom."

"You found her?" Meemaw's eyes were wide and filled with a look of horror.

"I went to see her Saturday night. Mom called and asked to see me. I dropped everything, because she said she only had until five and then she'd be gone."

Meemaw exhaled a shuddering breath. "Oh honey. I wish you would have told me your plans."

"Mom's a drug addict. The only reason she wanted to meet with me was to get money out of me."

Meemaw stood and walked to Aggie and grabbed her hands. "Honey, that's the drugs talking. I'm sure when she's clean, she really wants to meet you."

Aggie shook her head. "She couldn't remember my name. And she told me my dad was a guy who paid her twenty-five dollars to have sex without a condom."

"Did you tell Max all of this?"

"I tried. He didn't want to hear my reasons. He called them excuses."

"Because you ditched him for another man. He knows you left town with the new boyfriend in your life?"

"I don't have a new boyfriend. I was with Bill."

Meemaw squeezed Aggie's hands. "You should go to Max. Make him listen. If he's still of a mind to fire you after that, then that's on him."

"Trust me. He won't change his mind. He called me a fuckup. Said he should never have hired me. Called me the bane of his existence. Mom also called me the bane of her existence. That can't be a coincidence. There must be something inherently bad about me."

"Next time I see him, I'll give him a good piece of my mind. How dare he call you a fuckup? No one calls my granddaughter a fuckup and gets away with it all in one piece."

A small smile lifted Aggie's lips. There was the Meemaw she knew. The one who always had her back. "Don't be mad at him. I am a fuckup. I've been a fuckup. But I'm going to change all of that."

"What does that mean?"

"Remember my roommate my freshman year in college?"

"From Brooklyn? Theater major?"

"That's the one. She's said I can come and sleep on her couch while I search for a job. I'm going to move to New York City. As soon as I get a place, I want you to come and live with me. You'll have fun living there in your golden years. You can go to Broadway shows. People watch. Join clubs. Tell me you'll come as soon as I have my own place."

Meemaw walked back to the table and took a seat. "Honey, I can't give you that promise. I like it here. Please talk to Max before you make plans that can't change."

"I can't do that. He sees me as an unredeemable loser."

"Poppycock."

"He's partially right. I am a loser. But I'm not unredeemable. I'm purposefully choosing a fresh start at getting life right. At proving I'm redeemable. If you don't want to go, I'll send money each month to help you with your bills. I've been saving, and I have enough to cover at least two months."

"You're such a sweet child. But I don't want your money. I just want you to be happy."

Aggie popped off the counter. "I'm working on happy. I promise you I won't quit until I claim it."

Chapter Forty-Four

The sound of persistent knocking roused Max from his stupor. Grumbling at the interruption, he stumbled to the front door and opened it without glancing through the peephole to see who was there. Probably a neighbor, since the doorman hadn't buzzed first.

It wasn't a neighbor. It was the last person he wanted to see. Well, not the last person, but one of the last. His father. A man who'd only bothered to visit him once since he'd moved into the condo, and only then because Grandmother dragged him with her on a visit. Damn it. Was he here to gloat because Max was on the verge of losing the bet?

"Like what you've done with the place." He swept pass Max. "See you finally hired a real decorator." As always, his voice held a tone of arrogance, in case his words weren't suitably obnoxious.

He didn't wait to be ushered to the living room. Instead, he strode past Max and into the kitchen, where he poured himself a drink from a bottle of whiskey that had already had the neck and shoulders taken off it.

"A little early, isn't it?" Max asked and glanced at the clock. Noon. Which day he couldn't say for sure. But noon.

He'd come home after his fight with Aggie and hadn't spoken to anyone since. Not even Grant. Until today, Max had been drinking like it was New Year's Eve and a bachelor's party all rolled into one event.

"Says the man who smells like a brewery and locker room sweat." Dad made a production of opening the curtains and windows.

Max winced. "Why are you here?" He had the curtains drawn for a reason. He wanted the gloom. It matched his mood.

"Can't a father stop by and see his son when he's in the neighborhood?"

Max leaned against the refrigerator. "Is that why you're here?"

"Since you've not answered your phone or responded to any emails in a week, I came by to tell you good luck on the O'Reilly bid in person."

"Really?"

Dad walked into the living room and had a seat on the couch. "Why would I say something I don't mean?"

Max moved empty pizza boxes and Chinese takeout cartons off a chair, along with an empty whiskey bottle, and flopped down. "Because I know you're also in the running on the project. The last thing you want is for me to have good luck."

Dad shifted and pulled an empty wine bottle out of the seat cushion. "Not true. I hope you win. I want that for my only son. Your success is my success."

"Since when do you want good things for me?"

Dad scowled. "I've always wanted good things for you."

Max propped his feet on the ottoman. "You want good things for me unless it meant letting me live with Mom growing up. Or hiring me out of college. Then it wasn't what was good for me but what was good for you."

Dad rubbed the back of his neck. "Son, it's time you learned the truth." The words came out sounding weary. "Your mom didn't want you to live with her. She gave me custody without a fight."

Max recoiled. That couldn't be true. Mom said she fought for him and lost. Grandmother would have told him. She wouldn't have allowed him to blame his father, her son, all these years if it weren't his fault. "I have enough going on in my life without your lying to me."

"If you don't believe me, ask your mom and watch for her tell. When she lies, she rubs her left cheek."

Max glanced toward the kitchen. He wished he had a drink now. This wasn't a subject he could carry on sober. His insides were too raw. "I'd prefer you tell me the truth, and I can watch for your tells."

"Fair enough. The reason I forced you to cancel all those weekends with your mom was because I would rather you blame me than to know it was your mom who actually did all the cancelling. I just came up with things for you to do so you wouldn't know the truth. I let you believe I was the villain."

For the life of him, he couldn't remember what Dad's tell was, so he had no way of knowing if he lied. Except, of course, he lied. "So I'm to believe you're the good guy?"

Dad took out a handkerchief and cleaned his glasses. "I'm just a dad trying to do the best he can as a father."

"That's a fuck-ass thing to say about Mom. Did you dummy down your bid so I could win?"

Dad smiled sadly and shook his head. "Of course I didn't. If you win, you win on your own. I would never help you win a bid against me."

"Exactly." His stomach grumbled, reminding him he hadn't yet eaten today. Hell, it may have been days since he last ate. "My feelings have always been secondary to your own."

"I just explained to you that's not true."

Was it the cleaning of his glasses? Was that his tell? "You might explain Mom away, but you can't explain away your refusal to hire me after college."

"Actually, I have a solid reason for that. If I'd hired you right out of college, everyone would have said you were handed your success. That I paved the way for you to move up through the ranks. By forcing you to go out on your own, I've given you the opportunity to prove yourself. I goaded you into that bet to put a fire in your belly."

Max didn't believe anything Father was saying. He couldn't. Not until he talked to Grandmother. "I need to shower."

"Do that," Dad said. "And then we can go to lunch and kill time while we wait for the winner to be announced this afternoon." He picked up the remote and turned on the television.

Max peeled off his T-shirt, smelled it, and grimaced. "You want to have lunch with me?"

Dad nodded curtly. "I do. It's high time you and I stopped butting heads."

Max studied him. "I didn't place a bid."

Dad pounded a fist on the arm of the couch. "What the hell are you talking about?"

Interesting. He didn't know. "My assistant screwed up, and my bid didn't get turned in by the deadline."

Dad swore. "What a complete incompetent. I hope you fired her ass."

Max stilled. "It's my fault. I should have never given her so much responsibility."

"The hell you say. When we get right down to it, this is Mother's fault for harassing you into hiring the tramp."

He jumped up and towered over his father. "Aggie's a lot of things, but she's not a tramp."

Dad leaned back into the cushions. "Don't get fussy like a girl. You know what I mean. She's not one of us. Ever since Mother's parents paid off the broke chap who wanted to marry her and forced her to marry Father instead, she's been determined someone in the family would marry across the proverbial track. When I refused, she set her sights on her only grandchild."

He knew part of Grandmother's story but not all of it. Knew about Johnny John. "There's nothing wrong with marrying someone who comes from poverty."

"Hell yes, there's something wrong with doing that. Their ways are not our ways, and once those types get a taste for finer things, they keep trying to climb the social ladder. They are always in search for a man with more money."

Max fisted his hands. "Just because Mom left you for a man with more money doesn't mean that's what every woman does. Besides, Mom came from money."

"Her money came from her daddy winning the lottery. Not heritage. I had to learn the hard way there's a difference. Your mom has poor people's ways, too. Find yourself a woman with old money."

He couldn't remember a time he'd ever wanted so much to punch Dad in the mouth. "Mom didn't leave you because you didn't have enough money. She left you because you didn't know how to show your love for anything but your money and your business and objects of your affairs."

"Aren't you full of contradictions?"

"What in the hell does that mean?"

"Tell me, boy, outside of your grandmother and mother, business, and the next big deal, what do you love? I bet you can't name one thing."

"You'd lose that bet. I love a lot of things."

"Name one."

Max didn't answer right away. Not because he couldn't, but because the answer that popped in his mind was one he'd been refusing to think of ever since banning her from his life. *Aggie.*

"See? You can't. You're a chip off the old block. And you know why? Because I raised you to be like me. Only smarter. Or at least I'd hoped smarter."

The thought of being like Dad sickened him. "I don't want to be like you. I want to love something other than money."

"Yet that's all you love."

"You know nothing about my life."

"You'll have to fill out a job application before you come to work for me. And you'll start at the bottom. Work your way up."

"Go to hell. I haven't lost the bet yet." He'd be damned if he went down without a fight. "I'm not thirty-one for another couple of weeks." He'd sober up, get his ass to work, and find another deal. A monster deal. If he landed a contract for the amusement park before his birthday, he might make that million-dollar mark.

"Son, I've made a lot of mistakes. Losing your mom was one of them. I should have chased her and begged her for forgiveness. Not judged her for her poor upbringing. Not let my own father's prejudices become my prejudices. So, if this"—he motioned to the mess of booze bottles—"is about your heart and not a business deal gone astray, don't make the same mistake I made. Even if the girl is that woman."

He ignored the *that woman* stab. "You and I are nothing alike. I didn't lose a girl. A girl lost me. She betrayed me."

"Are you sure about that? Did you give her a chance to explain? Your mom never gave me a chance to explain."

"I don't need to know why. Just that she did. And she admitted that much." Hadn't she? Of course she had. Fuck

Dad and his mind games.

Right now, all that mattered was the next big business deal.

"Call your grandmother. She will confirm what I've said."

Max leaned his head back on the cushion and closed his eyes. If Dad could turn out to be the good guy, what other things that he knew to be absolute truths were actually lies?

Chapter Forty-Five

Aggie sat in the Kansas City Airport and chewed on her fingernail. She'd not been a nail biter since middle school. Since the great race between her and all the other girls in her grade to see whose boobs popped out first.

But there was something about waiting on her flight, a flight that would literally give wings to her future, that had her fidgety, though leaving was the smart thing to do. Sure, she could have stayed and found a new job, but she needed more room to roam.

She pulled the crumbled-up napkin containing her life plan and manifesto out of her purse and reread her words.

…Always do the one thing that most scares you.

"I'm doing my new one thing that most scares me." She was searching, not for her soul's desire, but for her nirvana. Life taught her at a young age to hope for less than her soul's desires. Because her soul's desires were practically unobtainable. Having a normal mom, no matter how much Aggie's soul yearned for that to happen, never happened. And now, her soul desired Max would love her back. Which wouldn't happen, either. He simply didn't like her. And he couldn't fall in love with someone he described as the bane of his existence.

So instead of going after her soul's desire, she would search until she found the perfect job. And then, she'd start searching for her father. That she had complete control over. People were wrong when they said you only got one shot at a happy life. As long as you didn't place your happy in the hands of someone else to control, you got as many shots at finding happiness as you were willing to take.

Besides, leaving would take away all chances of running into Max. The guy who had her heart stuck to the bottom of his shoe, stomping all over it with every step he took. She reached for her phone to check the time, and it wasn't there. She'd not been able to revive it after the toilet bowl incident. As soon as she could afford it, she'd get a used one. But, for now, she'd have to adjust to life with an actual watch.

Listening to Meemaw call her a quitter had flattened her like three-day-old roadkill. Not once growing up could she ever remember disappointing her so supremely. To have given Meemaw reason made her even more determined to win back her admiration.

Living away from her would be hard, but she had done it while away at college. She could do it again. As long as their hearts were rooted to each other, they'd never really be apart.

She had heard nothing from Max. Without a phone, she had no idea if he'd tried to contact her after their blowup. She had an email, but he didn't know her email. She'd never gotten around to giving him a copy of Aggie's Assets, which contained that important factoid. All he had was her phone number.

And Meemaw's phone number.

But if he tried to call Aggie, and she didn't answer her phone, he wasn't the sort to call Meemaw. He'd assume Aggie wanted nothing to do with him. Which was exactly what she should want. But that wasn't true.

She loved him. Only he didn't love her back.

Never settle.

She had to get on the plane. She had to redeem herself in Meemaw's eyes. It was her opinion of Aggie that mattered. Not Max's.

Staying and fighting for her soul's desire would be heart-suicide.

But what if…

"We're now boarding for flight 1328. Passengers with boarding passes A1-A32 are now loading."

Chapter Forty-Six

Max didn't like to be rushed when deciding how to right a wrong. But when he received a text from Ms. Hazel saying Aggie had left for New York City, all of his foolish pride evaporated, and he realized begging for forgiveness was a small price to pay for a chance at eternal happiness.

He'd been a fool. Had known that ever since his father came to visit him. Probably before, but he'd stayed too drunk to comprehend that realization until the day his father showed up at his door, spouting, of all things, love advice.

Money and big deals weren't the key to happiness. What mattered more than anything in the world to him was winning Aggie's love.

Agnes Johansson was the key to every fucking thing that mattered to him.

He'd been trying to reach her, but all of his calls were sent straight to voicemail. Not that he blamed her. He deserved to be iced. Not that ice would stop him. Hell, a glacier wouldn't stop him. He kept trying. And while he waited for her to answer, he plotted what he'd say when they talked.

He hoped and prayed she'd find it in her heart to forgive him for all the horrible things he'd said.

Only his plot had no idea she really was leaving town forever. This piece of information meant his plan had to be put on fast forward. Which scared him because it wasn't perfect, and she deserved perfect.

Thank God, Grandmother and Ms. Hazel found it in themselves to interfere one more time in the lives of their grandchildren.

Luckily, the traffic lights were on his side as he sped toward the airport. He didn't know what he'd say to Aggie while everyone looked on, but hopefully the right words would come. If nothing else, he'd declare his love over the intercom system.

Thanks to Ms. Hazel's long text, he now knew all about Aggie's meeting with her mom and discovering she was a felon. Aggie had more than enough reason to space out and not do her job. He couldn't imagine how she must have stressed during the hours leading up to meeting her mom. And he'd been such a jackass. Nothing he'd said to her was forgivable. It would serve him right if she told him to go jump in front of the train that ran twice a day along the back of her and Hazel's home. Hell, he was on a suicide mission. And that's how it should be. When she needed him most, he hadn't believed in her enough to give her a chance to explain. He deserved whatever she flung at him.

At the airport, he parked in the no-parking zone and ran inside right up to the Southwest ticket booth. "I need to get an emergency message to a woman scheduled to board flight"—he pulled out his phone to get the number right. Ms. Hazel had sent it to him—"flight number 1328 to Newark."

"That flight has left," the woman said.

The hope inside of him disintegrated. "When will the next flight leave?"

"Not until tomorrow."

Son of a…fuck.

Now what? Was this an omen? In a movie, she would have been standing here waiting on him, having let the flight takeoff without her.

This obviously wasn't a movie.

"Will the passenger who left their car in the no-parking zone please move it, or it will be towed." The announcement came over the intercom system.

That was his car. He turned and dragged himself back to where he'd left it. With each step he took, an image of Aggie popped into his brain. The day of the interview when he first saw her in that tiny skirt and bomber jacket. The time she pulled him into the dumpster. Her in tiny little shorts running up a hill in front of him. Her holding Olivia and asking if he was going to die. Her wicked smile when they played strip trivia. Her fingers rolling a hot pink condom down his length. Her I-love-you expression on Bridge night. The sight of her storming out of his office after he'd told her she was the bane of his life. Little did she know, she'd left with his heart. She'd had the last laugh…as it should be.

Max drove back to work at a speed below the limit. Nothing seemed worth hurrying for if Aggie wasn't sitting in the car beside him. He'd really thought he'd get to the airport and find her waiting on him. He believed that after a ton of public groveling, she'd tell him she loved him as much as he loved her. He'd been a fool to believe in love.

She had left. She obviously didn't have it in her to love someone who'd treated her so poorly. And who could blame her?

When he got back to work, he realized he'd left in such a hurry he hadn't locked the office door. Frowning at his carelessness, he raced in and skidded to a stop. Someone was whistling. The hairs on his arms stood.

Somebody was in his office. The whistling grew louder. *You've lost that lovin' feeling.*

A smile stretched across his face. It was a somebody whose whistling could no more carry a tune than her singing voice. She hadn't left. She'd come back to him.

With a spring in his step, he hurried into his office.

The sight that met his gaze brought tears to his heart and eyes.

There stood Aggie thumbing through the résumés he'd left on his desk. Résumés for a new assistant. He stopped and breathed deep. He couldn't screw this up. This could very well be the most important moment of his life.

If this were a baseball game, they were in the bottom of the ninth, two outs, down by one. Bases loaded. And he was at bat with two strikes. And it was the seventh game in the World Series.

This swing had the power to elevate him to hero or plummet him to zero. "I thought you were gone," he said.

She glanced up. Her expression unreadable. "Looks like you're hiring a new assistant."

He advanced toward her. "I am. I screwed up and lost the best one I have ever had."

"Got her pregnant, did you?"

Meemaw must have taught her the fine art of a poker face, because he could tell nothing from her expression about what she was really thinking. Why had she come? To make up or to read him the riot act? God knew he deserved the riot act. "That's the rumor. And to make matters worse, I never even got a chance to grovel for forgiveness. I said things that were unforgivable. Things I didn't mean. Things I regret with every ounce of my being. Things that were spurred by foolish pride. Things she should never ever forgive me for saying. Yet I pray she will."

She winced. "That does indeed make matters worse. Will

those you interview be asked to take a test?"

He wanted desperately to grab her into his arms and kiss her senseless. He didn't. He couldn't rush things and screw this up. "They will." He'd been searching his whole life for someone like her. Hadn't known he was searching until she left.

She perched on his desk. "I thought you might still be up to that old trick, so I've reworked your test." Was it his imagination or did he just catch a twinkle in her eyes?

He was afraid to hope yet desperately needed to hope. "Why did it need reworking?"

"Because your old one had a major flaw."

"Major, you say?"

"Definitely. You need one that matches you with an assistant immune to all of your charms—not susceptible to them."

He certainly wasn't immune to her charms. He resisted the urge to touch her. Not yet. Not until he knew he wasn't foolishly misreading her signals. Which was quite likely. Hope could make an idiot out of a man. That and the fear of giving your heart away. "I don't suppose you'd be interested in applying for the job?" For eternity he stood in front of her, raw and exposed. Waiting for a "yes" or a "go to hell" or an "I've got a better idea."

She tilted her head to gaze into his eyes, poker face still in place. "Would I have to pass the new test? The one that doesn't allow for the falling for your charms?"

He briefly closed his eyes. He did not want her to pass that test. "I've been thinking, and I have another test in mind for you. That is…if you're interested." He waited for her to shoot him down. Tell him she'd just come back to give him a piece of her sharp-witted mind. She didn't.

Instead, she graced him with her slow-burning smile. The one that always scrambled his brain. This time was no different. The one she wouldn't give him if things weren't going to be okay. "A new test?"

He nodded and boldly stepped into her bubble, forcing her to open her legs to make room for him.

Her smile didn't falter as she laid the résumés down behind her. Neither did it falter when they missed the desk and fell to the floor. Or when she reached up and loosened his tie. "There's a distinct chance I might want to apply, if for no other reason than I do love to take tests. May I get a sneak peek at your new one?"

He yanked his tie off and unbuttoned the top buttons of his shirt. "It's not so much a written test as it is an action test."

She put her hands on his chest, sliding them up and over his shoulders before helping him to slip out of his jacket. "Like a skills test?"

"Exactly." His voice came out husky.

Her hands went to his waistband. "I'm listening." She unbuckled his belt.

He groaned. His wild, beautiful bird had come back to him. "It starts with a kissing test. And then progresses at an appropriate pace."

"I'm a seasoned runner, you know." Her hands undid the button of his pants. "And, as such, I like to do things at a reckless pace."

He placed his hands on either side of her on the desk and inhaled her perfume. The heady scent talked to him like a silent lover. "I can keep up with whatever pace you set."

She unzipped his pants. "And if I pass the test, is there a contract to be signed?"

The sweet sound of her sexy voice sent his blood pumping. "I'm a strong believer in contracts."

"Me, too. How many months would this contract last?" She pushed his pants down until they fell around his ankles.

God. It seemed like yesterday they'd stood in this room

and squared off on which of them would blink first about the job. Bless the Universe they were both too stubborn to blink. "Life." He kicked out of his shoes and his pants.

. . .

Aggie never knew her heart could soar while still throbbing with pain. But as much as she didn't want to bring anything negative into this moment, she had to. She needed to know the storm had passed and the sky would stay blue after the sex they were no doubt about to enjoy. *Lovers are in it for the sex. Period. Not your heart. Period.* "Does that mean I'm redeemable?"

Regret registered in his eyes. "Honey, you never needed redeeming or needed to be redeemed. You are a precious gem I found and foolishly lost. It's me who needs redeeming, and I promise, if you'll let me, I'll spend the rest of my life proving I'm worthy of your love."

She laughed. The first laugh since meeting Mom. "You're awfully pompous to assume I'm in love with you."

He reddened. "Are you?"

Was it possible he didn't realize how hypnotized she was by him? "As it happens, I very much love you." No need to be coy. "Can you ever forgive me for costing you the bid?"

"What bid?" He swiped everything off his desk and pushed her down on the clean surface. "The only thing on my mind is how very much I love you."

Sometimes lovers are in it for your heart. New period. "You do? Even if Mom's a felon? Which shouldn't matter and shame on you—"

"Agnes LaBelle Johansson, I love you. So. Fucking. Much. Your pedigree has never been an issue."

"And you're not saying that because you're after one of my world-famous blow jobs?"

Epilogue

Max's heart overflowed with joy. Aggie sat next to him in a booth located in the back of Vinos and Pinots. They'd met here with a client. Not any client. Max's pain-in-the-ass client. David Long. The one Aggie met with the day of the cat incident.

David had asked to meet with Max and insisted he bring Aggie. He'd just left.

"I can't believe everything worked out," she said, her voice full of awe.

Neither could he. Not the contract part, that was icing, but with him and her. "I still can't believe you came back to fight for us."

She fluttered her lashes at him. "You know...there comes a time in a woman's life when she realizes she really is capable of being *that* woman, so if a man says he likes-her, likes-her, he actually means what he is saying." She raised her glass of wine. "Here's to your newest contract."

"Here's to the wonder who turned one of my most difficult clients into my finest client." David had given him a contract so big, had he won the bid on the other contract—the one not filed on time—he would have had to say no. Together, they would turn the amusement park into a tiny-house community, complete with its own shopping center and business opportunities. A community for people who wanted a hand up in life instead of a handout.

"I am a wonder, aren't I?" She giggled and sipped her wine.

"In the office and in the bedroom."

She blushed. "I could say the same about you. I won't, because it will give you a second big head, but I could."

"Are you ready to get out of here and go home and celebrate?" He loved the fact his home now contained female touches and dresser drawers full of female things. Like panties. Lots and lots of panties.

• • •

Aggie's new phone rang. She glanced at Max. "It's Meemaw. What do you want to bet she's with Ms. Grace and they are in the midst of scheming something?"

"I know better than to take that bet."

She answered the call. "Hi, Meemaw. What's up?"

"I've got you on speakerphone. Grace is here with me. Are you, by any chance, with Max?"

She put her phone on speaker. "You know I am. Don't think we didn't notice you've both turned on the tracking apps on our phones."

"Oh. That. Well, it's for safety. You can track me, too, if needed. Unless I turn it off. In that case, be minding your own business."

"Hello, Grandmother and Ms. Hazel," Max said.

"Hello, darling," Ms. Grace said. "Hello, Aggie."

Max dropped an arm around Aggie's shoulders. "You're

cheerful, Grandmother. Is there something going on in your life you've failed to tell me about? Like the double-date you and Ms. Hazel went on over the weekend?"

Aggie elbowed him in the ribs. She'd filled him in on how Meemaw ended up with one date too many Saturday night, and she had turned a lemon into sweet lemonade tea. But that had been said in confidence. Good thing she hadn't told him the best part of that story. Halfway into the evening, the women realized they'd divvied up the men wrong. Ms. Grace was better suited for the police chief and Meemaw for Richard Harris. So they had swapped out dates right then and there.

Max gave her a very unapologetic shrug.

The grandmothers were silent for an unusual length of time.

"Grandmother? Cat got your tongue?" Max teased.

She gave a happy sigh. Not only did he like-her, like-her, but Pompous Ass was beginning to use some of her idioms. She'd conducted more research into the compatibility of a Reformer and an Enthusiast and came across a link that explained how the two types could actually be a really good mix if their values meshed and they were working for the same things in life.

"That's not what we called about," Ms. Grace finally said. "If you want to know what's going on in my love life, stop by and see me more often."

Max glanced down at Aggie and mouthed "love life." His whole face a picture of shock.

"I'll be there tomorrow."

"I'll come, too," Aggie added. If Ms. Grace had fallen into instant love, she wanted to hear the whole story from her, not Meemaw, who would leave out the sex bits.

"Aggie, darling, you're welcome to drop by any time."

"Thank you, Ms. Grace."

"You two be a peach and call before you drop by my

place," Meemaw said. "I just might be entertaining a guy."

Aggie laughed. "Meemaw, why did you call?" She and Meemaw were once again okay. Aggie discovered just because someone's mad at you didn't mean they stopped loving you.

"Bless your heart. You never have taken a hankering to the idea of my dating."

Her insides went gooey. Meemaw had put herself on the shelf for far too long worrying about being dumber than dirt. "You're stalling. What's up?" She tried to sound sharp and skeptical. Failed. It's hard to be either of those things when your life is a bed of roses stripped of their thorns.

"Are you two sitting down?" Meemaw asked.

"Sitting," Aggie and Max said in unison.

"Max, dear," Ms. Grace said, "Hazel and I have come up with the most delightful plan, and we need your help."

"What kind of help?" he asked.

He dropped a kiss on Aggie's nose. She loved when he did that. There wasn't much he did that she didn't love. Not that he'd suddenly become flawless. How boring would life be if you fell for a perfect person?

"We want you to find us a spot to open our new business. At a discount, of course."

"What new business would that be?" Aggie asked.

"We're going to open a new matchmaking business. It will be called Singles Mingle," Meemaw said.

"Or Love the Old-Fashioned Way," Ms. Grace chimed in.

"It will be a place for people to meet without the help of an app. Your fate no longer lays in the up or down swipe of a screen," Meemaw said. "We'll have a venue for holding singles functions. Grace and I will host the events, and with our eagle eyes for love, we'll guide those together who are meant to be together."

"Doesn't that sound delightful?" Ms. Grace said. "We're

hoping the two of you will give us permission to use your story as a testimonial of our skills."

"This is a wonderful idea. Meemaw, you're going to finally have a job that makes you happy." A tear landed on Aggie's cheek.

Max pulled her into his arms. "Aggie and I will be delighted to help."

She glanced at him. "They could set up business in one of the shops we're including in our new project."

"What's that about a new project?" Meemaw asked.

"We have some great news of our own," Aggie said.

The grandmothers laughed.

"Bless your heart, are you pregnant? Max, did you go and knock up my granddaughter?"

She rolled her eyes. That wasn't happening. She was determined to be the first Johansson to get the cart and horse scenario in the right order. In that vein, she'd recently purchased a new box of hot-pink condoms, and at the rate they were going through them, next time, she'd have to buy them in bulk quantity.

"Ms. Hazel—" he said. His cheeks were a bright red, and his Adam's apple was working overtime.

"Call me Meemaw."

"Meemaw, I promise to make an honest woman of Aggie before I make you a great-grandmother."

Aggie beamed up at him. They'd talked plenty about love but not marriage. Not that she was worried. As it turned out, she did indeed meet every one of his qualifications of the perfect woman.

"Maxi Treadwell, are you going to tell us your news or what?" Ms. Grace said.

Aggie placed a hand on Max's. "Yes, Maxi, why don't you tell them our news?"

He gave her a strange smile. "If you insist." He stood,

went down on one knee, pulled a ring box out of his jacket pocket and said, "Aggie the Horrible, Aggie the Lovable, Aggie the very most perfect bane of my existence, would you do me the honor of being my wife?" He opened the ring box, showing her an insanely large, square-cut diamond wrapped with tiny lavender-blue stones.

Sweet baby Jesus. She nodded, a tear dangling on her lashes. "Be a peach and slide that on my finger. Let's see how it fits."

Acknowledgments

This book is the brainchild of the fabulous Liz Pelletier of Entangled Publishing and me. I love that Liz makes herself available to bounce plot bunnies around with her authors. It is a perk of writing for Entangled Publishing that I do not take for granted.

Nor do I take for granted the wonderful editors who helped me whip this story into its sassy shape. During the process of bringing this book to the public, I had the privilege of working with editors: Robin Haseltine, Lydia Sharp, and Liz Pelletier. They are each a gem. And I have nothing but deep admiration for my copy editor, Jessica Meigs.

A big shout out to cover artist, Elizabeth Turner Stokes, who designed the fun cover. I am a firm believer it should be on display at every brick-and-mortar bookstore if for no other reason than that the cover just begs to be fondled.

My fabulous agent, Ann Rose, deserves all the accolades for believing in me. When I'm having a rough day, I remind myself she finds my writing fabulously funny.

Then there are my writing buddies: Barbara Huddleston

and Claudia Shelton. Via daily Zoom sessions, these ladies have talked me off more than one writing-related ledge during this past year and inspired me to write even on days the muse was not there. I don't ever want to go back to a life where I don't get to hang out with them Monday through Friday via Zoom.

And I need to thank my family for accepting me, quirks and all. They cheer me on every step of the way.

And lastly, I'd like to thank my writing angels who hang out with me during every writing session and help me come up with plot ideas.

About the Author

Lisa Wells always knew there would come a time in her life when she'd pursue her dream career as a romance author. This is that time. Before this moment, she's enjoyed a rollercoaster journey called—The Middle School Counselor—Dramas, Dreams, and Destinies. After many years of working with teenage girls, she knows when one comes in baffled because another girl hates her, the first question to ask is—"Did you steal her boyfriend?" Nine times out of ten the answer is some form of yes but... While Lisa enjoys working with adolescents, she writes for adults. Her books contain: Sex, Scowls & Sass.

Also by Lisa Wells...

THE SEDUCTION OF KINLEY FOSTER

THE ATTRACTION OF ADELINE

LIKE A BOSS
a novel by Anne Harper

As if it wasn't bad enough that her long-term boyfriend dumped her, Nell Bennett goes viral online for ranting in a restaurant about her perpetually single status. Thankfully a kind and attractive stranger offers to share his table with her...and their sizzling banter leads to a surprising kiss before they part ways. Now her tiny hometown of Arbor Bay is buzzing over their latest Internet celebrity, but Nell's no stranger to attention. Still, even she never expected to show up to work only to discover her brand-new boss is a very familiar face...

FOREVER STARTS NOW
a Forever Falls novel by Stefanie London

Monroe Roberts knocked "forever" off her wish list when the love of her life skipped town with the cliché yoga instructor. And good riddance. She's busy with her diner, trying anything to boost sales...until a hot Australian strolls in and changes everything. Monroe's restaurant is packed full of women who aren't there to order, unless Ethan is on the menu. This could sink her business. So—light bulb—what if they pretend to be together?

BACK IN THE BURBS
a Stuck in the Burbs novel by Tracy Wolff and Avery Flynn

In the span of three months, I lost my husband, my NYC apartment, my money, and frankly, my dignity. And then the only person who ever understood me died and left me her house in the burbs. First rule of surviving suburbia? There's nothing that YouTube and a glass of wine can't conquer.

RACHEL, OUT OF OFFICE
a novel by Christina Hovland

Single mom Rachel Gibson seriously needs a break, so color her less than thrilled when her ex backs out of taking their twin boys for the summer to his family's lake house. The next two months promise to be jampacked with juggling work, family, and some pesky new feelings for her ex-brother-in-law. Could he be just one more messy complication in the dumpster fire of her life, or is anything possible when she's out of office?

Made in the USA
Monee, IL
25 September 2022

14592141R00198